John Finbarr Buckley grew up in Cork, Ireland and still lives there today. A keen wildlife photographer who loves to daydream and create stories from memories. The ideal day for him is hiking in beautiful West Cork watching the clouds chasing each other till the Sun drops. Someday, he will actually find himself but until then he is enjoying the searching.

Also, visit the business accounts of *John Finbarr Buckley Writer/Photographer* on Facebook, Instagram and TikTok.

To my children, Hayley and David.

My friends:

Tina Pisco,

Fiona Buckley,

Kenneth Casey,

Linda Hanrahan,

John Brady

and the countless friends on Facebook who encouraged me to complete *Steeple City*.

John Finbarr Buckley

STEEPLE CITY

AUSTIN MACAULEY PUBLISHERS™
LONDON * CAMBRIDGE * NEW YORK * SHARJAH

Copyright © John Finbarr Buckley 2022

The right of John Finbarr Buckley to be identified as author of this work has been asserted by the author in accordance with sections 77 and 78 of the Copyright, Designs and Patents Act 1988.

All rights reserved. No part of this publication may be reproduced, stored in a retrieval system, or transmitted in any form or by any means, electronic, mechanical, photocopying, recording, or otherwise, without the prior permission of the publishers.

Any person who commits any unauthorised act in relation to this publication may be liable to criminal prosecution and civil claims for damages.

This is a work of fiction. Names, characters, businesses, places, events, locales, and incidents are either the products of the author's imagination or used in a fictitious manner. Any resemblance to actual persons, living or dead, or actual events is purely coincidental.

A CIP catalogue record for this title is available from the British Library.

ISBN 9781398446892 (Paperback)
ISBN 9781398446915 (ePub e-book)
ISBN 9781398446908 (Audiobook)

www.austinmacauley.com

First Published 2022
Austin Macauley Publishers Ltd®
1 Canada Square
Canary Wharf
London
E14 5AA

Chapter One
The Potato Peeler

I take the stairs two steps at a time to get to the bathroom before anyone else. It's a lot more enjoyable brushing your teeth before three other people. All the window opening in the world won't get rid of the smell of my family. I like brushing my teeth. My teeth like being brushed. I put a pea sized piece of toothpaste on my new toothbrush as raised voices come from the kitchen below. Paul is arguing with Granny. Someone's always arguing with Granny. She is centre stage in all the disputes in the house. They are still at it when I go back downstairs. Paul is sounding patient and sincere again. Granny is washing up the breakfast dishes with a scowl screwed on her face.

"Granny, the man is a senior lecturer at the university. He gave us a talk on philosophy. It's his job to ask questions so as to understand the meaning of life."

Granny wipes her hands off the hand towel over and over again. This is the first of many signs that she is getting annoyed.

"Fuck it, Paul. Run that past me again from the start."

Paul is fighting a losing battle, but he's not going to give in easily. He sits up and continues.

"He gave us an image first: Imagine that a man yells in the woods. No one is there. He is alone. Can his voice still be heard?"

"Yes," Granny snorts.

Paul, who is the smartest by far in the house, pounces. He has tons of brains but fuck all common sense.

"Who is there to hear him?" he asks.

Granny searches her apron pockets for her cigarettes. "Himself you fucking idiot. He hears his own fucking voice. Didn't he just yell! If I call out for ye and there is no one in the house, I can still hear my own voice. I don't need some prick of a professor to tell me that!"

Paul readjusts himself on the chair. He slows down his sentences and his voice becomes clear and careful. This drives Granny over the edge. She hates being spoken down to. The fact that Paul is so intelligent annoys the living day lights out of her.

"Granny, you're missing the point. Philosophy is the study into the meaning of life. Who you are and what role you play in affecting your own life and the lives of others. To see what's under the surface."

A cigarette is finally produced. "For-fucking-give me Paul, but we can't all spend our days like useless bastards talking shit. Sorry about that! Why do you go to university to listen to fucking loners talking about yelling in the woods? I'm no fucking expert, but I can smell something." Granny stares out the window at light clouds riding invisible airstreams. She gives a flick of her lighter and takes a drag on the cigarette. Then she sniffs the air and beams. "Horse? No? Sheep? No? Chicken? No? Definitely bull, Paul! Yes, I can smell bullshit. Amazing how I know the smell of bullshit and we don't even live near a farm. Must be a gift."

Paul sits, looking as if he can't understand the genetic link that bonds them together. "You see Granny…"

"One minute Paul, one minute," she says, cutting him off with a wave of her cigarette. "That Lecturer would be better off forgetting about that fucking idiot out in the woods and question his own sanity. If a man in the woods knew he was on his own, why in the name of God did he fucking yell in the first place? What the fuck is he? Some sort of sick, perverted, exhibitionist?"

Granny looks up, sees me standing in the doorway and strikes a savage blow just for me. She enjoys tormenting Paul more when she has her faithful audience.

"Maybe he was out in the woods collecting 'fruits of the forest' for that sissy yogurt that you enjoy so much? Now that would make sense! The over educated asshole was driven mad collecting bastarding blueberries, yelling out every time he found one. Blueberries, blueberries – whatever the flying fuck happened to the humble blackberry to be taken over by blueberries? I don't think I ever even saw a blueberry bush! Is there such a thing? They must be growing them in secret factories hidden away in the middle of that forest you are obsessed with."

Paul is not giving up. "Granny I think we've crossed wires here," he starts. They do have a genetic link – stubbornness. Placing his hands on the table Paul decides to use reason, but Granny cuts him down before he has the chance to talk.

"Stop insulting my limited intelligence. I might be getting fucking old, but I am not that fucking stupid yet." She puts the cigarette on the side of the ashtray and shrieks. "Sweetest fuck, try and be something in life! Learn medicine or architecture. Let the foxes and rabbits worry about the sick, fucking head-case, collecting those gay blueberries out there in the woods."

Time to leave. I lift my denim jacket from the back of Paul's chair and ease quietly out of the kitchen, into the hall and freedom. It is Christmas Eve morning, which means going into the record shops to check out all the new sounds. My pockets are crammed with change from a week of going to the shop for Granny. The world is mine.

Harpo is standing at the bus stop, looking like no one has ever loved him. His real name is Gerard Lucey. We call him Harpo because of an uncanny resemblance to the mute one in the Marx brothers. Unlike the real Harpo, he talks all the time. You can't shut him fucking up. It's like someone keeps pulling a cord in his back. Once he starts, he doesn't even stop for breath. Granny calls him the 'Harpo Express'. I am surrounded by nicknames in this family, but Granny is the only person I know who can add a nickname onto a nickname.

Dad calls Granny 'The Mad Mullah'. He mutters it under his breath when she annoys him. A while back the news was full of images of soldiers on open top trucks firing at demonstrators in the Middle East. One night, Dad's attention was caught by a Mullah whipping a crowd into a frenzy, shrieking and waving his hands around like Kermit the Frog. In between rants, he still ranted, not even slowing for a breath. When he turned and vanished into a nearby building my dad asked me, "Was that your Granny, the Mad Mullah?" Mullah sounds like the start of Granny's surname Mulcahy, so the nickname had staying power.

Granny often says, "Nicknames are life's great levellers." And so with the instinct of a wildcat she began to call Dad 'The Oak'. Granny believes in fighting fire with fire. Paul and I have different theories as to why she calls Dad 'The Oak'. My theory is that it's because Dad is always tanned and has a pretty impressive build and reminds her of an oak tree. Paul thinks it's because Dad is as thick as a plank.

Harpo looks up and sees me. "You took your time Fin. It's nearly eleven thirty. Have you got money? Stupid question, you always have money. Let's pretend we're only twelve. I know it's pushing it, but we don't look fourteen, do we? I'll do the talking to the driver. You can pay full price if you want, but I'm not paying them a penny more than I have to. It's better in my pocket than theirs." He hardly stops to take a breath. "The Police – that's who I am after. Zenyatta Mondatta is the album I want. It's unreal. I heard it on the radio. What does Zenyatta Mondatta mean?" Harpo pauses. He only does it when he needs an answer.

"Top of the world," I reply on cue.

He flicks his hair. "Yeah!"

Glad to be able to get a word in I continue. "I heard it on the radio yesterday. Disco Dave played a few tracks. How come The Police albums have such weird names? Like 'Outlandos d'Amour' and 'Reggatta de Blanc'. They're Brits, not frogs or Italians – granted one American – so what's with the titles? At least if The Beat's album 'Just can't stop it', is in the shop I won't feel like some up my own arsehole art student asking for it!"

Harpo takes no notice. He's back to one of his favourite subjects, which is my dad's taste in music. God knows why he cares. He talks about my dad more than I do.

"Is your dad still singing along to the Beatles and Elvis? I never felt comfortable with Elvis spelling evils! Your dad should give The Jam or The Police a chance and bury all that old time shit. The Beatles and Elvis broke ground in their day, but he should embrace new ground-breaking bands. Disco is dying. This is the eighties. Punk's not dead – it just smells that way."

That punk joke cracks us up every time. We fall about laughing as the bus comes around the corner.

Harpo comes from a different world than me; a world where a proper dinner is a luxury, not a guarantee. His house frightens the living fucking daylights out of me. Since his mum ran off it's gone from a normal home to a cesspit. His mum lives in Canada now. Last Christmas Harpo and his sisters received a massive box of clothes in the post; like the best of gear: Cool Canadian ice hockey jerseys, Adidas Sweatshirts and tee shirts; all top class.

Harpo used to talk about his mum sending him a ticket to come and live with her in Canada. Every conversation had Canada in it for no reason, just so he could say the word Canada. It got very annoying. The months passed and the ticket never arrived. So, then Harpo convinced himself that his mum was coming to collect him herself. Eventually the truth dawned on him, or at least part of the truth. His mum rang him at his aunt's house and explained that she couldn't come home because she had a partner. Sitting on the wall by my house, he proudly told me that he thought his mum had started a business. He was really excited that he could now tell everyone that his mum was a successful businesswoman. Then he started blubbering.

"I begged her to let me come work for them in Canada. I would do anything, any job, just bring me to Canada." He sobbed. Then he blew his nose and stood shaking his head in disbelief. "For ten whole minutes she spoke to me like I was a five-year-old, and then dropped the bombshell that she had a lover. A lover! When she said partner, she meant to say lover. Who the fuck uses a term like partner? She doesn't give a fiddlers fuck that life here is killing me, the selfish bitch."

What could I say? At least his mum was still alive. I wouldn't care where my mum was as long as she was still alive.

Since she did a runner Harpo's house has fallen apart. I'll do anything to avoid calling over to Harpo's house, never mind setting foot in it. Meeting outside by the green has become the norm. It saves us both the awkwardness.

Their kitchen never has any proper food. Most dinners come out of a tin. There's never any food you would like to eat instead of having to eat it. Jam sandwiches, beans, and spaghetti make up most of Harpo's diet; along with those poxy fish fingers and cheap burgers. Everything is just lobbed into a pool of fat in a frying pan. They don't even eat toast anymore. The bread is thrown straight into the pan and fried. The dirty dishes are left for days in the sink until they are needed again. The place is filthy. You know those ads on the telly where a woman who doesn't look like anyone's mother you've ever seen, is cleaning the house? They show us a 'dirty kitchen' and lo and behold 'Mrs I Never Lost My Virginity' throws on a pair of gloves, sprays some magic shit, and the place is suddenly spotless. Not one stain on her clothes, or a drop of sweat on her brow. If that silly bitch did the ad in Harpo's kitchen, she would need a massive fuck off flamethrower. She would have to burn the shithole down to the ground to get it clean.

Harpo has two sisters, May and June; both of them rides. May was sixteen in September, and June was fifteen in November. All three have to deal with the on-going nightmare that is their father. Even on a summer's day the house feels cold and lonely. Most nights, they sit silently watching the telly while Mr Lucey burps, farts, pisses himself, or throws up. On a good night he does all four. They have to clean it up, as he would never do it. Mr Lucey's life is a hamster-wheel of pub, home, pub, home, pub, on and on. The man tells the time by what drink is in front of him: Tea in the morning, fresh pints of stout in the evening, and stale pints of stout at night. A constant stench fills the house. Harpo says it's the damp. It might be, but his dad put it there. I've actually seen his dad pissing on the stairs.

One day I had to use their bathroom against all my best instincts. The odour was solid. It could actually be felt in the air. They don't have loo rolls. They use newspaper instead. Some of it was yellow where Harpo and Mr Lucey's aim was off. The bathroom window was nailed shut with a piece of ply-board. There is no frosted glass in the window, so when you take a piss, all the houses that look over the back of Harpo's house can clearly see you. At night-time with the light on, their bathroom can be seen right down to the end of the park. Maybe that's why Mr Lucey pisses at the end of the stairs.

The sink, splinter of soap, and towel were all the same greenish colour. The towel, which may once have been blue, hung stiffly with frayed edges. Out on the clothesline hung nice, fancy towels belonging to the girls, and the grimy bathtub was lined with expensive shampoos and conditioners. May and June go without a lot of things, but they get their hands on all the girlie things they need. Harpo says his sisters hide whatever they want inside their baggy jumpers. Shops that have all male staff are their favourite hunting grounds. Men are too shy to ask a young girl to lift up her jumper to check for stolen items. Sometimes the girls only spend a single pound in a store and come out with at least twenty pounds worth of stuff.

I couldn't bring myself to wash my hands. Leaving the bathroom, taking care not to even touch the door handle, I stop dead in my tracks. Mr Lucey was relieving himself at the bottom step. He gestured for me to come down. Then he shook himself, stuck his hand in his pocket, pulled out some change and offered it to me. His hands were damp from piss. I refused. He insisted. When he started getting boisterous, my hand unwillingly accepted the change. Warm, wet, unwanted coins touched my skin. My throat went dry. Gagging, I pushed past him and out into the summer breeze.

The coins added up to £1.90. I gave Granny back the £1.80 she'd lent me the week before. It could be my imagination, but Granny seemed to sniff the coins as I handed them to her. For days I got a smell of piss off my right hand.

The most frightening thing about Harpo is that he lives in a house that looks just like mine from a distance. If all this seriously fucked up shit can happen to him, then by the laws of the universe it could just as easily happen to me. After all, I'm more than halfway there. My mum is dead and my dad doesn't give a shit about me. The only person who cares about me is Granny and if she goes, well, that doesn't bear thinking about.

The bus pulls over at our stop on Patrick's Street. We jump off and run the twenty yards to 'Music Heaven', Cork's number one music shop. There is a massive poster stuck on the front window. It's the singles chart. The Human League are number one with 'Don't you want me'.

Harpo pulls me right up next to him. I push him away and go to smack him playfully across the back of the head. "Get off me. People will think we're queers."

He ducks and avoids my blow. "No, they won't, you're not a good enough catch to be my boyfriend," he says in a high-pitched voice.

The record shop is overcrowded and understaffed. As soon as we get in, I see a cassette slip up Harpo's jumper. First thing that comes into my mind is self-preservation. I move to the furthest corner of the shop where I felt safe to do my own thing. I know that Harpo is up to something behind me. Feeling scared, I turn and let my feet carry me back out to the street. Harpo follows, a smug smile between his ears. My head is spinning. If Granny finds out about this shit, I'll be dead. If Dad finds out, I'll be double dead.

My worst fears are confirmed as Music Heaven's massive security guard, in a drab, grey uniform, grabs Harpo's arm. "Alright lads, come with me. We need to have a word."

Harpo tries to control the situation. He pleads complete ignorance, which is the only defence in these situations.

"We have to go. My mum's waiting for us." Words are failing him. He tries to free his arm and shouts. "Leave me alone!"

Now we have an audience. The louder Harpo rants the more members our group attracts. The nosey watching the noisy. What appears to be the store owner pops up next to the Grey Uniform. My mind races around in circles, like a demented greyhound. What if a neighbour sees us? Or worse still someone from school! Thank fuck the owner herds us back inside. The four of us troop off through the shop to a tiny office at the back.

We can't be questioned or searched without a parent being present. Harpo doesn't have a phone, so my number is dialled. I pray to a mother I never knew that her mother would pick up the phone. Once again, the dead save the living. We can all hear Granny answering. In the tiny little office, not a word is lost.

"Hello?"

"Hello, Mrs Mulcahy?" asks the Grey Uniform.

"Yes. Who's speaking?"

"The head security officer for Music Heaven, Cork's number one music store."

Granny is confused. "Is this one of those telephone ads, or fucking mindless competitions on a stupid radio station? Holy fuck! I'm not live on the air, am I?"

The owner and Grey Uniform go bright red trying not to laugh. In a clear tone the Grey Uniform continues. "No, Mrs Mulcahy we are a record shop, right here on Patrick Street."

Granny cuts straight back in. "Thank fuck for that, you scared the living shit out of me. I was just soaking my feet. Fucking things are as raw as a duck's ass. Why are you ringing me, so?"

Both men are barely keeping it together. Harpo and I don't see the humour in any of this. Grey Uniform covers the mouthpiece and regains his composure. "Sorry, Mrs Mulcahy. We need you to come in here so we can search your grandson's friend. Harpo, I believe is his name."

Granny explodes. The blast is felt all around the office. "What do you fucking mean 'search'? Search for what exactly?"

"He was acting very suspiciously, and we need to search him. It's company policy."

Granny can be heard lighting a cigarette and wheezing on her first drag. "I am fucking telling ye, if this is one of these piss take things on the radio, I will fucking burn the radio station down. No fucking shit. All I want to be doing is enjoying my Christmas Eve in peace and fucking quiet. Do you get me?"

"I can assure you Mrs Mulcahy that we are not a radio station."

"Put my grandson on the phone."

A relieved Grey Uniform hands me the phone. I keep it short and simple.

"Granny, you have to come in right now, otherwise they will call the Guards. We haven't done anything honest."

Granny lets out a snort. "Keep your fucking mouth shut, Fin. Understood? See you in a jiffy!"

"Yes, Granny." I agree obediently, and hand the phone back to Grey Uniform who shakes his head.

"In all my years I never had a conversation like that."

The owner pats him on the back and they have a laugh about Granny. My blood boils to hear them mock her, but I promised Granny that I would be quiet and a promise to Granny is a promise that I don't break. Well, not lightly, or when it doesn't suit me, or if there is a possibility that she will find out. It suits me now.

We wait. A mug of tea and biscuits are placed on the table for Grey Uniform to enjoy. He shares the biscuits and insists that we take the chocolate ones. Harpo swiftly spits into the hot tea when no one is looking. Grey Uniform appears to be my dad's age and doesn't seem like a bad bloke. He's not threatening or nasty to us. Harpo just likes being an asshole.

It takes Granny forever to arrive because of the Christmas traffic, then the door swings open and she walks in, the toughest of us all. Grey Uniform explains what happened. He seems pleased to have foiled some sort of a robbery, like The Great Train Robbery. As the story unfolds, he paints Harpo as the main suspect with me as a witness.

Granny lights up a cigarette. Grabbing my arm, she says, "Thank you, I will take my grandson home, so."

"We need to search both of them," says Grey Uniform, not realising that he has stepped into a mine field.

Granny's eyes lock on to him as her false teeth come right out to the front of her mouth. "You just said my grandson was a witness, not a suspect."

"Yes, I did Mrs Mulcahy, but—"

"Shut the fuck up and get a proper job. Idiot!" Granny turns and clips Harpo across the back of the head. "Hurry up and get your jacket, jumper and jeans off. I have a dinner to prepare."

Each item is checked and rechecked by the Grey Uniform.

Harpo stands in his stained white Y-fronts, holding back tears. They find absolutely nothing on him.

The store owner gives Grey Uniform a pissed off look, as Harpo pulls his clothes back on. "I am sorry for dragging you in here, Mrs Mulcahy. Please accept our apology and a Merry Christmas."

"Fuck off," Granny answers over her shoulder as she herds us out the door.

On the bus back home, we sit upstairs in silence. We enter the flow of traffic and are soon out of the city centre. Peering into the distance I watch a flock of homing pigeons circling their loft. As the bus climbs one of Cork's many high hills the whole city comes into view. Grey church steeples pinprick the sky, casting their shadows on all the surrounding buildings. This is their city, my city, City of Steeples.

Harpo points his eyes to the top of the bus. "Check out the ass on that one!"

Sitting on her own is Sharon Lyons, and she is tasty, very tasty. She's the stuff of every schoolboy's wet dreams. We don't exist in her world. If a space craft were invented to get you to her planet, she wouldn't let it land.

"Shut the fuck up, Harpo. We are in enough trouble already."

Back home sit a hungry Paul with a hungrier Dad. They know something has happened. Granny throws on her apron and starts to prepare dinner, grabbing vegetables and clanging pots.

Dad pipes up. We all wished he wouldn't.

"Where were you Granny?"

"Out." She snaps, filling a pot.

"Were you out Christmas shopping?"

"No."

"Paying bills?"

"Aren't you the annoying bollocks all the same?" Granny slams the pot on the cooker to boil. "If you want to eat, shut the fuck up, be quiet, and let me get back to doing the dinner."

Dad doesn't like being berated. 'The Oak' isn't going to sway today. He rises from the safety of his chair and stands rooted to the spot, staring at Granny. "I was only asking a civilised question about where ye were, that's all. I was worried. It was out of concern, not hunger that I asked. Forgive me for noticing that you vanished out the door like the house was on fire, only to return with the boy."

The cold tap runs, and Granny washes the spuds. She doesn't even turn to look. "Leave him out of this."

"A funny thing happened after you left. A music shop rang. They were wondering if you were on the way in. So, I asked them why? Guess what? They had the boy in their office waiting for you. What has the little lying, stealing bastard done now?"

Shit he knows. This is getting way too serious. Granny spits back.

"Don't be annoying me about phone calls. Don't you fucking dare! Fin is my responsibility. He is my boy as much as yours. Just because I didn't carry him doesn't mean he's not fucking mine."

Paul and I are glued to the spot as Dad circles the table.

"Yours? What are you on about? Yours? He's your grandson just like Paul. They are my boys. I am their dad! Like it or lump it."

This makes Granny go full flow Mad Mullah. "Your boys? That's really fucking rich," she gasps. "They don't belong to you. They belong to my beautiful saint of a daughter." Paul and I exchange glances. What does she mean, 'they don't belong to you'?

"Yeah you, ye prick. Mr high-and-fucking mighty, laying down the law. It's not my daughter you're dealing with now! Do you fucking hear me?" she yells brandishing a potato peeler.

"The whole neighbourhood heard you, you old, demented bat," Dad snaps back.

The room goes quiet as the Mad Mullah glides up to the Oak, circling the potato peeler until it almost touches his nose. "Don't you ever forget I'm not my angel of a daughter. You ever speak to me like that again, and I'll fucking ram this straight into you," she hisses.

The Oak doesn't back down. Pride is a terrible thing. It's one of the seven deadly sins, and it's making him react with another deadly sin – wrath. Wrath is the sin that brings violence.

"Who do you think you are coming in here and ruling my home and my family? I can say and do whatever I want. It's my house. Your permission isn't needed." The Oak shoots a massive branch of an arm out and grabs me. "Now, boy – where were ye today?"

Granny rips Dad's arm off me. "Leave Fin alone."

Dad grabs me again. "He's my son and I can ask him what I want! Stay out of my business."

The Mad Mullah snarls, smirks and smiles. "Is he your fucking son? That's one for the record! Are you sure?"

My head is spinning. The Oak's face turns pure white. He looks frozen.

"What did you just say?" he asks through clenched teeth.

"Sorry I should have said – 'do you really think he's your son?' – slip of the tongue," she says in a sickly-sweet voice.

The Oak pounces. In a flash he grabs her by the throat and holds her face over the pot of hot water. A sickly smell of singed hair floats in the air. "The minute I married your daughter you had to get involved, didn't you? How could we ever get on with you hanging around like a bad smell?"

Steam covers Granny's face, turning it purple. She is calm and smiling her crazy smile. The one she saves for The Oak. Someone had to do something and Paul sure as fuck wasn't going to take on Dad, so I jump up to put an end to it, Dad catches me full force with the back of his hand. My nose goes numb and little drops of blood splatter my face. I fucking hate him with every single bone in my body.

The Oak pushes Granny away. "You sick tormented old hag. You talked her into having the boy after that excuse of a child, Paul. You claimed it would bring us closer together. We didn't need another child and you fucking knew it. She told me it was your wonderful idea. Then the useless little bastard killed her. I have to look at those two fucking failures of Sons every day. Why don't ye all fuck off and leave me in peace."

Granny stands next to me and protects me, while Paul just sits there crying. She places her hand on my shoulder. "I made yer mum, my daughter a fucking promise on her death bed and I will honour it. She begged me not to leave ye alone with yer father and to raise ye as my own. No useless fucker will stand in my way."

I keep trying to catch the blood that is falling from my nose. My head aches. The Oak won't give up. "There you go again – digging up your daughter to defend your craziness. Sick, that's what it is. According to you she never shut the fuck up on her death bed."

"Well, if you'd been at her deathbed, you could have listened too. You must have had more important fucking things to do? Like ride some cheap tramp."

The Oak raises a hammer of a fist. The Mad Mullah stands her ground. "A fist now, is it? Fucking beautiful! That's about all you're fucking good for – hitting women and boys. Lowlife that's what you are. A fucking, prick of a lowlife. Lowlife! Lowlife!" Granny sings the word Lowlife like an ambulance siren. "Lowlife…lowlife…lowlife…Thank God my daughter can't see what you have become!"

Granny goes back to her spuds. Holding each potato like it was a rock she peels off chunks of skin and drops each piece into the shining sink. Suddenly, Dad's fist connects with Granny's shoulder, sending her sprawling over the table, taking the knives and forks with her. He bends over her, as The Mad Mullah cracks that smile again. I try and grab him and unbalance him in the process. The Mad Mullah seizes her chance. Her right hand comes up and thumps into his left shoulder. The shock causes him to fling me straight off him.

He falls to his knees, clutching his arm, and screaming like a pig. There, driven straight into his arm, is the potato peeler. A thin line of blood runs down his shirt onto the lino. Shock is a strange thing. My first thought is, *Pity she wasn't cutting bread.*

Granny bends over him and with one swift gesture, the potato peeler is back in her hand. She pulled it straight out! She has the confidence of someone who has done this before. The Oak is lost in pain. Granny smiles again as she wipes the peeler on her apron. "Dinner will be a little late today. I hope that won't inconvenience you?" she says, biting each word.

Paul turns the colour of fresh cut grass. As he sprints for the toilet I get up and use him as an excuse to leave. Granny is back peeling the potatoes. Dad gets up and wraps a tea towel around his arm. Then he walks out the front door.

I sit on the lower bunk and pull off my jeans. Four cassette tapes fall out. Deep Purple, AC/DC, The Police and David Bowie land on my lap. Harpo was to get The Police. That was his price for distracting the Security guard. The other three were to be sold. Our luck nearly ran out today. Pulling up the loose floorboard under the bed I gently drop the tapes into their safe hiding place. I have three lads from school waiting to buy them at half price as Christmas presents. The enjoyment is gone out of this. I need to find a new way to make money.

Chapter Two
Condemned Fourteen-Year-Old

Five rows across, eight rows deep. That adds up to forty desks. My seat is halfway up the left hand-side, next to the window where I can watch everything. That's where I like to be: Hidden in with my sweaty, spotty generation who think that they're too smart for school.

The door opens and Mr Higgins walks in, right in on time. He is never late. If the world ended, he would be back here the next day, right on time. He never comes in early either. No sir, the government isn't getting a second free off Mr Higgins, or 'Beanpole' as everyone calls him. He is six foot three inches tall, and about one foot wide, so he looks like a beanpole. We all know his height because he likes to use it to terrorise the living shit out of us. He stalks between the rows of boys whispering, "Six foot three, that's me." He must have underlying mental health issues.

Beanpole is a bully who hates us all equally. If you don't fit the mould, Beanpole will recast you, press you and beat you into the correct shape. Beanpole doesn't do detention or extra homework. That would mean extra work for him. He prefers using fear and beatings. You can tell he really enjoys it. Eyes wide with excitement, mouth dry with anticipation, he will beat the first boy who is unlucky enough to grab his nasty attention.

This Monday morning, like every Monday morning, we start with an hour-long test. Some Maths, Irish and English questions to blow away the cobwebs that have built up in our minds over the weekend. When we are finished, we swap tests and correct them with a red biro while Beanpole mumbles out the answers. The most important lesson to learn in his class is to not involve him in any unnecessary work.

Beanpole wears an old jacket, a shirt that's never seen an iron, pants that look like he slept in them, and battered, dirty shoes. Mondays don't suit him.

Then again neither do Tuesdays, Wednesdays or Thursdays. Friday afternoons he is almost jolly, which is worse.

This morning, his bloodshot eyes, trembling hands and bad breath are a dead give-away. We all have dads and know what a hangover looks (and smells) like. Without raising his head from the desk he calls out:

"Harpo, my good man! How did you fare? What was your score on this beautiful morning?"

Beanpole knows Harpo's dad from the Horseman Pub, and always refers to him by his nickname.

"None, sir," Harpo mumbles.

Beanpole smirks. It is a joyful smirk; a jovial smirk, a jolly smirk. "None? That's beautiful. None!"

Harpo replies politely, knowing he is in serious trouble.

"Yes, sir."

Beanpole ignores him and continues. Beanpole likes to work the crowd and get the maximum attention before the real entertainment begins. The goal is to isolate the victim from the herd with laughter, to make the rest of the herd see that he must be sacrificed for them to survive.

"Nothing, zero, nought, big zero, zilch, big fat nothing. Will I go on?"

A shake of Harpo's head. "No thanks, sir."

The class becomes a chorus of nervous laughter. Beanpole sniffs the air as if smelling roses. The most beautiful sound to his ears is the sound of nervous laughter before the kill.

"How do you explain this extraordinary result?"

"I was up in Galway with my family, sir."

We all know that he's lying. I can't believe that Harpo went for such a massive lie. Fucking amateur.

"How about making a shorter journey on your own?" Beanpole quips, as he summons Harpo to the top of the class.

Harpo stalls for time. "Pardon, sir?"

Beanpole starts to wring his hands. This is not a good sign. "How about you get up here, now?"

We all laugh, like the spineless two-faced bastards that we are. I don't care about Harpo, my best friend, surviving an ordeal with Beanpole. I have enough on my plate caring about me.

Harpo approaches the desk the way you would approach a vicious animal, knowing that you are going to get mauled. He carefully inches closer, dragging his feet, head, and heart up to the front of the class Harpo drops his eyes. We all smell the fear.

Beanpole lowers his voice. He doesn't want to spook the prey once it is within striking distance. "You did not get one correct answer. What am I to do with you?"

"Sorry, sir. I was up in Galway."

Beanpole straightens himself.

"That's interesting, very interesting. When did ye all go on this magical trip to Galway?"

"Saturday, sir."

Beanpole rises from his seat. He towers over Harpo.

"Does your dad have a twin brother?"

Harpo looks confused. "What, sir?"

"A twin brother, who happens to be identical to him?" Beanpole roars.

Admitting guilt is worse than lying. Harpo gulps three or four times, then shakes his head. Walking around to Harpo's blind side, Beanpole causally remarks.

"Well, in that case it must be your dad I saw in the pub on Saturday. He hardly was in Galway and in the Horseman at the same time, was he?"

Harpo has nowhere to hide. Beanpole is closing in for the kill.

"Sorry, sir," says Harpo hanging his head.

Beanpole points out the window. "See that bird out in the schoolyard?"

Harpo looks up. "Yes, sir."

Beanpole fucking drags me into it. Pointing at me, he asks, "Fin my little pet, kindly inform us what kind of a bird that is? Your dad breeds those flying rats, so you should know."

Before I can reply, 'Chaffinch' Beanpole's right palm connects with Harpo's face. None of us see it coming, especially not Harpo. We were all busy watching the chaffinch. Harpo collapses on his knees, taking all of us with him. There for the grace of God and all that!

"Get up!" Beanpole roars. Harpo can't. He is too dazed. His eyes strain to focus. Getting annoyed Beanpole roars even louder. "Get up!"

Harpo uses Beanpole's desk to lever himself up. Climbing an invisible ladder of pain, he slowly rises. We all see the bloodied nose and watery eyes.

Harpo wipes the snot and blood on his cheap grey pants. He stands there staring at his hands. None of us are laughing. None of us move. None of us knows what to do. All of us are ashamed.

Beanpole sends Harpo straight out to the toilet to clean up, telling him to take his time. Inflicting misery has given Beanpole his much-needed fix. The aftermath, especially the crying annoys him. He doesn't need that carry-on in his class. The chase is over, the dead animal's body has been removed. We go back to whatever normal is supposed to be. I watch the Chaffinch as he flies away.

My history with Beanpole started back when Paul was in his class, way before he ever taught me. Paul told me that Beanpole insulted and bullied him regularly when he was a pupil of his. He'd called Paul a 'Sissy' or a 'Mummy's Boy', which was fucked up as our mum was dead. When Paul didn't stand up for himself in the yard Beanpole would leave the bully off scot-free. Most boys fight in the schoolyard. Paul doesn't. He has no interest in the animal side of being a boy. The need to prove your worth by picking on a weaker person never once crossed Paul's mind. Watching the other boys form a circle and shouting, 'Fight! Fight! Fight!' made him sick to the core. Beanpole was right. Paul was a 'Sissy'.

Paul's first encounter with Beanpole, occurred the week he joined his class. Paul was standing in the yard, minding his own business, eating his crisps, when a foot came up and kicked his hands. The bag of crisps went flying and landed to a chorus of laughter. No one tried to help him as the bully continued with three or four punches on the side of his head. Instead, everyone cheered. Paul bent over to protect himself, only to receive countless kicks. The cheering got louder and louder. Then it stopped and Paul could hear boys running away. Paul looked up to see Beanpole smirking. He pointed at the crisps all over the floor and told Paul to clean up his mess. Paul tried to protest, but Beanpole didn't have the slightest interest in anything Paul had to say, though he'd clearly witnessed the attack. He just turned and walked away.

My first day with Beanpole was one of the worst days of my life. Six times those long arms shoved hard hands against my back and head. He kept putting me down in front of the whole class, trying to provoke me. I wouldn't shed one tear for the fucking bastard, not a drop. If my queer for a brother could take the pain, then I had too as well. I did cry, but only when I was walking home with Harpo. He kept reassuring me that things would get better, just don't react. I didn't react and things just got worse. In a twisted way I began to despise Harpo at school. He could handle the constant aggression, whereas I found it all too hard to digest.

One night at home with Granny it all became too much. I broke down sobbing and told her. She listened and listened and held me while I sobbed uncontrollably. Then she made me a milky cup of coffee and said not to worry, that everything would be okay. Like a class 'A' dipshit I believed her. That night for the first time in ages I slept soundly.

The next morning, she kissed my cheeks, as I ate my cornflakes. Smoking a cigarette an inch away from me, she wheezed. "You should have seen his fucking face, the long string of piss. He didn't know what to do! The whole bar didn't have a fucking clue how to react."

"What did you do, Granny?" I asked. I pushed away the bowl. A sick feeling was starting in my stomach.

"Well, when you and Paul were asleep last night, I took a walk down to the Horseman. It's a busy fucking place for a Tuesday night. There were a lot of lucky women in Cork last night, getting a break from the depressing bastards sitting in that shithole. Our maggot of a friend Beanpole was there, watching the soccer. I bought two pints of stout, went over to his table and thanked him for teaching both you and Paul. I told him that there was a pint from each of ye. Then I fucked the two pints over his head, which wasn't easy. Even with that pile of shit sitting down, I could barely reach over his fucking head. The owner barred me, but I don't give a shit. It's not like I want to go back down there."

"Granny he will kill me. Honestly, he will kill me," I moaned, hanging my head.

Granny dismissed me, as she took another drag. "Get the fuck out of it. Kill you? I told that prick that if he ever touches you or Paul again it won't be fucking two pints of black stout. It will be two cups of boiling black coffee. Don't be worrying. The asshole got the message, loud and fucking clear. You know all the other assholes in there got the message as well, including that rat of a Father of yours. Over in some corner like a sex mad fucking pervert with some whore. I don't know where the fuck he finds them, under some stone. Yeah, a whore stone, ha-ha."

Beanpole is teaching us History. None of us are listening, except for Coleman who has an arse licking expression on his face, like he's really interested.

"Today we are going to discuss The Battle of Stalingrad. Page fifty. At this time, in 1942, Hitler controlled nearly all of Europe. All the good bits anyway! Which was an amazing feat for a country the size of Germany. Britain's Empire was a mishmash of third world countries. The only real problems the British army encountered were climate, landmass, diet and the odd Zulu or Afghan rebel. No denying it lads, the Germans are up there with the Romans in terms of having the ultimate killing machine. Any country can have an army, like those useless French and Italians. My God, those sneaky, slimy two-faced Italians sure left the Germans down when the Allies landed in Sicily. Madness it was. Pure undiluted madness." Beanpole walks up and down in front of the class as he continues his rant. "The Germans defending the island kept running into Italian troops fleeing the fighting. The Italians actually hid in their own country! In lots of ways the Germans not only equalled the Romans, but they also bettered them."

Coleman raises his hand. The fucking dope will never learn that you can't impress Beanpole. Even if your dad fought in Stalingrad, was a Luftwaffe pilot, had an Iron Cross, knew Rommel, and hid in the bunker with Hitler, Beanpole won't be impressed.

"What now Coleman? Make it quick."

Coleman stands and mumbles like a trapped bumble bee.

"You said British third world countries, Sir. The British ruled us too, Sir. Wouldn't that make us a third world country as well?"

Beanpole wipes his wrinkly, white face with his wrinkly, white hands.

"Are you winding me up Coleman? Are you? Was Ireland a third world country? We are one of the oldest races of people in the world. We were building New Grange long before the Egyptians ever started building the pyramids."

Coleman has touched a raw nerve. Beanpole turns even whiter. I decide to wind him up some more. Despite the excitement with Harpo, I am very bored.

"Sir, didn't we have a famine like a lot of African countries we collect for during Lent?" I ask without raising my hand.

Beanpole squints at me and then puts on his girly voice that he only uses when addressing me.

"The famine was caused by the Brits taking food out of Ireland to Britain, to feed the Prods."

Coleman leaps back in, panicking that his point is being hijacked. He moved to our class three months ago because his class was overfull. They picked the first name on the class roll sheet. It was 'C', it was Coleman. "Sorry, sir, but didn't—"

Beanpole cuts him off. "Sorry for what exactly Coleman? You and Princess Fin here are disrespecting the heroes of 1916: Pearse, Connolly, Clarke…" Beanpole waves his arms around the room, as if they were all right here in class with us. "I will make life a misery for any boy that disrespects this great land of ours, dripping in culture and the blood of heroes past and present! Michael Collins, our true saviour, died for you lot!"

Coleman won't leave it alone. A bit of old-fashioned ass licking is called for. Coleman's dad drinks with Beanpole in the Horseman pub. They're old college buddies. Maybe that's why Coleman thinks he's safe. Or maybe he just has a death wish.

"Sir why are some of the Germans in black uniforms and some in grey on page fifty?" he asks sweetly.

Beanpole grins. "Mother of God, finally a good question!" Praise from Beanpole is like watching a dog wag his tail before ripping your arm off. "A miracle someone asked a relevant question. Well done!"

The door opens. Harpo is back, his pants wet where he attempted in vain to wash out the blood. No one looks at him. He doesn't want to look at us either. Beanpole ignores him as he shuffles back to his desk.

"Black is a nasty colour used to frighten people. It's a colour to hide behind. Everyone in the group appears the same in black. The individual melts into the background. When people saw these uniforms, they knew death and misery weren't far behind. Those SS soldiers brought the biggest armies to their knees."

All that is missing is Wagner playing in the background and flowers thrown at a victorious Beanpole, saluting the class. A soft knock rings out. Without skipping a beat Beanpole calls, "Come in."

It's Father Collins, dressed in black like one of Hitler's henchmen. Beanpole leaps up and holds the door open as Fr. Collins marches in. Kissing ass doesn't come easy to Beanpole. It is awkward, forced and unpleasant to watch. They whisper together like Hitler and Himmler discussing the troops. Boys start chatting as we enjoy this small interlude from the constant threat of death.

"Quiet please, boys," says Beanpole calmly.

The class goes graveyard. Beanpole's rare use of manners stuns us all into silence. We all know what is coming. It's a regular farce we all perform together. Fr. Collins comes in and casts out an easy question across the classroom. Beanpole tries to pick a safe pair of hands to catch it. Question asked. Question answered. Farce over.

Fr Collins' eyes dance around the room. I try and make myself invisible. Fr Collins and I have a colourful history. It's actually more like Fr Collins and Granny, but I get caught in the crossfire. Just last week Granny and I were walking through town when Fr Collins appeared out of thin air. It must be the black clothes. They make him hard to spot. Anyway, he makes chit chat with Granny and then asks her if she reading the bible with me? Granny nearly choked on her cigarette and snapped back:

"He's getting too big for fairy tales now, Father. Thanks anyway."

Fr Collins' eyes roam the classroom. Clapping his hands to get the crowd warmed up he asks, "Who here would like to tell me what yesterday's sermon was all about?"

Harpo grabs his attention before Beanpole can pick someone else.

"You! The Lucey boy! Harpo, isn't it?" Fr Collins actually thinks that Harpo is his real name. We all gently snigger.

Still a bit dazed from Beanpoles right hook, Harpo springs to his feet, and begins to ramble around, and around and around in circles.

"Yesterday's sermon was the loaves and fishes. Christ led the people up the hill. Or did they just follow him? Maybe they all arranged to meet somewhere first? Anyway, they didn't have any food. Well, they had a small bit. There was some loaves and fishes, but not enough for everyone. The people begged Christ to feed them. He wouldn't at first, which confused me. Why didn't he want to feed them? They kept begging him and it was doing his head in. So he got the apostles to round up all the food. Then Christ blessed the food and…"

Harpo stops talking. He hasn't a clue where he is. His eyes are fixed firmly on Beanpole. Fr. Collins stands there staring at a spot on the floor by Beanpole's desk. The silence jerks him back to reality. "Good boy, do you have any questions about that sermon?"

This is a cue to shut the fuck up and sit down. Harpo can't read cues.

"Yes, Father. I was wondering how did they gut all those fish? They didn't have knives! There must have been some smell! When my dad comes home from fishing his hands smell of fish for days. My sisters May and June go mad. They hate the smell. It drives them potty. Dad says when he drives them mad it's not a long journey, because they are nearly there already. Petrol! My dad washes his hands in petrol to try to get rid of the smell. There wouldn't be much petrol around back in Christ's days, Father!"

Harpo wipes a tiny drop of blood from his nose. There are a couple more drops of blood on his desk. He is talking shit for Ireland.

"Very interesting," says Beanpole, his eyes promising a lifetime of beatings.

Fr. Collins sees that Harpo isn't right and goes back to staring at the floor. Harpo sits down, then stands back up. He sways a bit and has to steady himself on the desk. Then he raises his hand. Maybe he's completely lost his mind?

"Father," he says, "how did they cook all these fish? Another miracle would have been needed for all the wood for the fires. I know because, when I go camping with my dad, building a fire isn't easy. You need a lot of small twigs first. Then you slowly build it up with bigger sticks. Not everyone can light a fire, Father. It's an art, a dying art. It's a hard trade to learn especially if you haven't got matches. A lighter makes it so much easier, but if my dad caught me with a lighter he would kill me. They really…"

Beanpole knows that this is getting out of hand. He cuts Harpo off with a wave of his hand. "Thank you, Harpo. Sit back down. Good boy. Well done."

Harpo wobbles and falls into his chair. I am struck dumb. Fishing? Campfires? It's all complete and utter bullshit. Harpo's dad never brought him further than the front fucking gate. Beanpole looks at Harpo like he was deserting the frontline at Stalingrad. A bullet in the head would be too good for him. We wait as Fr. Collins raises his eyes slowly from the floor.

"Mr Higgins did you enjoy chatty young Harpo's description of yesterday's sermon?"

"Yes, Father, it was most enjoyable." Beanpole shines like a star.

"You heard all about the loaves and fishes too?" Fr Collins beams back.

"Yes, Father."

"Then you and young Harpo here must belong to some other Catholic Church. Because the sermon I gave yesterday, and all Catholic Churches gave yesterday, was The Ten Lepers."

Blood and alcohol drain from Beanpole's face. Someone is going to pay for this. I figure that someone will be Harpo. Fr. Collins points a firm finger at the floor. "Is that blood Mr Higgins?"

Beanpole cast an eye over the spot with a false shrug of surprise. "Sorry, Father?"

Fr Collins digs his heels in. "Right there, blood."

Beanpole isn't going to start lying to a priest about an obvious fresh blood stain on the floor. He shakes his head in amazement, like it just fell from the sky.

"Make sure it is cleaned up Mr Higgins. I don't expect to be greeted with blood stains on the floor. It is a given that the boys are treated with respect. If any foul play comes to light in this or any other classroom the school board will demand explanations. Do I make myself clearly understood?"

Beanpole nods, "Yes, Father."

Nazi fighting Nazi isn't pretty. But Hitler left Himmler off the hook in front of us all. Why didn't Fr. Collins ask whose blood it was? I guess Hitler didn't care what Himmler was up to as long as he wasn't dragged into it one way or another. Fr. Collins is just covering his ass. Beanpole smirks back at him as he holds the door open to release Fr. Collins from any more responsibility. There's still plenty of fighting to be done in Stalingrad, plenty more innocent soldiers to be sacrificed.

Fr Collins raises his right hand. We stand. He blesses us, and then, like the Holy Ghost, he vanishes. Beanpole is still very much here. Staring at Harpo he growls, "Up here. Now." Beanpole is vexed. A baffled and disorientated Harpo struggles to find something, anything besides Beanpole to focus on as he shuffles back to the gallows. Beanpole leans right into Harpo's face, "Where's all the chat now? Well! Where is it?"

A large wiry hand shoots and takes a generous helping of foxy hair. Harpo is dragged over to the spot where his blood stain is. "Clean it up. We will have a proper chat when Fr. Collin's is gone from the school."

Chapter Three
Paying to Be Pitied

I am sitting, drinking tea, and wolfing down chocolate biscuits while Granny sucks all the cancer out of one cigarette after another. My mouth is in overdrive. Biscuit after biscuit is plucked out of the gleaming gold tin. After about ten biscuits I call it a day. It's important to know your limitations when it comes to chocolate. Then again, fuck it! I grab two biscuits wrapped in blue foil. They must be good if they are that fancy.

This place is really nice. No money spared. All the mod cons, like those trendy lights under the cupboards to brighten up the worktops. There are gold fittings on everything: Handles, knobs, switches, hinges, even the screws. There is definitely a gold theme. I am bored, really bored, and I need to go for a leak.

Earlier, when I came home at seven o clock, Granny instructed me to wash my hands, face, brush my teeth and go to the bathroom. Rushing I did only the first three. Granny has her nails varnished and wears matching lipstick. This type of grooming means that we're off somewhere important. She never tells me where we're going. God forbid I might have something else to do instead of tagging along with her. I don't, but the principle remains the same. Going somewhere with Granny is like death itself. You can't plan it. It just happens.

We trotted for the seven-thirty bus. We only went five stops, before we got off. Granny then informed me that I might not be allowed into the room with her. I had no idea what she meant until we got into the house. Susan, the fortune teller, lives in a normal house just like the rest of us, so it's not obvious. I wonder if she knew that she would live here when she was a kid? Dad would freak if he knew where we were.

Unwrapping the blue foil, I am not disappointed. This is a serious biscuit. I throw the foil into the overflowing ashtray and slip the second one into my pocket for later. There is only one rule when going out with Granny – shut the fuck up. She detests small talk or people over-hearing her business. If I were mute, she would be the happiest person in the world.

My stomach feels bloated from too much tea and biscuits. My ass is numb from sitting for an hour. I really need to pee. Still, we wait. Granny is really nervous. When she is stressed out, she constantly adjusts her jewellery. Gold rings are twisted around fingers worked to the bone. More comfort is found in the crucifix dangling from her neck. Her lips move and I realise that she is praying. I don't think I've ever heard Granny pray out loud. Her love of Christ is strictly private. She gently rubs a thumb over Christ's body as she says the words to herself. If Christ ever returns, I wonder if he'll want to see all these crosses everywhere. Hadn't he enough of crosses the first time around? Please God, deliver me to a bathroom.

A door slowly opens, and a low voice calls out, "Next." To my utter amazement Granny squeezes my hand and brings me in with her. The room is a huge disappointment. It's just a normal front room like anyone else's (except for Harpo's cesspit). A really voluptuous woman beckons us to a large round table. This must be Susan. She is all smiles as Granny slips her some notes. Her chest is fucking massive. I thought it couldn't get better after the chocolate biscuits, but it did literally big time. Her huge breasts are perfectly rounded and rest on her left arm as if she is holding them back.

Granny's palm is lit by a lamp hanging about two feet over the table. Susan, the fortune teller with the giant chest, examines the lines and wrinkles like someone who has all the time in the world. The whole scene is presided over by a picture of the Sacred Heart. Even in our most sinful of practices we call upon Christ to protect us.

This is getting serious. I really need to go for a leak, but I can't miss a second of this. Susan leans into Granny and inquires, "So, Mrs Mulcahy, how are you?"

Granny does her best to impress and leaves the bad language outside in the street. "Not too bad, Susan love. Not too bad."

I feel the whole string section of the London Philharmonic Orchestra start warming up. Susan shakes her head sadly. She exchanges a glance with Granny, and they both shake their heads at the tragedy of life.

"Are you suffering Mrs Mulcahy?" asks Susan. She sighs heavily, which lifts her breasts for a second, before they settle back on their perch. "I understand. I have pains in places you don't want to know!"

A cold shiver jerks my spine. Not women problems! Please God no! I have to stop staring at her chest as her head swings in my direction. "Is this one of your boys?"

She's meant to be a professional who is getting well paid to tell the future. Did she think Granny just picked me up off the street on the way over here? This is proving to be way better than sitting at home watching TV. Granny answers as if I'm not there.

"Yes, Susan, love. Fin is my daughter's youngest. He is my rock. I don't know where I would be without him. I've reared him as my own since my darling daughter was robbed from me. He only got to spend a couple of hours with his mum after he was born. It's very, very sad."

Looks of pity are bought and sold. The currency of suffering and misery is all that old women have to swap and trade. Susan's eyes peer into Granny's palm; in and past the cracks, wrinkles and small scars.

"Mrs Mulcahy, are you under a lot of pressure?"

I don't know what pressure Granny is under, but the pressure on my bladder is starting to be a problem.

"Yes Susan, love. I am. But as my late husband used to say: Pressure is for tyres. Please, call me by my first name—"

Completely ignoring what Granny just said, Susan cuts back in. "You need to take time for yourself, Mrs Mulcahy. You have to slow down. There are only so many hours in a day."

The circle of 'Sure, God love us!' bullshit is up and running and Granny is sprinting out ahead of Susan. "Susan, I try, love. I really do. But taking care of my boys isn't easy."

"Mrs Mulcahy, I can only imagine." Susan murmurs, "Only imagine."

Susan's eyes hunt down the future skin cell by skin cell. Something seems to have caught her attention and she isn't letting go. Her forefinger cast a long meandering line up and down Granny's palm. "Mrs Mulcahy, I have news for you and lots of it. You know that I can only tell you what I see. It's up to you to live it."

Even at my age I understand that if you pay someone to tell your future, you're not going to start arguing about it. This could be over soon. My legs cut into each other as I try to block the need to pee. Susan adjusts her breasts to get more comfortable, for which I am very grateful. Granny speaks. She sounds a bit scared. "I understand, Susan. I have to be brave."

Susan sighs again, and then speaks loud and clear. "There is a man coming into your life. He is known to you and you to him. There is a lot of sadness in his heart: Too many women, too much money and too much of the demon drink. Now he is clean of the sins of the flesh. He is a changed man. A heart of light now beats where once a blackened heart was. His intentions are good and holy. When you meet him, it will rain. The rain will be lashing, but you won't feel a drop of it. Remember that in life there are two types of people, those who only live the moment and those who actually feel the moment. Learn to feel the moments again, Mrs Mulcahy."

Granny looks bemused. Without an ounce of shame she says, "Susan, love? I have one quick question. It's about the sins of the flesh part and that he's changed. Do you mean that he won't want me that way? It won't be much of a relationship without a bit of the other. I'm only human."

My body switches from wanting to go for a leak to nearly vomiting. This is too much information. Susan looks embarrassed. She gives a quick glance in my direction, and then returns to Granny's palm. "If there is love then the physical side will be just as fruitful."

Then, with no warning, Susan breaks down crying. Granny shrugs at me. We don't know what to do. Susan sobs unashamedly. Then she reaches for a nearby box of tissues. I smell a set-up. Everything is too perfect. The tissues are a little too handy.

Granny looks worried. "Are you okay, Susan?"

Susan sniffs, and swiftly gets back on track. "Yes thank you, Mrs Mulcahy."

"What's wrong, love?" asks Granny.

"Sometimes when I see it the future, it frightens me."

This is getting tiring. My bladder is bursting. Toilet, please God.

"This man Mrs Mulcahy, you know him from your past. He will love you through thick and thin. At times you might not be able to understand or see his love for what it is. Money isn't a problem to him. He's doesn't seem to need it. Very shortly you will be reunited. You will never ever meet a person with so much love for you. But be careful. Don't go rushing into the arms of the first man who beckons you. You are a great catch, Mrs Mulcahy. An exceptional catch, so be careful. Treat him right and return his love unconditionally. There is a lot of love bottled up inside of you. Don't waste it. Now that's the good news. You paid your money, so I am obliged to share the bad news as well. Otherwise, it wouldn't be honest." The mention of bad news gets both Granny's and my undivided attention.

"Suffering will visit you and have no pity. Darker nights will be visited by darker days. You have to be strong. This man will help you deal with it. Accept him, for it will be too much on your own. Black moods will bring on blacker moods. A lighting candle will fall, and a beautiful flame will suffer and die. A candle is only alive when the flame is burning. The flame dancing in the darkness, licking the air, casting light onto everything it touches. Be brave. Love God and put your trust in him. The tragic death of a loved one is near."

The pressing need to go for a leak disappears. The bit about candles dying has me freaked. Without asking Susan pulls my hand up onto the table. Thankfully, it's clean. She reads the faint lines quickly. "It's not him. He is as strong as a horse mentally and physically."

Granny looks relieved. "Thank God for that, Susan. If anything happened to Fin, I would be lost forever. He's my baby. But who could it be?"

Susan shrugs. "Mrs Mulcahy, I don't know."

Granny sits in silence, taking it all in. I'm still dying to have a leak. It distracts me from the other dying. Susan looks at me. It makes me feel uneasy.

"Fin, isn't it?" She waits for my nod, then continues. "The fallen candle, you will see it fall but not pick it up."

"Susan, love, what does that mean?" asks Granny.

Susan ignores her. She rubs her thumb into my palm as her voice rises loud and clear. She focuses on my eyes and won't leave go of my hand. "Fin, you hide your love for music out of sight. You sleep over your love of music. Your love of music will get you into trouble."

I am terrified. Granny is baffled. I am so scared that a tiny warm trickle of pee burst loose. How does she know? Did the lines on my palm tell her that I have a secret stash of robbed music tapes?

"Susan love, I was following pretty much everything till the music part," mumbles Granny.

Susan lets go of my palm and dismisses her with a wave of her hand. "Don't worry Mrs Mulcahy. Fin knows what I mean and that's all that matters. Isn't that right Fin?"

I nod like a condemned man. After some parting chit chat, we head out the door. I walk back to the bus-stop like a zombie. There are some bushes, so I finally go for a pee while Granny takes lookout. She's not very good at it, because just as I'm finishing two figures catch my eye. May and June are anchored to the spot staring at me. They saw enough of this shit at home but seeing me peeing seemed to shock them into silence. I don't even have time to shake.

The bus journey home is like a trip into the unknown. Granny sits, trying to figure out how to handle all the happiness and sorrow that is coming. I settle back in my seat and watch the condensation roll down the bus window. Tiny drops roll into bigger drops and fall on the thick rubber on the edge of the glass. It's not right to mess with the future but saying it to Granny would be like throwing salt on an open wound. She loves me more than anyone else in the whole world. My granny is my mum. Anything my brother gets, I get better. Bigger birthday parties, Christmas presents, more pocket money and above all the most precious thing to Granny, time. I get more time with Granny. Mind you, if I do something bad, she'll beat me harder than she ever hit my brother. After smacking me Granny won't talk to me for days. She resents me for making her punish me. The punishment is to show the world that Granny isn't weakened by love. Love makes Granny stronger. I wonder what will happen when Mr Wonderful comes along. Will I be left behind at home? No one ever speaks about Granny's dead husband. Not even Granny. Who was he? What was he? Where did he come from? Why did he go? I don't even know where he's buried. Dad's parents are long dead. Both died in their forties. They are never spoken about either. 'Once dead soon forgotten', should be our family motto.

As the bus nears home, I start feeling angry. I didn't ask for my palm to be read. I feel cheated and used. Not once were my feelings taken into account. Not once was I asked how I felt. Not even about the fallen candle and dying. I will know the person as well as Granny, so it will affect me as much as her. Especially since Susan said I will be around when it falls. Now I have to deal with all this bullshit that I didn't ask for.

The next few weeks are strange for Granny and me. Everyone becomes a candidate for sudden death or sudden love. Trips to the hairdressers are followed by trips to the clothes shop. New glasses with matching sunglasses are bought. She even drags me through the Lingerie section of Dunne's. I am totally mortified that someone will see me. Granny used to look like she just got out of bed all day. It was a look perfected over the years by not giving a damn about what people thought of her looks. Things have changed. Now she looks like she's going out somewhere important all the time. I guess she wants to be ready when Mr Wonderful makes his appearance. All this getting ready takes time. Granny neglects the house. She only does a quick tidy now and then, and meals are just as quick and uninspired.

Granny inspects every man she meets for clues that he might be the one Susan saw in her palm. A man from the gas board comes to fix our meter. He is a tall man who's seen better days. He checks out our meter and enjoys the best tea and chocolate biscuits money can buy. As he scrambles amongst the mountain of crap under the stairs, Granny quizzes him about his life. He speaks with love and pride about his wife and kids. Granny grabs the chocolate biscuits off the plate and returns them to the tin. No point in wasting Cadbury's finest on a married man, especially on a happily married man.

The same thing happens when our gutters need cleaning. The gutter man seems to fit the bill. He is grey haired and single. He also speaks well, which is a huge bonus with Granny. Then again, he speaks so much that Granny can't get a word in, so she quickly loses interest. The biscuits are put back in the tin and the search continues.

Paul and Dad click that something is seriously afoot but can't put their fingers on it. They have other fish to fry. Granny isn't the only one acting strange. Paul has started to go missing every Saturday and Sunday, only surfacing for meals. Dad tries his best to find out where he's going but fails. Whatever Paul is up to, he's keeping it to himself.

Mr Wonderful never appears and Granny slowly sinks back into domestic bliss. I am happy that once again, the house is clean. The laundry is ironed, and dinners are on time and delicious. I am also happy to be the centre of Granny's attention again, even when it means going into to town to get my hair cut. It's better than following Granny around the lingerie section.

I am sitting in the barber's chair when I spot a tramp's reflection, staring at mine through the window. His weather-beaten face inches closer to the glass. His dark hairy hands scratch under his tee-shirt. I feel extremely uncomfortable. It takes me forever to get the courage to look back. When I do, I realise that he isn't staring at me, he is staring at Granny. What the fuck does he want? He steps back and just stands there waiting. He is still there when we leave the shop.

Granny stops and looks at him, as if waiting for him to ask her for directions or something. The tramp smiles and gives a little shake of his head.

"I'm sorry, Missus. You remind me of a lady I once knew," he says in a rough country accent. He looks her up and down. Granny stands there and says nothing. "Exactly like her. Sorry for troubling you."

I tug at Granny's sleeve, and she turns and shuffles a few yards up the street. I want to get away from the tramp. Suddenly, she shakes me off and walks back to him.

"Conor? Is that you? I don't believe it! How are things with you?"

That sounds like the dumbest fucking question ever asked. He looks like he's living on the street. I would throw out a wild guess and say things were pretty shite. Before he can answer, Granny puts her arms around him and hugs him. He just stands there smiling. I pray for the ground to please open up and swallow me. He finally hugs her back and they look like they'll never let each other go, despite the constant current of people walking past. As I step back and lean against a wall, I feel the first drops of rain begin to fall.

Chapter Four
Timmy the Bull

There's nowhere to hide. The sun seems to know every time I swap seats that I'm trying to hide from it. Sitting directly beneath a massive pane of glass doesn't help. Granny and I sit quietly, waiting to see Conor. He lives with other homeless men in a huge building run by a religious order. Every morning all the homeless have to leave the building by ten and aren't allowed back in till six in the evening. I know all this because I read it on a sign straight across from where we sit. There are signs everywhere. They plaster the walls: Big black and white signs warning people not to smoke, drop litter, loiter, make noise, to respect each other, along with mealtimes, and visiting times. My favourite sign is the one which reads 'No female visitors after 8 pm'. Thank God for that. It means that we won't be stuck here all night.

It's ten past six on an August evening, one week since we bumped into Conor. Granny insisted we come here to meet him, as out on the street would be very impersonal. A homemade fruitcake, wrapped in countless layers of tin foil rests on Granny's knees. She wrapped it up so well it was like she was afraid the cake would escape. Hope he likes fruitcake – being one himself.

The urge to scratch is overwhelming. I am covered in imaginary itches. A large Nun stands and watches me scratch. It seems to annoy her.

"Be careful that young fella doesn't bring anything in here with him," she says to Granny, who thankfully ignores her.

Nearly everyone who staggers past us stinks of drink. When they see us, they produce a token 'Hello' like we might be here to visit them; like we might be a long-lost relative who wants them back in their lives. As soon as they realise that we're not there for them, they vanish down a corridor. One of the signs proclaims, 'No drink permitted'. I figure this means that they are not permitted to carry drink in a bottle, but it's okay to carry it in your bloodstream. This place is full of people who look like they would rob your eyeballs and come back for the brows.

Conor strolls in, acting like he works here instead of being a lodger. There isn't any smell of drink off his breath. Granny leaps up and gives him a kiss on his weather-beaten cheek. A schoolgirl grin appears as she hands him the cake. Conor thanks her and says that he will share it with everyone. That's the Christian thing to do. Granny looks impressed.

Conor asks me to do him a favour as Granny disappears with the nun to cut up the cake. We slip out a side door and find ourselves under a massive palm tree in a small garden. It's really peaceful and quiet. He hands me a blue biro and plastic change bags from the bank.

"Would you mind helping me count out today's earnings? Put the coins into the right bags and write the amount on each bag. Thanks kid."

With a nod I sit down next to him and get comfortable. At least this keeps me away from all the riff raff and nut jobs.

I start to count out the one, two, five, ten and fifty pence pieces. Conor sits humming to himself, like I'm not there. Then he speaks, and a thick country accent fills the air.

"Never trust a chicken. Never boy."

Our eyes meet and I wonder what type of a fucking nutter I'm dealing with? My head stays bowed as I count the coins.

"Chickens are busy little nobodies, who spend the day waltzing around spying on each other. You don't know where they have been, and more importantly, who they have been talking to. They're always trouble."

He picks a few blades of grass and plays with them. Is he actually talking to me? This is getting a bit uncomfortable. Then again, he's not checking my counting. He seems totally uninterested.

"Never let a horse drive your car. Their blinkers cause them to only drive in straight lines. That's deadly on the road to Mallow. There are fifty bends on the road on the way up to Mallow, but only forty-nine on the way back. I know because I've counted. You can't talk to a horse. It's a waste of time. They have a blinkered outlook on life. They know it all. Best you stay clear of horses boy."

He is definitely talking to me, the fucking nutter. Head down I write amounts of money on each bag. I look up and realise that he's not playing with grass. He's making a long daisy chain.

"Never ask a cow for directions, no matter how lost you are," he continues. "They don't know their right udder from their left. You being a city boy wouldn't know what udder means. It's a tit boy, their udders are their tits. You get involved with cows and you're fucked. Fucked I tell you. Their possessive and menacing boyfriends will flatten you down into the ground. I have seen a bull kill."

Now he has my undivided attention. This story sounds genuine.

"Timmy was a gentle bull. We hand reared him, and he used to follow us around the farmyard like a puppy. Timmy would lick the molasses off your hand. He was big and beautiful with a pure black coat, like a water buffalo. He was as affectionate as any dog."

Not wanting to miss a word I put all the bags of money on my lap. He senses he had my interest and continues.

"He had a copper ring in his nose. We got it from Buddies Co-op. If a bull charges, the ring will stop him dead in his tracks. Dad always said we would get our money back from Timmy a hundred-fold because he was so pure breed. He was right. My dad was always right. Farmers from all over North Cork paid a pretty penny to have Timmy service their cows."

He checks to see if I am following. I say nothing.

"By service I mean, riding, you understand?" He adds with a wink.

I nod.

"Timmy was our pot of gold. Dad got a new Massey Ferguson and Mum got a second-hand car. We were the first people in our parish to get a television, would you believe it! Summer was his busiest time. Every day a different truck collected Timmy to fuck the brains out of as many cows as he could. Boy, did he enjoy it! Dad would have to beat cows into the back of the trucks, whereas Timmy bolted straight up the ramp. He knew the score, all right!"

The daisy chain is getting longer. His massive thick fingers work like a jeweller, piecing together the delicate thread-like stems.

"It was a Saturday night. A wind picked up that evening, and by nightfall the rain was falling like marbles. Thunder and lightning fought the heavens. You couldn't sleep through any of that. Our three sheep dogs pissed all over the back-kitchen floor with fright. As the night went on the storm got heavier. Our yard was one big pool of water by midnight. That's when we all heard a dreadful banging, like a huge door being slammed, over and over. My mum thought that it must be Timmy, afraid of all the noise. I ran and got Dad's raingear for him. Timmy paid all the bills, put food on the table and we were all fond of him." Hood pulled up, Dad followed the shelter of the farmhouse wall till he reached Timmy's shed. It was a collection of rubble. Timmy had knocked it right down. He weighed more than Mum's car and was well over six foot in height. Dad couldn't see Timmy in the darkness, but he could hear Timmy's chain rattling. He couldn't figure out where Timmy was until it was too late. There wasn't anywhere for Dad to hide, he was pinned in one corner of the yard with Timmy blocking his only escape route. Our sheep dogs sensed the danger and ran out barking and circling Timmy. With one kick Timmy killed Spot, our oldest sheepdog, clean dead.

"I didn't see Mum with the rifle, so the first shot was a surprise. Mum got Timmy behind the left leg. Sure, it only tickled him. We were all stuck at the window bawling and crying. The dogs were barking. Timmy was bellowing and the storm was howling and crackling with thunder and lightning. Taking aim with the .22 rifle, Mum waited for a flash of lightening to take a shot again. She missed and hit Dad's shoulder. Mum shot again, hitting Timmy in the nose."

He inspects his daisy chain as I hold my breath waiting for the rest of the story. Conor doesn't sound insane anymore.

"What was Mum to do? Dad was shot. Timmy was at the other end of the yard blocking the way back into the house."

Conor adds the last daisy to the chain. It is now a complete circle. He sounds upset.

"Mum was worried about our future, and it clouded her vision. If she killed Timmy, how would she pay the bills and feed a family of seven? Timmy should have been finished there and then. Sure. No farmer would want a crazy bull like that on their land. While Mum was deciding what to do, Timmy had his mind made up. He charged across the yard. You see, boy, the bull only does what the bull knows."

We all stopped watching after about twenty seconds. Timmy threw my poor beautiful mum across the yard again and again playing with her lifeless body. Nature is a whore! Mum fed that fucker by hand since he was five days old. His own mother turned on him. Maybe she sensed something wasn't right with him. Animals can see, smell and sense things that we can't. Maybe Timmy's mother after tens of thousands of generations knew that this calf wouldn't bring any good to the herd. Nature exists because nature is ruthless. That's why my mum was killed. She stood there thinking, Timmy stood there doing. Timmy didn't have a decision to make, my mum did.

Conor stops and looks off into the distance as if his mum is still lying dead in the yard. Then he sighs and continues.

"The following morning the Dairy truck driver pulled up and opened the gate to the yard. Spot lay with his tongue hanging out dead by the gate. Mum was in a lifeless ball by the old water pump. The two other dogs protected Dad, who had climbed up onto a piece of roof that was still standing. They wagged their tails in a frenzy of excitement when they saw help was near. The truck driver told the Guards that he thought there had been an explosion because of all the rubble. It was only when he spotted the rifle that he realised something out of the ordinary had taken place."

The sun was disappearing behind some buildings. Conor sat with the daisy chain resting on his lap.

"That rifle saved the driver's life. Seeing the rifle stopped him coming into the yard. He hopped back into his cab and drove the dairy truck back down the lane. That was the most frightening part. We were all hiding upstairs in case Timmy got into the house. The loss of our mother hadn't sunk in. We hadn't a clue where Dad was, but we did know that the Dairy truck had left."

Granny appears out of thin air. She's delighted with the daisy chain. Conor takes the bags of coins from my lap and offers me two quid for my work counting. Two quid is twice my pocket money. If he's trying to buy me it's working.

As I thank Conor, I can see Granny fill with pride. The Mad Mullah is nowhere in sight. She never curses around Conor. She smiles more and is way more relaxed. It's like a new woman has taken over her body. When we get home the Mad Mullah is back again, telling Dad lies about where we were, and complaining about the state of the house. It's like turning the key in the front door also turns a key inside her.

I'm dreaming that I am on the ferry to France. There is nonstop shouting. People are swaying with the sea. The warm weather only makes things worse. The toilets are full of people getting sick, throwing up everywhere. The stench is unbearable. There's no escaping the smell of puke. My mind keeps prodding me to wake up, so I do.

Above me Paul leans over the side of his bunk and heaves. My bunk gets most of it as he jumps off his bed and lands right next to me. His T-shirt, jeans and hands are covered in a greenish puke. So is my bed, the carpet and his record collection.

A light appears through the door and a large hand grabs Paul by the hair. Dad hauls him out and throws him into the shower. Granny is on the landing, protesting. She claims that it must be a stomach bug.

I look at her in disbelief. Paul has been missing nearly all day every weekend. It doesn't take a rocket scientist to figure out that he's up to no good. Realising that arguing Paul's corner is a waste of time, Granny starts to strip my bed. She then cleans the carpet, and put everything with puke on it, including Paul's records, into various buckets of water outside the backdoor to soak.

Paul is way too young to be getting pissed. Dad tells him that he isn't allowed out after six o'clock for a month. Paul pleads for a beating instead, but Dad says that he's too big to be hit.

This morning Granny gives me the nod to get washed, brush my teeth and go for a leak. It's been a week since we made the twenty-minute bus ride, and ten-minute walk to the homeless hostel. This time Conor is waiting for us in reception. Every time we meet him, he looks cleaner, or maybe I'm just getting used to him. After a few minutes of making small talk with Granny he politely asks me to help him bring some chairs down to the canteen. Granny finds that schoolgirl smile again as I helped Conor carry the chairs down the long corridor.

"I'm very impressed with you, boy," he says when we are alone.

I don't have any idea what Conor is on about.

"You're a class act alright. You have your Granny well fooled."

I look up to see his face darken.

"Robbing off a homeless person is fairly impressive alright."

My knee's turns to jelly. How does he know? Who told him? No one could have because I didn't tell anyone. Was he bluffing?

"How much did you rob?" he asks.

I notice that we are not in the canteen, but in a large, dark, storeroom. Conor has hands like shovels and shoulders that could carry the world. He could pack some punch. Why, oh why, did I steal from him? It must be force of fucking habit. I can't stop myself.

One of those massive hands grabs me by the hair. Conor pulls me up until I am standing on my tippy toes. It really hurts, but I won't cry. The last thing I need is to have to explain tears to Granny. Grinding his teeth, he whispers into my ear.

"Keep up the stealing, boy, and before too long you'll be in here with the rest of us. Your Granny led me to believe that you're something special. Ha! She never shuts up about you, you little, two-faced shit. Tell the truth kid. How much did you rob?"

"Three pounds and fifty pence," I reply.

My hair is pulled tighter. The honest approach isn't working out the way I expected. He seems angry that I gave in so quickly.

"Well, I hope you enjoyed it – you spoilt little brat. Think you are better than all of us in here? Don't you? Well surprise, surprise! You are only a few slip-ups from ending up in here with us. All you need is a run of bad luck. The smartest, wisest, most talented people end up under this roof, mostly through the actions of other people, but you kid will get in here all by yourself. Well done."

"Please Conor, can we be friends? It won't ever happen again."

He releases my hair, and my feet are back flat on the ground.

"No, Fin, we can't."

"Please, give me a second chance. Please, I'm begging you."

He shakes his head, then he chuckles to himself.

"I knew exactly how much money I gave you. When you are sitting there all day long begging, you don't have much else to do besides count the change. I knew you had robbed me. We have to go. By the way – your Granny has enough in life to deal with besides you being a thief! We are going to keep this between ourselves."

I nod. That suits me fine.

Chapter Five
It Burned Like Acid on Her Skin

The doorbell rings. I run to open the door and Auntie Mary prances into the hall, ignoring me, and looking her usual stuck-up self. She just can't be bothered making conversation with the likes of me unless she has to. Auntie Mary is a snob, plain and simple. No matter what is said she very rarely shows even the slightest bit of interest. She handles any news with false surprise, whether it's a death or a marriage. They are both just an inconvenience, as if she's been informed that there was a rat in her garage. She doesn't want to be dragged into anything that's beneath her. It's all too common for her.

She floats straight into the kitchen taking care not to touch anything. Walls, door handles, cups and especially the kids are all avoided like the plague. God knows what she might pick up off us. Auntie Mary is Dad's younger sister. It goes without saying that Granny and she are like chalk and cheese, with Granny obviously being the cheese, because it smells. Auntie Mary views everyone and everything like they're dirty and smelly. Years ago, at Dad's cousin's funeral she flatly refused to shake hands with any of the mourners. Auntie Peg, who was as old as the hills, unexpectedly hugged Auntie and she broke down sobbing. Auntie Mary was sobbing because Auntie Peg touched her, not because she was overcome with grief. Now she's standing in our kitchen on the spot where Dad bled after Granny stabbed him with the potato peeler. She must be on a mission, or she wouldn't be here.

Dad throws out a forced 'welcome', while Granny throws on the kettle. Granny isn't making tea for Auntie Mary. She's boiling water to soak her feet. She always soaks her feet when Auntie Mary calls around on a mission. Granny pulls her tights off, sprinkles some Radox into an old basin, and eases her bunions and pastry white skin into the hot water with little gasps of pain and pleasure. She started this to spook Auntie Mary so that she only stays the bare amount of time, but it's become like a mental trigger. One night Dad just mentioned Auntie Mary's name and Granny instinctively threw on the kettle to do her feet. Sometimes I think that maybe Auntie Mary is right about us being the great unwashed.

I'm not in the mood to sit and watch Granny light up one cigarette after another so as to blow more smoke over Auntie Mary as she soaks her feet. I slip out of the kitchen and take the stairs two at a time and flee to the sanctuary of the bathroom. It's the only place with any privacy in this house.

I sit on the toilet and think about how fucked up Auntie Mary's story is. I know how fucked up her story is because Granny told me the whole thing. Granny knows because everyone in Cork knows everyone else's story. Granny says that, "Cork city is big enough to get lost in, but small enough to be always found."

Granny said that Auntie Mary wasn't the brightest candle in the box growing up, but that she did have the most beautiful flame. Auntie Mary was not just the prettiest girl in her class. She was probably the prettiest girl in the whole school. Everything was going swimmingly until the entrance exams for college. Four times she did them, and four times she failed.

Auntie Mary ended up working full-time in the local petrol station. That's when the trouble began. Auntie Mary fell in love with the Deli counter. Staff had one free meal a day from the Deli – two if they worked overtime. The first meal was always a massive fry with all the trimmings, extra toast included. The second meal always consisted of chicken. Auntie Mary didn't care whether it was barbequed, roasted, stir fried, or sweet and sour. If it was chicken, she wanted to eat it. The pounds slowly crept on. People who saw her every day didn't take much notice, but school mates who hadn't seen her in a while had to adjust their eyes to make sure it was her. Horrified they would make small talk when paying Auntie Mary at the till, and just gawk at the size she had become.

Pounds became stones. Her self-confidence shrank in direct proportion to the weight. More and more she found herself wearing the same clothes because nothing else would fit. Depression crept in like an unwanted guest and refused to leave.

Mick worked in the garage out the back, repairing punctures. It was a soul-destroying job, which he did to pay his way through Night College. Mick was so easy going he could fall over. Nothing seemed to faze him or wind him up. One day he invited Aunty Mary out hill walking with his college club.

Reluctantly, she agreed. To her surprise she enjoyed both hill walking and Mick's company. Auntie Mary never missed one hiking trip for the rest of the College year and in doing so took the first steps in burning off the unwanted pounds.

Within six months she had lost three stone and gained an army of fans. By the following September she had only a stone to lose. Mick was so proud of her. He loved the ground she walked on.

As she lost weight, she took up tennis. Tennis became an obsession with Auntie Mary. She loved looking fantastic in her tennis whites and destroying her opponents. She joined the Hillside Lawn Tennis club and paid a small fortune taking lessons from a local semi-pro. Auntie Mary was living the dream. It was at this time that her voice changed. She began to speak with a higher tone. Certain words were dragged out for special emphasis when she had to make a point. The tone of her speech varied greatly depending on the subject matter. Granny said that Auntie Mary started speaking like she had something stuck up her ass.

As Auntie Mary got leaner and more popular, Mick's role became more and more blurred. Auntie Mary began to resent Mick for having loved such a fat cow. How could any man love what she had been? The nearer she got to her ideal weight the more she began to despise him. His love disgusted her. A real man worth his salt wouldn't be seen dead with the woman she used to be.

Dr Hughes was a prominent tennis club member. He had a collection of cars, including a three litre BMW that looked like it cost a fortune because it did. He was no oil painting, but he had education, money, and most importantly, his wife had passed away five years earlier. When Dr Hughes asked Auntie Mary out for a drink one night when she finished work, she let him wait for a whole five seconds before saying, 'yes'. She rushed home, picked out her favourite dress and phoned Mick to say that she was breaking up with him.

Her marriage to Dr Hughes was a quick affair. Dr Hughes' chances of fathering children were very slim, but that didn't bother Auntie Mary. In fact, she was delighted. No losing her figure, no selfish brats to rear and all the time in the world for herself.

The wedding was a no expense spared affair with the best food and drink money could buy, freely available to the 250 guests. The cake was seven tiers tall. The honeymoon was to Australia.

Life was like a dream except for one little thing. Dr Hughes never touched Auntie Mary. At first this bothered her, but after a few years of fighting they settled into two completely separate lives that only crossed paths at the kitchen, the tennis club and hill walking. Sometimes they didn't even know if the other was in the house. It did dawn on Auntie Mary that maybe Dr Hughes married her for the same reason she married him: To get out of a situation that needed getting out of.

Remember Mick? Well, Mick had come a long way from fixing punctures, a very long way. He had become a well-respected lawyer in one of Cork's top legal firms. One day they bumped into each other, went for a coffee, shared a chocolate éclair and ended up in the nearby Atlantic hotel.

I guess it was an odd story for a Granny to tell her teenage grandson, but I relished every word. I listened and never ever said a word when Granny told me these stories. She never seemed to worry that she was telling me the most secret details of people's lives and I was only fourteen. I was delighted to know who was up to what and with whom. I loved it that my stuck-up bitch of an Aunt was no better than any of us.

I go back downstairs just in time to hear Auntie Mary ask Dad if Paul can work part-time after school and at weekends at Hillside Tennis Club. Dad thinks that's a great idea. Paul is summoned and thanks Auntie Mary, who forces herself not to smile. Granny told me that even when our mother died she wouldn't hug any of us at the funeral. Auntie Mary just patted our heads like puppies and said, "Sorry for your loss." As if we'd kicked a ball into the neighbour's garden.

Auntie Mary is leaving, so I open the front door for her. Just as she is rushing away and shouting goodbye, Conor appears all dressed up. Avoiding any contact with Conor she drops her head and paces past him. He stops and looks pleased.

"Mary, is that you?" he asks.

In one movement she turns and smiles.

"Conor how are you? It's been years," she says sweetly.

Conor reaches out and touches her arm. "Good thanks. You're looking well girl. All that tennis?"

Auntie Mary blushes. He must be somebody important to make her go red. "Thanks Conor. Sorry – got to fly. Talk properly next time." Auntie Mary leans over and plants a kiss on Conor's cheek. My jaw is on the ground. Conor takes it in his stride. It's his first visit to our house, and already he has me freaked out. Patting me on the shoulder he walks past me and into the kitchen. This is all too confusing. I decide to go over to Harpo's.

I sit on the wall waiting for Harpo. The Lucey house looks empty. No one is home except for Vincent, the cat, who is stretched out on the warm concrete of the path, soaking up the morning sunshine. Vincent and Harpo live parallel lives in this strange and fucked up Universe. They are both foxy, both their mothers abandoned them, and they always land on their feet. Vincent is named after Van Gogh, on account of his ginger hair and wonky ear, which was bitten off when he was a kitten. He is a lean, mean tomcat who hunts down mice and rats and is always getting into fights with the other cats on the estate. Vincent sits up and gives himself a little shake. Then he takes off around the back of the house. I'm bored waiting for Harpo. I decide to go back home, hoping that everyone has left on whatever business they have today, and I'll have the house to myself for a while.

My wish is granted. The house is empty. I'm up in my bedroom, when I look out the window and catch some movement in the garden below. It's Vincent! That foxy flea ridden manky bastard of a cat is in our garden.

Vincent spots something and stops. Someone has left Dad's bird room door open. It's not my problem. I hate those poxy birds. The bird room is Dad's and Paul's thing. It's the only thing they share. I have nothing to do with the fucking place.

Every spring Dad and Paul pair up the birds to get the best bloodlines to breed with each other. All the birds bred are carefully planned. Once the eggs are laid, it's Paul's job to fill out the paperwork as to what date the eggs are due to hatch. Once hatched, he feeds the parents twice a day with a mixture of boiled egg and a special bird food which is very expensive. Dad lets Paul have the great privilege of putting the metal rings on the seven-day old chicks' left legs. These rings carry the chick's unique identification number from the Irish Border Canary Association. Once they leave the nest, Paul prepares the cage with a new clean nest bowl for the next round of chicks. The independent chicks are placed in special nursery cages. Paul spends an hour before school out in the bird room, making sure all the birds are cared for before he has his own breakfast. Paul does all the hard work, but Dad gets all the glory. Dad just uses Paul the way he uses everyone. He doesn't ever thank Paul and he gives him a bollocking over the slightest mistakes. The door being left open is a massive fucking mistake. This is going to be fun.

Vincent starts to inspect the open door. Stop, look, listen and sniff the air. Tip toe right up to the door. You've got to hand it to the horrible little bastard, he is extra careful.

Standing at the door to my prick of a father's bird room Vincent peers in to observe the scene. Dad designed the bird room to keep the likes of Vincent out. The main door leads into porch and an inside door as a double protection to stop cats getting in and birds getting out. It's not much use if it's not closed properly. Curling his back around the door Vincent slips in. He's in predator heaven. A wall of singing fills the entire room. Canaries bounce from perch to perch. The smell seems to intoxicate him. Then all the singing stops. The bird room is silent. The canaries have been domesticated for hundreds of years, but something in their tiny brains still tells them that a cat is trouble. Once Vincent has been spotted, they are silent. They know Vincent is trouble. How much trouble he is, they will soon find out.

I don't want to miss a second of this. The bird-room is designed so that it can be fully observed from the house. This saves Dad and Paul having to walk up and down the path all day checking the birds. I sneak downstairs and hide by the kitchen window to get a better view. Plastic drinkers are clipped onto the cages next to the perches, while seed hoppers hang below. Everything is neat and tidy the way Dad demands it from Paul. All the birds are stiff with fear. Vincent sits and plans his next move. On the radio, Disco Dave plays, *The Doors – When the music's over*, which is really appropriate.

Vincent smacks the front of the first cage with his paws, extending his claws in between the bars. This works to perfection. The frightened canary lands against the cage front and clings to the bars. It is met by razor sharp claws. The canary falls, cut clean open from head to tail. Vincent goes from cage to cage. In fifteen minutes over sixty birds are dead. The silence is deafening. One after another, they fall onto their backs shredded. Blood forms pools where they land. It splatters against the white wooden sides of the cages. Some have seizures before dying, flapping their wings as the life leaves them. Feathers float around. Vincent is surrounded by death.

Suddenly the wind picks up and the bird room door slams shut with a bang. I'm as surprised as Vincent. He freezes and sniffs the air. Wrapping his tail around his back Vincent crouches down to plan his next move. I can't risk letting Vincent out as Paul or Dad could appear at any moment. Anyway, I don't want to miss them coming home to this.

I wait in the unfamiliar silence for an hour until Dad walks around the back of the house. He immediately senses that something isn't right. It's strange not hearing the birds singing. He goes straight up to the bird room and stops dead. The place is decorated in blood and feathers. He stands there like the prick that he is, wondering what the hell happened. The inside door is open. The outside door is closed. It makes no sense.

I watch him suffer, enjoying every second. He opens the door and Vincent slips past his feet like the silent assassin that he is. Dad jumps back in shock and watches him scale the back wall. Vincent takes off in the direction of the yellow house where the Luceys live.

Dad takes a few steps into the room. There are bits of birds, blood and feathers everywhere. Only five canaries were spared. Five out of seventy! Vincent wiped out a whole generation of prize winners in ten minutes! Dad doesn't know what to do. He just stands there.

Paul appears around the back and instinctively knows what's up. He walks into the bird room and stares the destruction. I go into the garden and pretend to have just arrived. I don't want to miss a second of this.

"It was Vincent, the Lucey's cat," Dad mumbles. "He only did what he is designed to do, but you helped him by not locking up properly, you careless fuckwit. Clean it all up!"

Paul is distraught, surrounded by all this death. Dad points at the five remaining birds. "That's the future. There is one outstanding cock bird and four hens. They are this year's best birds. You're lucky that I put them up high to be able to see them properly from the kitchen."

Paul works late into the night to clean up the slaughter. First, he has to scoop up all the dead bodies, heads, guts and feathers. The feathers are everywhere. It takes him all day to paint the cages. I keep well out of it. He asked me to help him. I told him to go fuck himself. Granny drops down tea and sandwiches to him. She comes back into the kitchen and gives me a funny look as she lights up a cigarette.

"Where were you when all this shit happened yesterday in the bird room?"

"I was out at Harpo's."

Granny takes a long drag and shakes her head.

"Bit convenient you were over there when their cat was over here!"

I trust Granny, but not enough to say I was in the house. Bottom line is that Vincent only did what Vincent does. If he didn't come into the bird room that day another cat would have. Paul left the door open. It's not my fault, so fuck them all.

The smell of fresh paint fills the kitchen. The bird room is sparkling white. The remaining five canaries don't make a sound. They're still in shock. Dad strides past us and goes down to the bird room to inspect Paul's work. The place looks brand new. Paul couldn't have done a better job. Dad casts an eye over the five remaining birds and ignores Paul as he walks back out. Then he stops at the door.

"Once you're finished you are never to set foot back in here again," he tells Paul and fucks off, presumably down to The Horseman.

I fucking love it.

Chapter Six
Sharon

There she sat in my kitchen on a Sunday morning eating cake. Sharon, 'Prick Teaser'. Since she could walk, she has been playing people. Not a single gesture or word is ever wasted. If Sharon Lyons were a boy she'd be called a 'Prick', being such a great creation of God, society has given her the 'Teaser' part as a double-edged compliment. Sharon is headed for greatness. You couldn't see Sharon in ten years' time wasting her life with some dead-end loser. Matter of fact, you couldn't see Sharon in ten days' time with a loser. She's not really eating the cake. She's playing with it. She takes a bit on her fork, then puts it back on the plate, on the fork, back on the plate, until I want to yell, "Just eat the fucking thing like a normal person!"

Granny sits there, marvelling at Sharon's fanciful tales about the beautiful world she inhabits. Paul sits across from her, excitingly joining in when she mentions someone he knows. A tight blue shirt covers her incredible breasts. Sharon has the breasts of an eighteen-year-old woman trapped in a fifteen-year-old girl's body. They push and heave their way out to form womanly curves on a teenager's frame. Everyone has noticed. You would be blind not to. Granny, Dad, and even Paul, have all commented on how grown up she had gotten. I notice how grown out she is.

Paul looks as gay as Christmas with his legs crossed, in a blue shirt, emblazoned with a tennis racket and ball, with 'Hillside Lawn Tennis Club' in gold thread on the left chest pocket. Paul enjoys Sharon's little forays into humour. That's all they are. She can't deliver a punchline to save her life. Sometimes, she repeats the punchline twice if the level of laughter isn't sufficient. Granny and Paul laugh again to appease her. Jesus, I even join in! What is it about beautiful people that we have to appease them more than smart people?

Sharon is centre stage, like a conductor with a baton. We are the orchestra following her slightest hand gestures. Every time she makes a point, she emphasizes it by touching her bottom lip. I count her doing it sixteen times. My eyes can't peel themselves away. They follow her thumb up to her mouth and back down to her knees. Sometimes I get stuck on her breasts. This only makes it more difficult. I am getting harder and harder. Looking away doesn't help. Even her perfume gets me aroused.

Granny offers more cake and tea. Sharon politely refuses, remarking on how absolutely yummy the cake is. She insists that it must be from Lazy Liz's Cafe, though she knows full well that Granny baked it herself. Granny is so delighted that Sharon Lyons likes, no loves, her almond cake that she actually blushes. She doesn't seem to notice that Sharon didn't eat much cake to begin with. Sharon's plate is full of tiny little pieces, creating an illusion that the cake was enjoyed.

Sharon's dad is my dad's boss in the post office. Granny never mentions this to Sharon, in fact we never discuss it among ourselves, but it plays a massive part in all our lives. Her dad decides the overtime chart, which means easy money for whoever gets asked to do the extra work. You get overtime by not annoying Sharon's dad. It's that simple. On that basis my dad gets a lot of overtime, which thankfully means the prick is missing a lot. All the extra cash means we do better than most. It gives Granny the spending power to keep our house a classy home. Dad and Granny clash on many things, but money is one thing they never fall out over. Every Friday Dad hands Granny a small brown envelope. She takes money for the bills, food and everyday needs, and hands him back the remainder. Dad then hands Granny back some extra cash to do her hair, or buy flowers, or a new dress or whatever. Granny treats herself to something small and cheap every weekend, but on a Monday, she divides what's left and lodges it into our Credit Union accounts.

Paul says something about being late for work and off they go. I watch Sharon Lyon's perfect form leave the house as Granny tidies up the plates. She looks up, catches me watching Paul and Sharon, and gives a little shake of her head. I know what she's thinking. It's never said, it doesn't need to be. If anyone else had walked out the door with Sharon Lyons, Granny would have made a little comment like 'lucky boy', or that they would make a nice couple. Instead, she gives a shrug and goes back to clearing up.

Nothing is said, because if it was, then we would all have to deal with the fact that my brother is openly displaying the signs of being an out and out fucking queer. None of us like these signs but they are getting bigger and brighter as he gets older.

Paul spent the morning ironing his shirt for work. I'm wearing the same t-shirt I slept in last night, wore yesterday and am probably going to wear again tomorrow. Paul blow dries his hair, polishes his shoes endlessly and wears aftershave even though he doesn't shave. Paul always strives to be spotless. I find it creepy. Not once growing up did I ever see Paul climb a tree, enjoy a fight, or want to get up to mischief. I have to endure endless slagging from my so called friends regarding my brother 'the queer'. I am so fucking tired of the unwanted attention. Paul is a pain in the hole, an annoying queer who is happy to sleepwalk through life. His new friend Cider helps with the sleepwalking.

I settle into the front room to watch TV. The mantelpiece is covered in small marble squares that hold up plastic gold covered shapes that range from chess pieces to soccer balls. They are Paul's trophies. All these trophies are Paul's, and he doesn't a flying fuck about any of them. I would have given my right arm for just one of them. My two tiny trophies for running are placed out in front by Granny. The harder I try to be picked for the school teams the more I fail. All that asshole Paul has to do is turn up to play whatever game he fucking wanted, and he gets on the team. Like, how the fuck is that fair? To add insult to injury he doesn't even want to play on any of the teams. He just plays out of spite, to piss off people like me. And boy is he good at pissing people off. The bullies can't be beaten up, so he takes what they prize most, which is a place on a school team, be it soccer, relay, basketball or chess.

Like for example – take last year, Paul didn't forget about the boy who kicked his crisps out of his hand and beat him up. That boy was the striker on the school soccer team. All summer long Paul practiced and practiced on his own, dribbling a ball around cones in the back garden.

When the soccer trails came up, he entered them with me. That match Paul scored three goals and caused a major argument between the coaches. Some argued he could play attacking soccer, they were right, his fast pace got him clear of defenders and scoring was natural to him. So, what exactly was the problem with the other coaches, well, Paul couldn't back track, defend, read the game, or really pass the ball. All agreed that he was lethal on his own with the ball, but no way was he a team player. Arguing went to and fro till the head coach put his foot down.

"He will play as long as he is scoring. He doesn't look like a footballer, act like a footballer or even wear his shirt like a footballer but he is scoring goals and goals win games. So, we play with an extra forward and drop a fullback."

Guess fucking what? Yes, you're fucking right, I was the fullback that was dropped to make way for that queer asshole. You couldn't make this shit up. I'd waited a whole year for the trials and bang my faggot brother knocks me and my position clean off the team and on to the bench.

On the first Wednesday of the soccer season a chill took the goodness from that sunny afternoon as we all sat waiting to watch the game. Thankfully, it was a home game without any away supporters. Paul warmed up, his long sleeves neatly folded up to his elbows, both sleeves squared and perfectly matching, otherwise Paul wouldn't go onto the pitch. His collar was pulled up to protect his delicate neck from the cold. He looked like he was going to a cricket match. All he was short was a jumper dangling from his shoulders. The game kicked off and Paul only managed to control three passes out of ten, but he still scored two fucking goals. I didn't know whether to laugh or cry.

During the half time every player except Paul was given a set of instructions. No point in asking Paul to do anything because he didn't understand the first thing about the tactics of football. Paul sat quietly eating his custard creams on the edge of the circle, not even watching as the coaches ranted and raved at the players. The game finished with the school winning three to two. Paul scored a winner in the last few minutes.

By Christmas, the school were topping the league. After ten games Paul had scored twenty-six goals beating the old scoring record by seven. There were still ten games to go! It would be natural to think that the soccer team would be on cloud nine with this achievement, but they weren't. We had become a laughing stock in every school in Cork. We had a star striker who was a fairy. Before long Paul got the nickname 'Twinkle Toes' and it stuck.

By Easter, the league had been won and the school were in the Cup Final. A record crowd turned up to watch us win a historic double. Because of Paul I only got to play three matches as a sub. You need to make five match appearances to be entitled to receive a winner's medal. All my training was for fucking nothing. On the awards night Paul stood on stage and received six trophies! You read it, six trophies: One for the League Cup, top scorer League (forty-four goals), top scorer Cup (twelve goals), School player of the year, player of the year Cork City and County. All of this from a guy who never ever even went to see his local team Cork Celtic play, never watched Match of the Day, never supported any English soccer team, and couldn't name one player on the current Irish team. Oh yeah – and never ever once kicked a soccer ball on the green with his own brother. It was pretty mind blowing!

Needless to say, the only Dad missing on the awards night was our prick of a dad, who was probably too busy down the Horsemans with some tart to attend. The chicken suppers were handed out after the awards ceremony and Paul quiet happily sat and ate on his own, placing his can of coke in among his trophies as he slowly nibbled at the chicken leg. I watched him, consumed by jealousy and hate. Thanks to Paul, I only got to play three games, just fucking three games! Not one medal for me, never mind a fucking trophy. I couldn't get on the team as long as that cocksucker was playing.

He did the same thing with chess. Last year, Paul was walking past the school's top rugby player.

"Queer," the rugby player called out.

"Thanks!" Paul smiled back, as if he was glad of the attention.

This made the rugby star angry. "You like that, you Queer?"

Paul produced a camp wave. "Thank you very much."

All night he planned his revenge while bitching to me about the rugby star. No way could he play rugby. Not a chance. It wasn't soccer and sooner rather than later he would be caught in a maul and get seriously hurt. I thought that sounded like a great idea, but he kept saying, "I'll find something else." Then he got it, the rugby star also played on the chess team. Paul found my old chess set, which was covered in dust and made me teach him how to play. In a matter of weeks Paul grasped the nettle that is chess. He got better and better while I still made basic stupid fucking mistakes. The more I tried the more I failed. I told him I didn't want to play chess with him anymore and took back my chess set.

One of Paul's Christmas presents that year was a shiny new wooden chess set. Over the holidays he carried it daily to the local Community Centre where the old folks were happy to play for hour after hour. By the last week of the Christmas holidays, Paul was playing three pensioners at once. He used to brag to me that he averaged forty games of chess a day. His success rate according to him ran into the nineties. I told him that I wasn't impressed. He was only playing people who smelt of piss and only had half their senses left.

The school chess year started in mid-January. Paul entered the trials and was instantly picked. He took the rugby star's place on the team. Paul captained the team and only lost six games out of a hundred that year. The school won the coveted Cork City Chess Cup, which meant more to the school than any other cup. Paul received chess player of the year and best chess player in Cork City.

I've been sitting here thinking about Paul too long. I turn off the TV. I wasn't watching anyway. Maybe it's because Paul has recently been acting more strangely than usual, which makes it really, really strange. He has started to confide in me. I listen because I want to know who the local faggots were. If there are any other faggots in school, I want to be first to find out so I can direct the slagging that I get about Paul in their direction.

Last night he started to tell me about the chess team. He sounded upset. I thought I heard him crying, which is something very unusual for Paul. Even when we were younger, he never cried no matter how much he hurt himself. He began to choke up and explained to me, that he had a crush on a boy he called Brown Eyes. His crying was beginning to grate on me, but the prospect of hearing who else was gay kept me interested.

He said he'd met Brown Eyes when they played against each other at an away chess match. Paul thought that Brown Eyes must be gay. His suspicions were confirmed when Brown Eyes gently touched Paul's hand after he lost the first game. Then Paul lost the second and got another touch. Game three and again Paul lost. No touch, just a firm handshake. Paul was confused so he went up and thanked him for the games. Brown Eyes, the queer, accepted Paul's thanks and suggested that it would be nice to meet up somewhere in town at the weekend for a hot chocolate. A time and place were picked. Paul counted down the minutes till he would meet Brown Eyes again.

Saturday at one pm Paul finally met with Brown Eyes in a cafe off Patricks Street. He went on and on about it like it was a movie: His heart raced as he saw Brown Eyes waiting for him. They were both so nervous. Emotions were well hidden as they chatted over coffee and mini buns. They spoke, listened and enjoyed being themselves all afternoon. Not once were their secret gay lives discussed. No, the fact they were here was enough of a statement for the two of them to make. When Paul went to pay the bill, he was told that Brown

Eyes had paid it earlier. Then without an ounce of shame Paul told me that they'd met up four other times, and that on the last meeting they kissed goodbye in a doorway. At sixteen it was Paul's first kiss and boy he couldn't wait to tell me, fuck knows why? I kept hoping he'd just tell me the name, so that I could have a quiet wank, thinking about Sharon's tits before going to sleep. Instead, Paul started crying again. Brown Eyes had stood him up on the fifth date. Paul was sure that there must be a reason. Maybe he was sick, or had to help his mother? Maybe he got knocked over by a car?

Long story short, today he had to go into town to buy a schoolbook. On the way home he decided to get the bus. As he waited, propped against a shop windowsill, something caught his eye. No way! Walking towards him was Brown Eyes! Brown Eyes: Smiling, strutting, stunning and holding a girl's hand.

Brown Eyes stopped and introduced Paul to his girlfriend as someone he played chess against and then just walked away. Paul was gutted. I began to wonder was it ever possible to get a bedtime wank in peace and quiet. So, you know what I told him? That he would have been better off not fucking bothering with chess in the first place.

Chapter Seven
Pets for Profit

I'm sitting on my own at the Hillside Tennis Club. From my seat outside the club house, I have a great view of the whole place: The bar, the courts, and the club house. Paul is busy serving bar, as Sharon tidies up. Auntie Mary drops me out a free coke. Auntie Mary must know that Paul is gay, but she never treats him any differently. Maybe having a queer for a nephew is fashionable nowadays? Sunday is the busiest day of the week at the club. Countless games of tennis are played followed by drinks and a cold buffet. Sunday is the day to be seen by everyone and to see everyone.

Auntie Mary's husband Dr Hughes is warming up for his first game. Mick, her secret lover had won his match earlier and was fresh out of the shower. Auntie Mary and Mick stand on the balcony above me and plan their next rendezvous in front of the whole club. Trying to hide the fact that they are up to no good will bring unwanted attention. As Granny told me – "The longer an affair stays out in the open, the longer it will last." They were just friends, sure that's all they are. Why wouldn't Auntie Mary enjoy Mick's company? He is an easy going guy who could charm the birds down from the trees. He disarms everyone who meets him. This makes him above suspicion when it comes to his dirty, little, seedy affair with Auntie Mary. Their past romance was just that, past. Auntie Mary had hit the jackpot with Dr Hughes, and lightning doesn't strike twice. To have a secret lover of the calibre of Mick would be absurd to even contemplate.

I eavesdrop on their conversation, as I pretend to watch Dr Hughes panting through his match. The sneaky fuckers plan to meet the following Tuesday, in a nice hotel outside Clonakilty. Then Auntie Mary gets paranoid and goes back to the ladies at the bar. I sit back and savour the sun. Dr Hughes plays like a man with a disability. He can't serve, return a ball, or volley; but as the club's main donor and the man responsible for keeping the club finances in order, he holds a lot of power at Hillside. Tennis isn't the only game played at Hillside. Members include lots of professionals like doctors, lawyers, teachers, and civil servants, with a healthy dose of builders, tradesmen and small business owners. Hillside has all the big shits, as well as the little shits who yearn to be bigger shits.

The women run the show, relentless in their pursuit of self-gratification. Like farmyard hens, the have a strict pecking order which has nothing to do with one's tennis ranking. It's all about the money. Hillside's foundations are built on the steely knowledge that their members are the richest members of any club in Cork. Forget rugby, golf, GAA or soccer. The money is at Hillside. No doubt about it. Over five hundred members and a waiting list of a hundred to join, Hillside is for the elite. That isn't a secret. It's a fact.

Paul keeps himself to himself, collecting glasses and wiping down tables. Sharon does as little as possible. She is helped in this by a constant stream of questions from the members on how her training is progressing. Sharon loves the attention. She is the club's very own poster girl. Sharon leaves Paul to work on his own and disappears out to the courts to watch a game. I have to head off home to help Granny with the housework. I've had two free cokes. Auntie Mary wasn't going to give me a third.

It is getting dark when Paul and Sharon arrive back in our kitchen. They both sit while Granny makes them tea. Sharon looks so beautiful it hurts. She chats happily, as Paul and Granny hang on her every word. Does she ever fucking tire of being centre stage? I leave them and go in to watch the GAA on TV. After about ten minutes, I hear a shout from Granny in the kitchen: "Fin, come out here!"

Sharon has her jacket on and is saying her goodbyes. I stand in front of her as if she were a great cathedral, overcome by the beauty of it all.

"Walk Sharon home," says Granny. "Paul is knackered."

Sharon pipes up. "I'm okay thanks…"

Granny slaps my arm. "Walk her home, Fin. Be a gentleman."

I grab my jacket and off we go, into the dark night without a word being said. Sharon's house is only around the corner. The journey is shortened as the pace is fairly fast. I am over the moon when Sharon asks me in for tea. Her house is the opposite of mine. The place feels like it isn't even lived in: No mountains of clothes to be ironed, no jackets left lying around. No smell of boys. No noise!

Her dad is down in the Horseman, pinting. Sharon's mum died five years ago. They pay a cleaner to come in every day to cook dinner and run the house. The fridge is full of delights. Sharon takes out a chocolate cake and cuts me a thick slice. She is the perfect hostess. As the kettle boils, Sharon takes the cling film off her chicken dinner.

"Yummy!" she says smacking her lovely lips. "I love chicken! I love roasters. I love my gravy!"

My jaw drops at the passion with which she tears into the meal. Her jaw opens and closes, as chunk after chunk of chicken is devoured.

"I'm starving, Fin. What a fucking day!" she says, her mouth full of chicken.

I am in love. This is a side to Sharon that I never knew existed, and it drives me mad.

"Eat your cake," she says. "My dad will be home in a while. Then I have to go to bed."

My appetite is gone. I find myself playing with the cake. My senses seem to pick up every girly thing about Sharon. Her hair smells so nice. Maybe it's because I don't have a sister. Boy, can she eat! She goes back to the fridge for more chicken. My eyes are locked on her breasts as she moves.

"I do love my food," she declares as she sits back down. "It's been a long day, and I didn't get a chance to eat a thing! Do you want to touch them?"

"What?" I say, gobsmacked.

Sharon touches her breasts. "Them!" She laughs.

Unsure of what to do I fumble. "Them what?"

She sticks her chest out and puts more chicken in her mouth. "My tits you fucking idiot. You're staring at them."

"Sorry, I'm sorry," I mutter, going bright red. I want the ground to swallow me up.

"Go on. I don't mind. They're just my tits."

I freeze. Sharon puts her hands under her round breasts and lifts them up.

"What's wrong, Fin? You don't like girls either?"

Wiping the chicken from her lips, she opens her top button. Then she reaches out and grabs my hands. She is in charge, which is good, because I don't have a fucking clue what is happening!

My hands rise up to touch her chest. She pushes them down on her. Sharon can see how horny I am, which gives her a fit of the giggles. "I had to see for myself if you were queer as well. The girls in the club dared me to see if you were like Paul."

I am confused. I don't know whether to be angry, sad or bitter. I'm not the one in control. My hands drift away from her as an awkward silence fills the kitchen. Sharon can tell that she upset me. She continues to eat. Then she smiles and says: "Sorry, Fin."

Not knowing what to say, I say nothing. Sharon grabs my hands again and carefully cups them under her breasts. I watch her chew her chicken as I grope her tits. I don't know if this is normal, as I've never felt a girl's tits before.

"If you want more of this, you can take me to the pictures next week," she says swallowing the last bite of chicken. Then she smiles again. I nod and drop my hands off her tits. I am very confused. I move into the conservatory to try and compose myself as Sharon tidies up the kitchen.

A movement catches my attention in the conservatory. Socks and Boots are two purebred Siamese cats that Sharon got three years ago for Christmas. They cost a fortune. Her dad bought them as a present and an investment. He has a pet for profit thing going on. Both cats are female and never get further than the back garden. When they're in season they are under house arrest for weeks on end. Mr Lyons had a plan to make big money by breeding them to a top class Siamese tomcat and selling the kittens.

Harpo and me often watched Vincent trying to get into Sharon's conservatory. The window was eight feet off the ground from the garden level, as the garden was two steps below the house. Vincent kept trying to get in. He jumped for hours on end, smacking up against the window only to slide back down again. He was a good two feet short each time. From Harpo's end wall it was possible to see right into Sharon's bedroom, and from Sharon's wall it was possible to see Harpo taking a piss in his bathroom if that took your fancy. We used to watch Sharon get changed or dry off after a shower. It was the highlight of our week. Those memories of Sharon drying herself off helped me get through many a night! We would often sneak down by the wall and wait till Sharon had to shower or get changed. Harpo and I were convinced that she knew we were watching. Why else would you dry yourself right next to the window? Now, I hadn't just seen those perfect, beautiful breasts, I had also touched them.

Harpo and me often saw Mr Lyons watching Vincent try and try again to get into the conservatory. Each time the cat ended up sliding back down. It was like a cartoon. Thinking that his precious Siamese were safe, Mr Lyons would leave the small window open all day long when the house was empty.

Vincent didn't give up. He finally figured it out. Why try and jump up to the window when he could easily drop down on it from the roof? That's what he did. Harpo nudged me as he noticed Vincent climbing up on the conservatory roof. He slowly followed the supporting metal beams down to the small window. Socks and Boots suddenly got frightened. Their sixth sense was telling them they were in trouble. They started to whimper, but to no avail. The house was empty. Vincent leant over the edge into the small gap between the window and the frame. He dropped in silently. Full of pride, Harpo smacked his hands off his thighs. "That's my boy. Go on you good thing!"

Vincent landed right in the middle of the floor. Harpo and I leaned over the wall to get a better view. Socks hid under the wicker chair as Boots was left to fend for herself. Staring at the ginger tomcat she didn't realise the trouble that lay ahead. Sniffing her Vincent got aroused. In a flash he mounted her. Fighting him off was useless. The harder she strained to escape the harder he fought her. Biting her back caused Boots to push back into him and then it was over. Boots ran to the corner of the room yowling.

It was Socks turn. She hissed, stuck out her claws and spat. Vincent frightened her into leaving the safety of the wicker chair. He swiped at her and chased her around the room. Blood dripped onto the pearly white tiles. Pieces of fur were flying around. Bloodied Socks fought bravely but was no match for Vincent. He caught and mated with her too. Suddenly Vincent released Socks. Something spooked him. Like a flash he was up and out the small window. As Vincent crawled back out the window, he had to lean on the window frame to push himself back up on the roof. This caused the window to shut, eliminating any theories whether there was a strange cat intruder. A few seconds later the cleaning lady walked in and surveyed the mess.

Sharon came into the conservatory and sat next to me. Her scent made me swoon. She started to tell me about her cats. I sat next to Sharon, trying to hide my erection and all she wanted to do was tell me about the problems with the Siamese tomcat. She explained about how he serviced both Boots and Socks. Surprisingly, they never fought or refused to be mounted. Mr Lyons and the Tom cat owner stood and observed. After discussions they both agreed that it was very unusual that they were so easily mated. With a blank expression I acted interested. She thought I was being extremely thoughtful and was super impressed. My hand crept up and landed on her right boob. Sharon didn't seem to notice as she rambled on about the cats. As she spoke, I rubbed her right breast, being a bastard is a full time job.

Within four weeks Socks and Boots couldn't eat enough. All day long they made the journey from conservatory to kitchen to empty their bowls. Mr Lyons started buying the best of fish for them. After a week, the house stank of fish, but he didn't care. His babies were going to have babies, though the size of Boots and Socks were slightly alarming him. This must be a good thing that they are so big, extra kittens!

By week seven Socks had got very aggressive. The pregnancy was driving her mad. She was nearly twice her normal size. With labour only ten to fourteen days away Sharon prayed it would come as soon as possible. Boots spent all day hiding. It was like she was terrified of the birth date arriving. Still, they ate. A pint of milk only lasted them a morning now. Their cat litter had to be cleaned twice a day. As the pregnancy neared its full course, Boots and Socks constantly sought out Sharon's company. She was always there for them. Nights were spent sharing her bed, with days following her around the house, until she settled on the sofa. Then Boots and Socks would lay on her lap while she watched TV. Socks would scratch the front door when Sharon left for school.

Sharon was getting emotional as she told me about the night the kittens were born. Reluctantly I stopped rubbing her tit. Boots was first to give birth and it lasted the whole night, followed by Socks whose labour lasted the whole day. Both mothers hurt and bled. Beaten by the experience they fell into a deep sleep while their new families drank from them. Six kittens each. Mr Lyons was elated. One kitten from each litter was for the owner of the tomcat and that left him with ten. Sharon slept on the wicker chair, night after night for a week tending to the mothers and kittens. All day long Boots and Socks would lick their babies and re-arrange them to get the most from their teats. There never seemed to be enough milk to feed the kittens. Even Mr Lyons, who isn't a cat breeder, knew it wasn't right. The kittens seemed massive, very powerful for a delicate breed like a Siamese, so he rang the owner of the tomcat. As Sharon started telling me what happened next, I wondered if I was going to have to listen to this shit all night. Then again it was worth it. My hand was still on her right tit.

Seems that the tomcat's owner saw the kittens were ginger, and not Siamese right away. Mr Lyons declared that it must be the tomcat's fault. He must not be purebred. The owner insisted that his tomcat had serviced many females without any problems. Then he pointed out the window. "My guess is that big ginger tomcat sitting in that Chestnut tree halfway down the garden," he said. "My educated guess is that he's the dad. Has he been around a lot lately?" It was obvious that Vincent was the culprit.

Sharon explains through blood shot eyes what happened next. Mr Lyons now had twelve worthless kittens! They had to go. He gathered up the poor little things and put them in a thick plastic bag tied with a strong knot. He filled a bucket, pushed the bag into the water, and placed a heavy rock on top. Sharon cries her eyes out uncontrollably, as she recounts the horror of those twelve cute little kittens struggling in the bag. I nod and try to look sad. I couldn't care less about what happened to the kittens, I just want her to keep talking, so I can keep my hand on her tit. Sharon wipes her eyes and stands up. My time in heaven is over.

Walking home from Sharon's I am lightheaded. A strange warm feeling comes over me: I had felt Sharon Lyons tits! Probably the best tits in Cork and they felt great, like firm jelly. Not what I expected. Come to think of it – what are tits supposed to feel like?

As soon as I get home, I start to panic. I know Sharon Lyons is out of my league, but one date with her would be worth a million dates with normal girls. I could say that I dated Sharon Lyons, even if in reality Sharon Lyons was dating me. She asked me out. She was in charge. I'd had no say in what had happened in her house. Did it really happen? Had I really rubbed her tit, while she told me about her cats?

Paul is asleep when I crawl into bed. I have a quick wank and fall into a restless dream. Sharon is next to me. She is warm, and close, squirming and jerking forward. We eat red meat. Our mouths open and suck blood. All around us are the lifeless bodies of the kittens. Thousands of larvae are devouring the fresh meat. It's a race to see which one of us larvae can turn into a fly the quickest. We eat and grow. We eat and grow. Sharon eats more than me, developing quicker than me. She is so white, so beautiful, constantly shedding her skin to produce a cleaner whiter skin. I felt useless because my skin is dirty from all the blood. She would never date someone as dirty as me!

Slowly Sharon turns brown. She is changing into pupae. A hard shell protects her from the outside world. Within this shell she begins to change, developing those beautiful wings, and those six sexy legs that hold up that black perfectly shaped body. I haven't even started to change. Sharon breaks free from her shell. Her body needs to dry quickly for her wings to be able to work. Using her six legs she crawls out into the sunlight. Sharon is reborn as a beautiful jet-black housefly. A breeze takes her off into the garden, lifting her up, up, and away. She vanishes into the blueness of the sky. I have lost her.

Chapter Eight
The Flowerbed Team

It's Sunday evening. Dad is down drinking at the Horseman and Paul is working at Hillside. Granny sits with her feet on the couch, noisily chewing gum. It's spearmint gum, and smells fucking horrible. She's been chewing gum since she went off the cigarettes. She takes a piece of gum from the packet, tears it in half and starts chewing. When all the taste is gone spits the gum into the bin in the corner of the room and starts in on the second half. Her aim is often off, and I have to pick up the warm, sticky, little nugget, and put it the bin for her. The TV is at full volume to drown out her chewing.

The theme music for Little House on the Prairie comes on. Paul, the faggot, loves this show. Granny hums along: Do Do Do Do…Do Do…Do Do Do Do…Da Do…She's not even in the same ballpark as the tune. We watch the last little girl fall over as she runs down the grassy hill. Granny gets worried and says, "I hope she didn't get hurt." She says it every time.

Nobody can ever actually explain an episode of Little House on the Prairie because nothing ever happens. I watch it because there isn't anything else to do on a Sunday at 5pm. That's not entirely true. I also watch it because of the Mother. Boy, I would love to fuck her brains out. This perverted thought keeps me going during the whole episode.

The smell of melting cheese wafts into the room. I run out to the kitchen and bring back two piping hot cheese, chicken, and onion sandwiches from the sandwich maker. The cheese is so hot, it's like a nuclear explosion. Dad bought it two weeks ago and we have been enjoying red hot, toasted sandwiches since. My mouth had blisters the size of marbles for the first few days. Granny takes out her gum and places it on the edge of her seat for later. She blows on her sandwich and takes a bite of the lava cheese without even flinching. Her mouth must be destroyed from all the cigarettes.

We watch Little House on the Prairie in silence. Nothing actually happens for ten minutes. I mean nothing. After twenty minutes, still nothing has happened. By the end of the show, I am none the fucking wiser for watching it. All I get out of it is an erection watching the Mother doing absolutely fucking nothing. Granny's eyes are tearing up. Something must have struck a chord with her in among all the nothing in the Little House. She puts the hard gum back into her mouth and chews. I think about getting her some tissues to dry her eyes, but I'm too late. She wipes her eyes, mouth and nose with her jumper, leaving a sliver line of snot ran neatly up her arm. At least the Muppet Show is on next. Now that's entertainment.

There's a knock at the door. I go answer it and find Conor. Granny doesn't want him to see her upset from watching Little House on the Prairie, so she sends us both out to tend to the flowerbeds. Conor instantly agrees and leads me out to my own back garden.

Conor bends over, carefully working the soil. He takes great care not to damage any of the roots of the delicate plants. The heat is cruel. The dark, damp earth changes to a lighter shade within minutes of being exposed to the dry air. They call heat like this in the Autumn an Indian summer. Do they call it an Irish summer if it rains all summer in India? Conor's hands work to a set pattern: Weed, weed and then turn soil. Slowly he transforms each untidy flowerbed into a work of art. Once a flowerbed is finished, Conor sprinkles snail pellets around the base of the plants saying, "That will sort the little bastards out."

The flower beds are massive; row upon row of flowers stretching up to the sky. They are Granny's pride and joy. Once upon a time the flower beds were her escape. Day after day from March to September she would toil the soil between the household jobs. As we got older, she got us to clean and hoover the house while she took a well-earned break tending her seedlings. She would get us to dig up the beds in late March and rake the moss peat into the earth. As she got older, she got us to weed the beds, on account of her knees. She counted on us to keep her beds perfect. Now, Conor had joined the flowerbed team. He was slowly edging me out of the way in my own home. As we weed Conor starts talking:

"Exams came easy to me Boy. No tight stomach or loose bowels. My head wasn't crammed or overburdened walking into the exam hall that hot May Day. Final Business exam and then off yonder into the working world. No surprise when the results were announced that I came first. No one could argue I didn't deserve it. A combination of hard work, and never missing a lecture, meant I had the knowledge and the teaching staff on board. I had a gift for repeating whole lectures to paper in exam conditions. Let me tell you Boy, it's not intelligence that gets you through – it's being smart, and you need to be smart to survive in this world. There was a job waiting for me within a week of my grades being announced. One of my lecturers tipped off a friend at his local golf club about my high grades. Job in the bank sorted."

No one could accuse our Conor of being modest. Fucking hell, I never thought someone living in a homeless hostel could have such a high opinion of themselves. Jesus, it was a miracle Granny could love him when he was so fucking busy loving himself.

He bends over the flowers and picks the weeds like a cow eating grass as he continues, speaking just loud enough to be heard. I figure he must have picked that up from living in the city and people hearing your private conversations. It was hardly from growing up in the countryside. Your neighbour isn't going to hear you when he lives a fucking mile away!

"Tell you what Boy, the week waiting to start work wasn't wasted. God no! I spent the days drinking, and the nights riding some lucky woman in a friend's empty flat. Nothing was ever left to chance with me. You've got to be cute, really fucking cute, so fucking cute that you don't realise you're cute."

I'm not sure what he's talking about, but there's a mention of riding, so I'm listening. A large pile of little weeds is building up next to him. I add a few more. Conor stares into my eyes and finds my conscience trying to hide from the sunlight. His voice stays low. Then he says seven words which frighten the living shit out of me:

"I was once just like you, Boy."

He pauses to let that sink in. I don't look up. He pulls a few more weeds, and then starts talking again:

"Cute to the fucking bone. Now here, boy, is where the cuteness caused a serious flaw in my character. The pubs that I drank in gave me credit. The principle of how I managed to obtain this credit ran exactly opposite to everything I studied at college. The credit was used, or more correctly, invested in a night's drinking; starting with cold bottles of German beer, and changing to Russian vodka an hour or two before closing. By the time the vodka and Cokes arrived some local beauty would be perched beside me, enjoying my undivided attention, and free double vodkas. You see, Boy when you're really, really good at something you never have to say it, because everyone else will say it for you."

I have to stop myself from pinching myself. Sweetest fuck this guy is up his own arse so far, it's frightening. The Muppet show is on and I'm out here listening to this bullshit. He rabbits on.

"Once a bar manager asked for the credit to be repaid, I had to show my creative side. Seeing as the managers didn't own the pubs, and hence the money wasn't theirs, they could be bought. We all have a price. The trick is finding this price. I have a knack for finding a person's price. I had a friend who sold stolen cigarettes. If a manager requested cash, I would hand over five cartons of cigarettes. If the bar manager smoked, then he was delighted, if he didn't smoke, he sold them and was delighted. It was a win-win situation."

He stares straight at me. "I hope you're taking this all in, Boy?"

Shit! This is one of these adults to kid chats with a fucking moral story thrown in. I nod my head, and he continues his weird Sunday lesson.

"I loved the drink, but more importantly, I could handle my drink. Mixing with the evening crowd I threw back cold German beer. After three quick bottles I usually slowed down. By half nine I would be nursing my sixth bottle. The carefully crafted illusion was created that I could really drink. This illusion was based on my first three quick bottles. After that people stopped counting the amount I drank."

I sit on the edge of the raised flowerbeds and pick at a blister on my palm. Where the fuck is this story going? He sounds delighted that he was a drunk. I keep nodding. The more I nod, the more he talks. The more he talks, the more he weeds, and the less I have to do.

"Ten, when the night crowd arrived, was the signal to order my first Russian Vodka. It was all for the crowd. All show. At the end of the night, doubles would be ordered; especially if some female company had arrived. All show. Often the next day, I would be told that I had drunk ten bottles of beer and ten vodkas by a friend who wasn't even in the pub! That was the secret to my success. Always create a positive image. You don't have to be positive, but your image does."

I still haven't a clue what the fucking hell he is on about, but I keep nodding and he keeps weeding.

"First day at work, I was introduced to all the people that mattered. All these people had one common thread joining them – Ashmore Golf Club. The bank was joined by the hip to Ashmore, both financially and morally. To work in the bank meant automatic membership to Ashmore. It wasn't free or even cheap. It was three months of my wages. Then there were the expensive suits and shoes that had to be bought, along with two long, wool coats to defend against the year-round rain. I also needed a car, and the car needed tax, insurance, and a service before I had even sat behind the wheel. I was in serious debt before I ever earned a penny. After my first week at work, I owed two years' salary."

Conor looks at me to make sure that I'm listening. Maybe he is telling me all this to keep me away from stealing. Happy that he has my attention, despite the blister, he continues:

"You'd think that I would have a payment plan, to slowly chip away at this mountain of debt. No! Not me Boy, sadly not. I just got into deeper debt. I even took out a bogus loan from my own bank for the car insurance pretending the cost was twice as much as it was. The extra cash kept me in drink and women for a couple of months. I was supremely confident, and this confidence was my fucking downfall. I really loved the banking system where someone like me never had to save for anything. Everything I purchased including drink was on the never-never. That meant I never actually had a debt free day as a man. Owing money on a mortgage is one thing and considered good debt. Owing money for drinking five nights a week can only be considered pure madness."

Conor loves the sound of his own voice. He's not really talking to me. He's talking at me, loving the flow. If this story was going somewhere, I wish he could hurry it up.

"Within six months I made a massive impression. I had a touch for connecting with clients. Mixing with shop owners in the morning, and farmers late at night, I closed deal after deal. Charisma was the secret to my success, and by God, I used it freely. The men liked it, and the women loved it. I can't describe the high of closing deal after deal. I drove up and down country lanes night after night wooing farmers to invest in offshore bank accounts in countries they couldn't find on a map. By the end of year one I had made enough money to pay off all my debts and even buy a new car. Not that I bothered to actually save any money! More money meant more drinking. More drinking meant more women, and more women meant more good times. I regret the drinking alright, but not the women. Don't ever deny yourself the joy of holding a beautiful woman in your arms, Boy. You can go without a lot of things in life, but make sure women aren't one of them. They put the oxygen into your blood, make the heartbeat faster and drive you fucking mad. A woman's touch is worth more than all the tea in China, or diamonds in Africa."

Conor collects up the bundles of weeds. The blister is doing my head in. I follow him around my own back garden like a puppy. He dumps the weeds and leans on the back wall in a spot of sunshine. He shakes his head as if he's really sorry.

"Things got fucked up one night and my luck changed. Whatever the hell was covering my ass before just disappeared. My destiny became unclear. As a sailor friend of mine down in the hostel would say. I found myself in uncharted waters."

"Was it the drinking?" I ask, surprised at how small my voice sounds. He winks as if to say yes. Then he rolls on with his story.

"The craic was mighty as I ordered my first pint of stout. I was in a country pub, so no fancy German Beer in tankards. There's no fancy stuff in the country pubs. Sitting at the bar I got caught up in the banter with the regulars. For a Tuesday night the place was packed. The local Football team had won their league, and the whole parish was out to celebrate with free pints given out by the pub owner to thank the team for dropping in. When the cup, filled with whiskey, came around I was already after downing at least four pints. By the time I turned the ignition in the car, I was at least three times over the legal limit. I drove the twenty miles back home like a deluded fucking idiot. Within a mile of my destination, I noticed that a dark car was tailing me. When I turned left, the car turned left. When I turned right, the car turned right. Then I saw the blue lights flashing. Pulling over I knew that I was in very serious shit."

Conor looks broken. The humour and buzz of the story has faded. He spreads his massive hands on his knees. They are so tanned they are bronze.

"'Do I smell alcohol?' the Guard asked me. I told him that he is right. Then I look at him and realise I know him. It's my old school friend, Gary. Sweetest Christ I was relived. I got out of the car and shook Gary's hand. The conversation turned to old times playing rugby at school and ended up with Gary giving me a playful bollocking about being over the limit. So now, I'm sure you're wondering how was this bad luck? Simple – I couldn't shut the fuck up and we stayed talking for ages and at some point, I offered Gary an offshore account, where his investments could be safe from prying eyes. I don't know whether it was the drink, or pure fucking stupidity. Only God knows why I did it because I sure as fuck don't know why. Gary was a guard. He knew this wasn't one hundred percent legal, but more importantly it wasn't completely illegal. Two days later I had Gary's account up and running."

I'm still not sure what he's talking about. He keeps sounding like he's going one way and then takes off in another direction. This time he goes from Gary the Guard to golf.

"Ashmore golf club became home from home for me. I never played golf, in fact the slowness of it drove me distracted even watching it. No, the reason I was in Ashmore Boy was to play the money market. While the members worried about their swing and par, I concentrated on their portfolios. The bank was dumb struck by the calibre of the new customers I kept recruiting. Straight up I was averaging four times more sales of policies than my nearest rival. You know what Boy? There is always someone smarter than you out there. The bank manager used to build me up no end."

Conor examines his nails. Dirt is after getting in under them, and this seems to irritate him, but it doesn't stop him talking.

"I sold my soul to the bank, lock stock and barrel. As far I was concerned the masses were ill informed about the greatness of the establishment. Get in now I would insist when selling a policy and beat the rush. The policies were great value if – and this is important, Boy – if they were off loaded in five and not ten years. After five years the government wanted a slice of the action, leaving the customer caught to pay the bank charges and state taxes for money earned. So, I created offshore bank accounts for any policies that I sold. Once a few people bought into the concept it spread like wildfire. Most of my sales were at Ashmore Golf Club. Nearly every single member had a policy that I sold to them. Five years had passed, and I was earning more than the Branch Manager through commissions and kickbacks. On paper I had still had uncontrollable debts, but not one single person in top management ever thought of doing a simple check on my personal finances. Complete fucking madness."

He chuckles and rubs the back of my head, and I can't help thinking that Conor shows me more affection than my own prick of a father. Conor can relate to doing wrong things. As if he's read my mind he repeats: "I was once just like you, Boy."

Silently I wait for Conor to continue. We watch a bumblebee buzzing around. He takes a deep breath, waits for it to land, and sighs.

"The drink was taking its toll. On a drunken Friday night, I managed to piss off half the bar. No surprise that I received a long overdue punch. Blood flowed down my face. I was a mess; an out-of-control mess who drank more and more to hide from himself. Sore and shocked I tried to adjust myself against the wall. A sweet voice took control of the situation. She put me in her car, drove me to her house and cleaned me up. Next morning totally dishevelled I sat there absorbing my surroundings through blood shot eyes. My whole body hurt. A mug of tea was placed next to me. A man the same age as my late dad stood next to me and slagged me off. Looking down at me was Michael Davis the local garage owner. Sipping the welcome tea, we swapped tales. Michael had to explain to me that his daughter had picked me up off the floor. A figure caught my attention despite the hangover. She leaned at the door frame with hair as black as midnight tossed in a bun. Her eyes were blue and tempting. At that very moment I decided two things: First, I was going to marry her as soon as I found out her name. And second, that I would give the drink an overdue break. I stuck to my word and did both. Within two years, and with the grace of God, I found myself standing at the altar waiting for Michael Davis to give his daughter's hand to me. At the wedding reception I toasted my new bride with orange juice and never felt so blessed."

He sure as fuck doesn't sound like a man who was so blessed. In fact, Conor sounds tired of life. He shrugs and starts cleaning out his nails with a broken twig.

"We were the perfect couple. Louise worked as a teacher in a girl's school and did endless voluntary work. I kept getting promoted in the bank and doing endless shady deals on the quiet. An awesome house on an acre of land was bought and filled with loving children. New deals replaced old deals as the offshore accounts mushroomed out of control. Looking back now I can see that the cause of my debts changed from alcohol addiction to love addiction. Anything Louise wanted, she got. Like the rest of the world, she thought that I was doing unbelievably well, but I was just about managing to keep afloat in a market that was taking a tumble. The policies were affected by international forces. When the Six Day War started in nineteen sixty-seven, the constant stream of oil slowed coming into Europe. This single event gave the market the jitters. All shares and policies got sucked into the abyss and everything tumbled down the chart. I slaved nonstop, cooking the books, hoping to turn a disaster into profit."

Conor stares at his shoes as if they are telling him something.

"I was just about holding everything together when a knock came at the front door. Standing in a dark blue suit was Gary, the Guard who left me off the drink driving charge many years earlier." Gary explained briefly that the money tied up in his fake account needed to be released. Pen in hand he did the maths. Gary had been saving four times what he earned per annum. Something didn't make sense. Gary must have been laundering money on a large scale. This meant that he was just the middleman.

"I talked to him about the nature of the beast, how the stock market rises and falls. How it's all about risks. Gary didn't care. If I didn't get him the money by the next week, he would sell the debt for half price to a loan shark. Working in the force he had the pleasure of meeting countless colourful characters. I had no doubts that he was serious. My world was imploding. Gary wasn't bluffing. So, the next day I walked out of the bank with my briefcase stuffed with money for Gary. Handing it over, I knew that it would all catch up with me. Wouldn't it have been a lot easier if the Guard who pulled me over that night was a complete stranger? Maybe a year off the road might have reigned in all my madness!"

He shuffles back to the flower beds, and I follow, eager now to hear what happened. Conor seems more upset talking about his own stupidity than the time he told me about Timmy the Bull killing his mother.

"It was a junior clerk who spotted the unusual withdrawal. Two days later a special team from the main office in Dublin confirmed her findings. The bank stood to lose over five million pounds. I was forced to take responsibility for everything."

He begins weeding again, head down, avoiding all eye contact with me. A lonely canary slices the air with song. A slight chill takes the goodness from the air.

"Sadly, it didn't pan out like that. I decided to let the bank take the hit. Well, that's not completely honest, I had to let the bank take the hit, otherwise I wouldn't be able to set foot outside my front door again. This produced a couple of scenes never before witnessed in Cork Courthouse. In a room off the main corridor my lawyer scolded me to take a deal while the prosecuting lawyer stood by the door and glared straight through me. It was left known in no uncertain terms that I would go to prison, and I would stay in prison for a long time. By fuck I held my ground, come here Boy, sure I had no other choice. Upon entering the courtroom, I was terrified to discover that there weren't any members of the public allowed in. They were going to stitch me up in private."

Conor's story is proving to be better than The Muppet Show. My blister bursts. I try to ignore the stinging pain.

"Justice James Owens explained that the issues were sensitive to the bank and therefore, he respected the banks wish of privacy in their internal financial matters. I was shitting myself knowing that my lawyer, Justice James Owens and the bank manager were all members of Ashmore golf club."

As the Justice began to speak his words echoed around the deserted courtroom:

"Conor Flynn you find yourself before me on a very serious charge of tax evasion. How do you plead?" I was terrified, but I had to stand my ground. "Not guilty your honour." He eyed my lawyers. Then he turned to me and asked, "Is this your final reasoning?" I gave him a determined reply, "Yes."

"A day of defence argument and prosecuting argument began. It was nearly impossible to tell them apart. Both sides fought valiantly for the bank. A blind man could clearly see the writing on the wall. Nervously I watched the stenographer – that's the person who types everything down – stop when anything that cast a shadow on the bank was mentioned. The whole system was stacked against me. My own lawyer briefed the Justice as to why I wasn't taking the stand! This was a fucking bombshell to me, but when I tried to interject Justice James Owens banged his gavel on the sound block. By three forty-five the whole song and dance was completed. I got eight years."

I was super fucking confused. Was he guilty or not? I thought that he was selling shit he shouldn't have been selling. So how does he feel hard done by? Hans Christian Andersen couldn't explain what the fuck was going on in Conor's fairy tale of misery. He was finished weeding and sat down on the small stone wall which kept the flowerbeds separated from the grass.

"Cork prison is nicknamed the Hotel on the Hill. But this must be one of the most ironic nicknames ever thought up. It was chaos. I arrived just before lights out. A large prison Guard led me to a three-man cell where four other men were already bedded down. Four pairs of eyes locked onto my every move. It was the longest night of my life. Cramped between two bunk beds I silently let the tears roll down my cheeks. Boy all around me I could hear the other cell mates snore, cough, talk in their sleep and masturbate. I made myself a promise that I would get through this ordeal and be a stronger person."

The light was fading, and the sun was moving on to other parts of the world. Conor seems to realise that he needed to wrap it up and speeds up his delivery.

"My wife Louise was fighting a different battle. The house was repossessed by the bank within four months of me being locked up. The whole community had turned against her. She was spat at while out clothes shopping one day. Our kids weren't welcome in any of their friends' houses. It was impossible to venture out without getting abused. After six months, Louise let me know that we were finished as a couple. Only my youngest son ever came to visit after that."

He looks upset and hangs his head. I'm starting to get really cold.

"I waited, knowing that the tide was turning. Finally, on a frozen February morning postmen all over Cork City and County dropped large brown envelopes through post boxes. Astonished addressees opened them to find a statement of their savings. Enclosed and attached to the bottom of the page was a cheque. They say that by the week's end more new cars, kitchens and holidays were bought in Cork city and county than the rest of year save at Christmas. Some of them felt ashamed of how they all incorrectly assumed I got locked up for turning my back on them. By the following March I was averaging two visits a day from people who had sworn they would never speak to me again. I accepted each and every apology. Not everyone called, but those who did make the journey were friends worth taking back into the fold."

This story was taking a lot out of him. Trying not to think about Sharon Lyons is taking a lot out of me.

"Louise my ex-wife was now getting positive attention everywhere she went. Free hair dos and makeovers. Once she touched any clothes for herself or the kids it was automatically reduced. Her presence made people feel guilty at how judgemental they were to her and our family. But she wouldn't visit me. I waited day after day for a visit I never got. Only my youngest still visited. Louise poisoned the other kids against me with endless nasty jibes. It didn't matter. All I wanted now was my youngest son who was growing up very quickly. This boy was a dream child. He excelled both inside and outside the classroom. That boy cycled in rain, winds, frosts and snow to see me."

Darkness, like an unwanted guest, is on the way. The chill is now turning to cold. If he doesn't finish up soon, I'll have to make some lame excuse to go in or freeze to death, which means I would never get to touch Sharon Lyon's right tit again. I start to fade out Conor's voice, when something he says brings me back.

"My boy was starting college, studying law, and got himself a part time job repairing tyres in the garage by the service station. Money was so tight. Louise never got out of the debt we had acquired. We named him after his grandfather Michael. Because of the obvious confusion we all called him Mick. I was so proud of him, studying law, cycling between UCC, the prison and his job. He was the son every dad dreams of – not a sports hero, but a great hillwalker all the same. He's still fit as a fiddle. He plays at that fancy club your brother works at. I remember I just beamed when he told me about one of the girls at work and how sweet she was. I never asked what happened. I figure she broke his heart, because he never married – or even had a serious relationship, after that one."

I'm choking trying not to laugh. You couldn't make it up. Conor's son and my Aunt Mary. Holy shit! I have a fake coughing fit to cover it up. Conor doesn't notice anything strange. Conor stretches his massive frame. His hands hang loosely by his side. Then he shrugs as if shaking off something heavy. He turns to me.

"Well, that's about the long and the short of it. We'd better get back to Granny." He has a little chuckle to himself and adds, "There's one thing I forgot: How I met your Granny? Well, remember that the greatest aid to selling policies, were the housewives who could smell the good deal. Well Granny tore strips off your grandad and demanded he buy one there and then."

That night I dream that Sharon and I are flies again. She is lying on her back, legs sticking up to the ceiling. What can I do? I creep along the silver outside of the Zapper and push myself gently below the blue light. Inch by inch I get closer. Close enough to touch her. I stop and clean my two front legs vigorously. The pads at the end of my feet stretch out and grope Sharon's chest. Pleasure fills my body. Excitedly I arrange my body so that I am on top of her. Gripping her harder, and harder, I can't believe how lucky I am. Her eyes open. Startled, I stop. She wants me to mate with her. There is an enormous clatter of metal against meat. Frightened, I fly up and touch the blue light. Zap! I fall down next to her. She rises from beneath the blue light and flies off, leaving me to go cold on my own. I wake up gasping as a thought suddenly strikes me. Am I dating Sharon or her chest?

Chapter Nine
A Beating Would Have Left Him with More Dignity

Friday is our first day back at school. Only in Ireland would they bring you back to school for the last day of the week. We sit in our usual rows; tanned, bigger, stronger, and full of the joys of summer. We all bob gently up and down in our seats like balloons. Then the prick to burst all these balloons walks into the room.

"Good morning boys," he declares with fake optimism. "Good to be back. Open the windows please. This heat is cruel."

Beanpole eyeballs the class. "I said, good morning, boys!"

"Good morning, sir," we reply in harmony.

I pretend to reply. The only thing on my mind is Sharon Lyons. Sharon Lyons, Sharon Lyons, Sharon Lyons. It keeps spinning around and around in my head. I have a date with Sharon Lyons tonight. Sharon Lyons! Drunk with lust I count down the hours into minutes, into seconds, like some sad, soppy bastard.

Beanpole sits on the edge of his desk, with the corner stuck right up his ass and calls out to me. I snap out of my erection fuelled daydream, and back to reality No more thinking about Sharon Lyons. We are straight back to work.

"Fin, my petal will you open your poetry book?"

"Yes, sir," I answer, ignoring Beanpoles gay jibes.

"Page one Princess. Read the poem by John Finbarr Buckley."

I fumble for the page. I can see Sharon Lyons tits everywhere; on the front of my school bag, on my pencil case, and even on the back of my hand. Those are real. I drew them last night. I find the book and stand up, taking great care to hide my erection. I turn to the page, trying not to flash the drawing of Sharon Lyons tits to the whole class.

"Black dots upon Chimney pots,
Black dots rest upon chimney pots,
Swooping, sweeping and spreading lies,
Down to the garden the jackdaw flies."

"Stop! What is the poet telling us in these lines?" says Beanpole, stopping me in full flow, just as I am getting the feel of it. What the hell? I only got to read for five seconds. Why the fuck do teachers ask you to read in class and then cut you short? Waste of fucking time.

A blanket of silence is collectively pulled over the class. I am still standing, so I may as well answer.

"That crows are not to be trusted!"

"Excellent. Continue reading," says Beanpole not even looking at me. His eyes scan the room. He is hunting. I soldier on:

"Strutting, striding, standing tall,
Feeding, foraging, finding,
Wings clap, heads bow and he's back,
Black dots upon chimney pots."

"Okay!" Again, Beanpole cuts me short. This is very fucking annoying. His eyes come to rest on his favourite prey. "Harpo! Can you enlighten to us what exactly happened in the poem."

Harpo doesn't know what happened all summer, never mind what happened in the poem I just read. Beanpole is highly irritated by Harpo's silence.

"Hello? Are you even with us, Harpo?" he roars.

Harpo looks completely lost. "Yes, sir?" he answers not sounding at all sure of where he is.

"Well then, answer my question!" Beanpole demands.

"I don't know, sir."

That isn't the answer to give. Any bullshit answer works in poetry, except that one. Beanpole points a white bony finger at Harpo.

"Get up here now," he barks.

Harpo slowly takes the twelve steps up to Beanpole's desk and waits. We all wait. Beanpole sits against the edge of his desk. He is flustered. A career spent hitting schoolboys has been stopped. This summer a European law stated that it was illegal to hit children at school. Hands cupped together, Beanpole digs deep into his arsenal of hatefulness.

"You are a waste of time, Harpo. Yes, a waste of time. The thought of having to look at your worthless face day after day depresses me. Even you standing here is a waste of that floor space." He turns his attention to the rest of the class, appealing to us in a sweet, fake, tone. "Let's all be honest. Does anybody here think I am wrong about Harpo?" The blanket of silence gets warmer. We all pull it tight up over our heads. "Come on lads! One of ye geniuses must have a good word to say about Harpo?"

Another year and all we are is older and wiser cowards. Beanpole eyeballs Harpo with disgust. "You see Harpo? You are worthless. That's it in a nutshell. You are worthless. You are worthless now and you will be worthless in the future: A worthless worker, a worthless friend and a worthless husband. Any questions Harpo?"

Harpo shakes his head in stony silence. I hope Beanpole is finished so that I can get back to Sharon Lyons, but no such luck. Beanpole is only getting started.

"Why God put the likes of you on this planet I don't know. Maybe he did it as an example for the rest of us what not to do in life. You are the youngest child in your family Harpo, aren't you? Do you know what they call the youngest child? A mistake."

Beanpole laughs at his own joke. He thinks it's priceless. No one else laughs. This is getting uglier than usual. I wish Harpo could just get a smack on the head and be done with it. Beanpole shakes his head sadly.

"All you are doing here is wasting my time. This is where my life has brought me to, educating a halfwit whose own Mother doesn't even know he exists. Or maybe she does, which explains a lot. Why would she waste her time with such a waster for a Son?"

Harpo is crying. "I will tell my dad what you said."

"Don't bother. I will probably see him down in the pub tonight before you will at home. I will save you the bother and tell him myself."

Harpo sits back down. I don't know about these new laws about hitting school children. A beating would have left him with more dignity. The law might have changed, but that won't stop Beanpole beating up school children, one way or another.

I shower, dress, brush my teeth three times, and comb back my hair twice; my head swimming with delight. Tonight, I'm going to the pictures with Sharon Lyons! We are going to see E.T. It better be good. I spray on more deodorant, just in case.

Taking two steps at a time, I glide into the kitchen. Granny produces a five-pound note and slips it into my hand. She gives me a cuddle and says the money is to pay for Sharon and myself at the pictures. Dad sips his tea.

"She won't lose you anyway that's a given. I can smell you over here," he says, adding, "Fin keep your hands to yourself." This from a man who spends night after night drinking beer and pawing old whores.

"Leave the boy alone," says Granny. She kisses my cheeks and tells me sternly to enjoy myself.

As I walk out the backdoor, my attention is drawn to the bird room. I stop for a moment as the one surviving cock canary starts to sing. Dad still won't allow Paul near the birds. I don't feel an ounce of sorrow for either him or the birds. Fuck them! I am off out to enjoy myself. My new runners feel awkward as I walk over to Sharon's house.

As I turn the corner I stop, confused. Harpo is at Sharon's front door, joking with Karen Quinn while Sharon puts on her denim jacket. My heart sinks. She must have invited them along. Otherwise, why would they be all smiling and waving at me to hurry up?

I pretend to be pleased and we all walk off together. The girls walk ahead, and Harpo informs me in hushed, excited tones that my Sharon had arranged this double date, because Karen Quinn fancies him. I couldn't care less who fancies him. Now I'm stuck with two extra people on my date. I couldn't care less if Harpo is my best friend. I don't give a shit whether he lives or dies. My main concern is having a good time at the pictures with Sharon, which will hopefully include touching her in some shape or fashion. Even to hold her hand would be enough. Now I won't even get that far!

At the cinema, I go to pay for Sharon with the money Granny gave me, but she discreetly pulls my hand down and pays for the both of us. As we walk into the foyer she whispers, "Fin, get the popcorn and drinks."

As I wait to order, I wonder what that was about. Then I realise that Sharon is making it look like I had paid for her and was now buying the treats. Why? A light bulb goes off in my head. Granny says that a woman would trample all over her best friend to better them. As Karen walks up to us, I can see that she is impressed by the illusion that Sharon has created. Harpo has noticed and calls out: "Fin is Flash. Leader of the big spenders!"

We all laugh, but each one is a different laugh. Sharon laughs the confident laugh of someone who is in control. Karen laughs an envious laugh. Harpo sounds jealous under his jokey laugh. I laugh a relieved laugh that Sharon wasn't spotted paying on the way in. As I offer the popcorn around, it occurs to me that if Sharon could deceive Karen so easily. I should be very careful of her. I am so confused when it comes to girls.

A bright light leads us to our seats. E.T starts, and we all settle in. Sharon holds my hand and rubs it constantly. I can smell her shampoo. My hormones race as she begins to rub my arm. Even though I am living my best daydream, I can't relax. Maybe it's because I'm not in control. Sharon controls everything. She is a step ahead of me all the time. This shouldn't matter to me, but it does.

ET does his thing and goes back to his planet. I am none the wiser about extra-terrestrials, or human girls. As we walk out of the cinema, Sharon links arms and rests her head on my shoulder. The four of us head home in silence.

About twenty yards from Sharon's house, we walk straight into a gang of boys from school. They are at least two years ahead of us. As we stroll past, one of them spits at Sharon. It lands on her denim jacket.

Harpo turns and faces the boys who stand their ground as Harpo questions them. He doesn't seem to care that they are really big lads. Harpo isn't backing down. He starts shouting at the biggest one, calling him an array of names. Then Harpo jumps forward and hits him straight in the throat. The big lad gasps and holds his neck as Harpo's fist connects with his face, once, twice, three times. We all stare in disbelief as he falls to his knees. With a swing of his right foot Harpo connects with his nuts. The big lad doubles over and falls face down onto the footpath.

In a film that would have been the end of the fight. The big bully is beaten, the other bullies see reason, a moral lesson is learnt by all, and we all say goodnight and go home. Sadly it doesn't go like that in the real world. The other boys don't walk away. Instead, they smack me senseless. The girls shriek out as the punches rain down on me. I don't have a chance, so I don't fight back. I just try not to fall. Car lights shine down the road. Someone calls out to scatter, and they stop punching me. They're gone. It only lasted thirty seconds.

Every bit of me is sore. Sharon and Karen check my face. My head, nose, left ear and right cheek are bleeding. Harpo stands, panting. He is untouched.

Harpo gives me a brotherly hug and jokes that I will be okay. He sounds like he really cares about me. I wish he'd shut up. I'm not as tough as him, mentally or physically. My weakness eats away at me. To make matters worse, Sharon thanks Harpo for defending her with a kiss on the cheek. Talk about putting salt on an open wound. Harpo just shrugs it off. Jealousy engulfs me. If I can't be better than Harpo, who can I be better than? He has fuck all going for him in life and still he comes out of all the horseshit smelling of roses. Karen holds Harpo's hand as they walk away. Sharon and I walk home on our own. I don't even try to kiss her for fear that she would pull away, or worse, kiss me back out of pity. I go to bed, bruised, battered and broken.

Granny and Conor chat while she grills some sausages. The whiff of his Old Spice aftershave dances in among the smell of the sizzling sausages. Both of their mouths drop when they see the cuts and bruises on my face.

"What the flying fuck happened to you Fin?" Granny angrily demands. The old Granny is back. The Mad Mullah vanishes when Conor is around. But madness like sadness can't be hidden for long. Before I can mutter a word, she points again at me and shrieks even louder. "What the fuck happened to you? Are you fucking mute?"

I try to explain the night's events, but that only makes her angrier. Curse words bounce off the walls and ceiling. The neighbours would want to be deaf not to hear her. She is livid that I was attacked for no reason. Granny sounds like she would rather blame the whole thing on me.

Conor keeps well out of it. He slices his sausages down the middle, opens them out, and places three of them between two evenly toasted slices of wholemeal bread. Conor always has to make adjustments to his food: Cut a piece of fat off the meat, put butter over everything on the plate including the meat, chop vegetables into smaller pieces. His silence is louder than all of Granny's rantings. Munching on his sandwich, he winks at me. That's all I need to know. He'll sort Granny out.

He fills up Granny's mug with hot tea, and he gestures her to let the matter go. She frowns, unwraps a spearmint gum, and checks her varnished nails for chips. That is where I fit in her life nowadays, between a piece of gum and a nail check. Conor pours me some tea and gives me the other half of his sausage sandwich. Granny's chewing rings in our ears, as we try to eat our breakfast in silence.

Paul comes running in the front door. He is in a panic and has released his inner drama queen. "Auntie Mary is late, Granny. She's not here. Where is she?" Paul adjusts his shirt at least five times. I stop myself counting as it really irritates me. Then he sees my face. "What happened to you?" he gasps.

I can't deal with him. I turn my back, mumbling for him to leave me alone. Granny jumps in and saves me. "Get your bike and cycle to Hillside. It's a beautiful day, Paul. Go on, go!"

Paul nods and is quickly out the door. He doesn't enjoy arguing with Granny. He was 'too delicate for it' according to her. It made her fume when he refused to argue back. I think that he just can't be bothered lowering himself to our level.

The sausages taste nice. My mind is stuck on the image of Sharon smiling at Harpo. It was a well-earned smile that I couldn't see myself ever receiving. It's one of life's mysteries that your best friend can also be your worst enemy by just being themselves. I hate Harpo for being better than me at fighting. I decide to go round to his house after breakfast.

May opens the door. Wow, she is so damn cute! She gives me a warm welcome and shouts up the stairs to Harpo. I watch her perfect ass as she slowly walks down the hall. Does she know how sexy that walk is? Am I losing my mind? Even the slightest bit of attention from a girl and my brain goes to mush. The power they have over me both thrills me and scares me. I constantly worry that I am making a moron of myself in their company.

May sits inside the open kitchen door. Her arm is bent, scratching the small of her back. Slowly she scratches the same spot, over and over again. I just stand there mesmerised by her tanned hand, and the smooth, white, delicate skin on her back. Harpo drags me back to the real world.

"Fin, shit! Your face is in bits!"

It strikes me that May, for all her warm welcomes and friendliness, didn't ask me what had happened to my face. This girl thing was confusing. No time to linger. Harpo is on a mission.

"Fin let's go into town. Murph's burgers are doing free chips with a burger. Come on..."

I'm sold. Off we go to eat the mystery meat in Murph's burgers. Harpo relives last night's events over and over, on the walk into town. Each time the story is retold, I don't come out any better. After thirty minutes, I ask Harpo to stop talking about it because he is doing my head in.

Murph's is the kind of place that caters to teenagers and people with little cash. We join the people queuing for the Saturday Special. There are at least twenty people ahead of us. As customers trickle out, others join in behind us. It is weird. As if the queue never gets bigger or smaller. It's a constant.

Harpo doesn't know how to stand still and wait. He nervously fidgets with his jacket zipper. He shuffles his feet. He is really noisy. The noisier he gets, the quieter I get. At school he is as quiet as a mouse, but out in the big world he can't, or won't, shut the fuck up. We edge our way around the metal bar until only three people remain in front of us. I can tell Harpo is worried as he takes money out of his pocket.

"I need ten pence please," he says as he counts his money.

If I give him ten pence, then I can't get a can of Coke with my burger and chips. This is serious because Murph's adds lots of salt and vinegar. How can he embarrass me into giving him money in front of the whole queue? I hand over the ten pence and ignore his meaningless reassurances of paying me back.

Murph serves us our chips and burgers. He is huge, with a massive belly that seems to restrict his slightest movements. The weight has even slowed down his breathing, but he still commands respect. The staff jumps to his every word. Murph's runs the place like clockwork, with himself being the two arms of the clock, and all the staff being the second-hand racing around. He scans Harpo to check him out. Harpo comes up on most people's radar. Something about him seems to set alarm bells off in adults. They can sense he's different. Not bad, but different in an anti-social way. His face never seems to fit in. Today Murph eyes me with suspicion as well.

"What happened to your face?" he asks, panting at the effort.

"I fell," I reply. A chorus of laughter rises from the queue.

I grab our order and leave. Harpo follows. We sit on the windowsill of a derelict shop, and quietly eat our chips. The grease seeps through the paper. My hands are sticky and warm. The chips are perfect, and the burger is even nicer. All around us the aroma of deep-fried food fills the air. Discarded take away wrappers cover the street. This small part of Cork city belongs to Murph's.

We finish, throw our wrappers on to the street to join the rest, and walk slowly down the side street. Harpo puts out his hand and stops me. Coming directly towards us is one of the boys from last night. He doesn't see us as he stops to light a cigarette. Harpo grabs him by the hair. The boy struggles but does not fight back. He protests that he didn't hit anyone last night. I realise that he's telling the truth. He was the one guy who stayed out of the fighting.

"Don't bother Harpo. He didn't do anything," I say. "Let him go."

Harpo hesitates. Then a voice booms through the little street. "What the fuck are ye up to?" It's Murph, standing by his front door, smoking. He isn't impressed. We all run away together, down into Patrick Street. The other boy vanishes into the throng of Saturday shoppers.

We wander slowly down Patrick Street, feeling full and lazy. Up ahead, I spot two familiar figures. I try to duck, but they have spotted me. Harpo has seen them too and can't stop himself being a smart ass and waving at them.

"That's your Granny and the wino!" he says happily. "Is he going begging? Or is it his day off? Do winos get days off? Ha-ha!"

"Shut up, Harpo. You can be some fucking asshole, you know that!"

Granny and Conor stop to chat. I think that I might die of embarrassment. How can the ones we love embarrass us so much by their mere presence? Granny looks at Harpo like he has a disease and spits out a question at him. "Hope ye two are behaving yourselves?"

Terrified, Harpo mumbles, "Yes, Mrs Mulcahy."

"Fin, your dinner will be ready at six," she says, patting Conor's hand as if telling him to drive on. Why does she always tell me what time dinner will be at? It is always at six! Conor slips two one pounds notes into my hand. He nods, indicating that it's one each for me and Harpo. We are both over the moon.

As they vanish in amongst the Saturday shoppers we hurry to Tall Dan's amusements, a dark seedy amusement arcade down another one of Cork's countless side streets. I love Tall Dan's: A million mini flashing lights confuse the senses, ear piercing sounds shoot out of the games, followed by darkness once the games stop. Tall Dan's also has a nasty side. Menacing scumbags constantly patrol the place, asking for change. Why would any kid want to go in there? Space Invaders and Pacman is why. I'm not any good at them, but I still love playing. Harpo is a natural. His ten pence per game lasts him three or four times longer than mine. I often end up just watching him play after my money runs out.

Every now and again, some kid asks for some spare change. I know that behind this kid, somewhere in the darkness, lurk his bigger friends from the academy of lost causes. It's best to be polite, and just ignore them. Harpo never seems that put off by kids asking for money. He just keeps playing Pac Man. He's really good, eating all in front of him. Maybe the fact that he's always hungry, helps him relate to the game. I look up and my heart stops. Sharon Lyons is walking up with a friend. Sharon side steps me and glides up to Harpo. "How's Rocky today?" she asks with a flirty smile.

I want to die. Cool as ice, Harpo just keeps playing Pacman. I can't tell if he's acting cool, or just wants to play his game. Maybe he hasn't noticed her. Sharon tries to break the ice again.

"I feel a lot safer with you here, Harpo," she says, touching his arm. Harpo smiles, never taking his eyes off the game.

Sharon's dark haired friend stands next to me. I quietly fume at Sharon's behaviour, as I ogle her. She looks like she was poured into her jeans. The faded blue shows off her perfect ass. A large baggy jumper hides her tits, but I imagine that they are among the best in Cork. Her eyes have a tom boy glint in them. She smells like trouble; educated, upper class trouble. Suddenly, a weedy voice cuts in above the noise of the game. It's one of the pests that ask for spare change.

"Have you got ten pence? Thanks," he says.

Harpo growls back, "Piss off."

The Pest continues. "Ten pence, give me a loan of ten pence, boy."

Harpo's Pacman gets eaten up by one of the ghosts. He is pissed off. "Do you think I am a bank?" he snaps at the Pest.

"Yeah boy, an ugly bank! Give me ten pence," he answers with little conviction. The Pest seems to realise that he isn't going to get any money from Harpo. Slowly, he takes a step back. I exhale with relief. That was a close call. Then Sharon pipes up.

"Don't take that shit from him, Harpo!" she says, touching his arm again. "Go and annoy someone else," she adds, nodding at the Pest.

The Pest snorts. "Your old doll has a lot to say for herself. You have a mouthy one here sham," he says, pointing at Sharon.

Harpo is in deep, deep trouble, but all I can think of is that everyone is acting as if my girlfriend is Harpo's girlfriend. Sharon can't leave it go. She's like a dog with a bone.

"Why don't you run along, you little prick?" Her hand is still on Harpo's arm!

I feel a small tug on my sleeve. Sharon's friend looks terrified. She is staring past Sharon. A hand grabs Sharon's hair from behind. It pulls her down while the other hand smacks her head repeatedly. A skinny girl is yanking Sharon's hair back and forth. Sharon can't break free from this girl's grip. Her only defence is to grab the arm with her two hands and restrict the pulling. In a weird way I'm glad that Sharon is getting her comeuppance. I'm also glad to see that the skinny girl is no match for her. The endless tennis training has given Sharon a resolve that is well hidden. In one twist Sharon pulls the hand from her hair, and with a well-tuned back swing brings her prize right hand up and into the skinny girl's face. She wobbles as Sharon springs up and releases a kick square into her stomach.

Someone hollers, 'the owner is coming!' so we all run for the nearest exit. We run down the street as fast as we can, and find ourselves laughing, and gasping as we hide around the corner. Sharon smiles at Harpo. He smiles back, and then they both smile together. Sharon's friend makes some lame excuse about being late, and they both head off leaving me alone with Harpo. We walk away in complete silence; nothing said, nothing ventured, nothing risked. I resent him so much it hurts. My best friend is also my worst enemy.

As we pass Lazy Liz's Cafe, Harpo stops and points inside. My dad is sitting at a table, beaming an enormous grin at some woman. They giggle as Dad pours out tea. She tenderly cuts a piece of cake, and playfully places it in his mouth. Women love him. It's disgusting. They fuss and flirt with him. This woman can't take her eyes off him. She runs her hands through his hair and down to the edge of his chin. The cheap tramp gives him a peck on the cheek. She can't keep her hands off him. Whatever he has, women want it, the prick.

Harpo pulls my sleeve. He wants to say hello to them. I don't want to. No way am I playing the Father/Son game to suit Harpo, even if looks like he's bursting to get over to them. The more we stand there, the more I despise my dad. He's the man who left my mum to bleed to death while he went off out for the night. Harpo waves. My dad waves back and gestures for us to join him. Harpo is delighted. I walked past the café door, leaving Harpo to enter on his own. Dinner is at six and I'm not going to be late for Granny.

Chapter Ten
The Kitchen Is the Heart That Beats the Rhythm of the Home

The house is very quiet, which is unusual for a Sunday. No smell of the grill that Granny cooks for Conor every Sunday. Walking into the kitchen I have the sense to stay quiet. Granny looks too calm and too serious. There's a knock at the front door. I let Conor in.

He must sense that something's not right. No big grill waiting for him. Not even a cup of tea; just one very serious Granny smoking out the back door. She flicks the ash repeatedly in a well drilled motion. Conor evades the issue. He sits down and patiently watches Granny as she peers out into the steady rain, rubbing her crucifix over, and over again with her thumb. Patience doesn't exist in her world. There's no time for it. I know better and bury my head in my toast. Finally, Granny spits out: "You knew!"

Conor pretends that he doesn't know what was happening. I don't have to pretend. I don't have a clue.

"What do you mean?" says Conor.

The Mad Mullah is back, and not giving in to any old bullshit.

"You fucking knew all along."

Conor shuffles in his seat. He knows that this isn't going to be pretty. Granny has her teeth in him. He says nothing.

"I was worried sick, and you sat there in that chair and comforted me. There, right there and played the concerned worried friend."

Conor knows that he is in trouble. Real trouble. Silence is his best and only defence. I crunch the crusts and slurp my tea.

"Are you fucking mute?" Granny hisses.

"No." Conor tries to look humble. I try to look uninterested, but I'm dying to see where this is going.

Granny flicks the end of the cigarette into the flower beds. That's a mortal sin in her book. I notice that the kitchen is a mess, which is another mortal sin. Granny stands back, leaving a big space between her and Conor.

"You knew all along, and you never let me know! You knew from day one. What kind of a lying bastard are you?"

Conor hangs his head like a guilty dog. He can't meet her eyes. Tears are threatening. Granny lets loose:

"Get the fuck out of my house, and don't come back!"

She is interrupted by Dad, who wanders in from the back garden after feeding the birds. He washes his hands and pretends not to know what is going on. I swear this family should be up for an Oscar. Dad's lack of chit chat makes me think that Dad knows what this is about.

"I was just asking Conor to leave," Granny says sweetly, as if nothing is wrong.

Dad shakes his hands over the sink. "Good," he says as he dries them slowly with a tea towel. One word, but it speaks volumes. That's what I hate so much about him. He never ever cares about anyone ever.

Conor doesn't offer any reasons or excuses. I haven't a clue what is going on. All I know was that Granny is breaking up with Conor and Dad knows why. It must be something massive because Granny has gone all quiet. She is a woman who loses her nut over a dirty cup left unwashed in the sink, or crumbs on the table, or jackets left on backs of chairs. But with a major upset she never gets excited. She's just really quiet.

Conor leaves with a quick nod. Granny sits in silence; chipping flakes of nail vanish off her nails. I wait for her to start the blame game. She doesn't. Finally, she lets out a big sigh.

"Fin, go and clean yourself up. We are going out," she orders.

Ten minutes later, we're walking around the pools of water spread across the footpaths. The rain is falling heavier now. I feel the sleeves of my jacket let the wet straight through to my jumper. We pick up our stride as we march through the rain. Not a word is said. We get wetter and wetter. Granny hasn't told me where we are going. I figure it out when we go into the corner shop and buy three bags of mints. It's been months since we bought mints.

Five more minutes of getting soaked and we arrive at our destination. A huge arch spans the entrance. The front door is massive. It looks like it was built to welcome giants. A friendly lady in blue welcomes us in and guides us to a large room dotted with silent, motionless, ancient ladies. Only for the visitors there wouldn't be any noise. Our steps cause some white haired heads to rise. Expectant gazes look our way. We continue walking until we see a small, tiny, figure wrapped in a rainbow coloured shawl. Granny grabs a chair and sits down next to her.

"Betty how are you?" she asks, adding, "Look I brought Fin here with me."

My Gran Aunt Betty looks up at me. Her face lights up like a star. She is from Dad's side of the family, and needless to say he never ever visits her. Granny visits out of some sort of family guilt.

"It's been a while. Fin, is it still raining?" she exclaims.

"Yes, Aunt Betty it's bucketing down. How are you?"

Her old hands reach out and clasp my young hands. "Good Fin. Thank God."

We used to visit more regularly, but since Conor appeared on the scene Granny had only time for him. Maybe she figures it's time to catch up now that Conor is gone.

Granny has a set routine when we call in to see Aunt Betty. First the mints are handed over. Betty is always so grateful that we have thought of her. She holds our hands when she thanks us and draws little breaths of excitement like a little girl getting a surprise. Then Granny asks Betty all about her week and listens to every little detail no matter how boring. Thirdly, I read Aunt Betty the front page of whatever newspaper is nearby. Aunt Betty even likes me to read out the ads. She wants to know everything that is going on in Cork City, right down to the price of jeans or paint.

Aunt Betty smells of soap and mints with a hint of loneliness. Out the window is a colourful garden with countless flowers and shrubs. It's all so peaceful, and perfect. Nothing is out of place. All the old ladies seem untroubled in their own private worlds. It's like the whole place is too perfect to be true. Betty never complains. She loves trips to the countryside. She shows us the pressed flowers the bus driver collected for her. Granny takes each flower and admires it. Aunt Betty says a prayer to thank God for creating beautiful things. God plays a very important part in Aunt Betty's life. God supplies the helpers who care for and protect her. He also gives her something to do with her time. Aunt Betty prays every chance she gets, as God needs to be constantly reassured that she loves him. Granny and I never take a mint for ourselves as this would rob Aunt Betty. Each mint lasted at least ten minutes.

She doesn't suck or crunch it. She lets the mint dissolve on her tongue. Then she has another one.

I read the front page of the paper. My voice echoes around the room, rising high up into the rafters, and is lost in the vastness of the ceiling. Each news story is greeted like it personally means the world to her. God is thanked for the good news and asked for help to sort out the bad news. It doesn't seem to have occurred to her that God is responsible for the bad news as much as the good news. I fold the paper and return it to the rack hanging on the wall. We sit in silence, which makes the room feel even bigger.

Finally, Granny hugs Aunt Betty and nods at me to do the same. Aunt Betty thanks us for visiting and turns to face the big window. We leave in silence walking back under the big arch carved with the words – 'St Jude's Home for the Blind'. I pray that I never get old and dependent on others, as Granny leads me home, through sheets of cold rain.

I can't stand the silence in the house. I decide to pay a visit to Hillside and check up on Sharon Lyons. I'm not giving up my hopes of having another encounter with her. Also, I don't have anything else to do. The rain comes down in sheets. I get to the club half drowned. The place is full to the brim with the usual Sunday crowd. Paul shuffles between tables, removing dirty glasses and empty plates. Sharon floats around behind the bar and avoids eye contact with me. I love her and hate her at the same time.

The Club Chairman, Sean Harris inspects me, standing by the bar soaking wet. Then he turns away and exclaims to no one in particular, "Good God! We will get the tea and scone brigade in today, peering out the window and moaning 'Rain, rain go away!'."

Paul has vanished, so I have to put my hand in my pocket for a Coke. Sharon is ignoring me. It's as if I don't exist. I sip my Coke and gaze out the massive pane of glass covered in a million raindrops, I spot Paul. He is crispy dry and sitting in Dr Hughes flashy car. He spots me and pretends not to see me. Lovely, now he ignores me too. Soon the whole club will pretend that I'm not even here. Paul loves that car. Dr Hughes BMW is a status symbol that portrays success and class. Pity none of his secret queer friends can see him in this motor. They would die of homosexual envy.

Dr Hughes always has a smile for Paul. He's the only person in the whole club who actually has any time for him. Paul seems to annoy most of the club with his over-the-top prancing around, and continual talking. It doesn't seem to bother Dr Hughes. He just sits there and listens to Paul, rattling on as usual. I've never seen anyone that interested in anything Paul has to say. I figure it must be one sad faggot loner, talking to another sad faggot loner.

Watching Dr Hughes makes me think of my dad and our car. It's a good car, a Ford; but trips in the car are ruined by Dad constantly scrutinizing any unusual noises, or vibrations. It always ends up with Dad sticking his head under the bonnet, five miles from the sand and sea. "Ghost noises," Granny would mutter, as we other families whizz past to take the best spots on the beach.

I'm bored. Dr Hughes is parked in his reserved spot. It used to be right in front of the entrance door so that everyone was guaranteed to notice his motor, but over time scratches appeared and the odd mirror was broken. It became apparent that not all the peasants enjoyed viewing his wealth, so he took the captain's spot out of harm's way, further from the door. Dr Hughes insisted that the captain should get the best spot out of respect. The peasants applauded his unselfishness. The captain's car never gets scratched.

Paul looks really relaxed. So does Dr Hughes. They chat and smirk at the members they see scuttling past in the rain. The whole club and what it stands for seems to be way beneath them. Suddenly the car goes silent. Paul sits up and stares in my direction. I look around and see Auntie Mary, standing next to me. She peers out the massive window at the car. I can see by Dr Hughes lips that he has mentioned Auntie Mary. Paul looks uncomfortable.

This is prime time entertainment. Dr Hughes and Paul have been caught in his car, giggling like two little girls. They both jump out of the car and race through the rain into the club, without exchanging a word. Paul goes in around the back to help in the kitchen. Dr Hughes comes into the bar, shaking off the rain. He does not acknowledge me, or Auntie Mary who is tucking into a plate of scones. She pretends that they are having a conversation across the bar.

"These are really nice. You should try one. This is my second scone. Go on, have one and make sure to get cream," she says loudly. Auntie Mary is trying her best to wind him up. It isn't about the scone. She is showing the club that she can bully him. The pretence is long gone that they are a happily married couple.

Dr Hughes politely refuses. He walks to the bar counter and orders a black coffee. Auntie Mary watches his every move as she stuffs a fruit scone smothered in jam and cream into her mouth like a woman who has just discovered food. The pounds are creeping back on, after years of dieting. There was a new, slight roundness to her face. Members of Hillside call it the 'Hillside Stone'. All new members nearly always put on a stone in weight in their first year of joining because the food at Hillside is so good.

Paul comes in from the kitchen carrying a tray. On it is a pot of tea and a triple-decker sandwich. He looks as pleased as punch, as he serves Dr Hughes. They don't say anything, but their smiles speak for themselves. I remember Paul bragging to me that the minute the doctor set foot in Hillside, Paul would automatically pour out a soda water and lime for him. After his game of tennis, he loved a triple decker sandwich and a pot of tea. Paul would time it so that everything was ready when the doctor came out of the shower. I'd figured that Paul's devotion to Dr Hughes was because he was rich, had a BMW, and was married to our Auntie. Now I saw the whole disgusting spectacle for what it was: Faggot love. What I saw sickened me. It was faggot love and it seemed to go both ways. Paul goes back to the kitchen. Auntie Mary does not look inclined to be charitable. No chance of a free coke here. Sharon hasn't once looked at me. It's time to go home.

Chapter Eleven
A Quiet Drink and a Read of the Newspaper

Harpo's dad sat peeling the skin off an orange that had seen better and sunnier days. Every now and again I would get roped into the house by Mr Lucey when I called for Harpo. He was more confusing to listen to and understand when he was sober than drunk. For reasons I couldn't fathom, he would wear a tie all the time. Somewhere in his mind he reckoned that the tie would distract the viewer from the chronic alcoholic behind it. It was like trying to hide the iceberg that sank the Titanic behind an ice cube. His breath smelt or was it the house. I couldn't tell. So many odours and I had only one nose to take it all in. Beneath the smells lingered something more upsetting, an air of despair. The whole house was worn down by Mr Lucey. All the fixtures, furniture and fittings have been damaged, soiled or sold by him. Yes, even sold. Once Harpo came home to find a classy three-piece suit in their sitting room. He was delighted. A family friend dropped it off to them as a present. Next day after school the suite was gone, sold for drink money. All–electrical appliances suffered the same fate. My favourite is the living room door. Mr Lucey managed to sell the door one night in the pub to a fellow pisshead. Cash changed hands. Door was taken off the frame and left out the back. The door is still there uncollected.

The orange is divided into ten segments. Bits of orange and juice are everywhere. Impossible to tell what colour this table was originally. Like all the surroundings everything was painted and repainted by trembling hands and blurry eyes. A piece of orange is offered. I politely decline. One segment at a time is eaten. Every bite is savoured. Juice drops from a grey unshaven jaw. The conversation goes back to Mr Lucey, it always centres around him. He doesn't want to know about anyone else. This is because reality is something he can't handle. By knowing about me or my family would lead to comparisons with his family. Thus, the same old stories are dusted down and reinvented time and time again. All the tales consist of him doing ordinary things. But the way he spins the story, the listener is left in no doubt that only for Mr Lucey, the outcome would have being very different.

The time he won the Cork Senior Soccer League. It was his interception and pass that helped to score the winner. He didn't score the winner but takes the credit for it being scored. The player who did score the winner will never be able to forget that Mr Lucey gave him the pass. I wish he missed the shot on goal so we all would be spared the ordeal of having to relive it over and over again.

But there is one story he's never tired of telling. It was the time he was at work, yes you heard me, 'work', when a new machine worth a fortune was installed to carry metal from one end of the factory to the other end. It was massive, a series of rollers and beds where metal would be placed and carried automatically to its destination. The makers flew in from France and still the machine refused to work. A factory in Spain with the same machine sent its top engineer over to sort out the problem and he left bemused. For four months it sat idle. What could the company do? Mr Lucey asked permission to examine the machine. Senior management scoffed at the idea of an untrained or unqualified person touching their extremely costly merchandise.

Mr Lucey mumbled his way through the story. He always called me Fionn, the Irish for Fin, he thought it made him sound educated.

"Fionn," one person spoke up for me. It was the factory owner. He argued my case. "What harm can it do? We need that machine up and running or the cost of it in manpower and time will bankrupt us."

The owner joked that if I could fix the machine, he would pay me a year's wages. "Better still a year's wages in cash, an under the counter deal."

Mr Lucey panted into my face, his teeth yellow from cigarettes and his right-hand fingers-stained brown from nicotine.

"Fionn, my boy, this is where life gets confusing, this is where fate leads us for unknown reasons, and this is where it all went wrong. I offered to help from the goodness of my heart, no hidden agenda, never asked for a penny, I just wanted to help. So why did the owner offer the money, Fionn?"

Before I could answer Mr Lucey answered. He did that a lot, asks a question and then super quick answers it himself. Well, he does know all the answers anyway! It was his story.

"Well, it was a combination of two reasons, one, to actually try and get someone to fix the machine and two, to frighten the likes of me from showing the company up. Pride is a terrible thing Fionn, and the owner knew that he had spent a fortune so far, in bringing people in from abroad and the last thing he needed to find out was, that the solution was right under his nose all along."

Now this story was from Mr Lucey's angle. I knew that if the factory owner were standing in front of me here his story would be a lot different. Back to the man whose breath smelt of shit and whose house smelt of piss.

"There I was standing in the office surrounded by staff. All these college educated wankers staring at me. I once asked my boss how many years he spent in college."

"Fionn," he replied, "five."

"Well, I wasn't going to miss my opportunity to get one up on him, I told him two and half because a college year is around twenty-eight weeks. He wasn't impressed, Fionn."

"Anyway, I examined the drawing. Yes, I wasn't a tradesman or engineer. But I was a genius at constructing model aircraft. I could follow any drawing, no matter how complicated, I have been reading drawings since I was six. Eighty sheets lay out in front of me. By sheet five I returned to sheet one and started again. You have to read the drawing, then go back and read it again. It's not a book you're reading, you have to build the machine in your head before you build it on the ground." The Owner sneered.

"Have you any idea what you are doing, Lucey? Do you?"

Well, I just peered up from the table. Fionn, the crowd tightened smugly around the Owner. I could see them as they were, a pack of shits. So, I said to myself, I will call their bluff.

"I tell you what, if I sort this problem out, you pay me two years wages under the table."

The room erupted into fits of laughter. The Owner was acting the big boy now. He laughed condescendingly back at me.

"If you do it, I will give you five years wages under the table."

Now the arrogant pack of shits laughed uncontrollably Fionn, all the ass lickers around the Owner joined him in ridiculing me. Sitting as a quiet, well-spoken and dedicated worker I felt offended. It was my pride Fionn, they had really messed with my pride. I knew I could do the job. My head was getting flustered, so I asked the Owner.

"Give me two days…"

He freaked out.

"You'll get a day. Now, Lucey, get on with it."

Over the next few hours, the room emptied, the coffee poured, the sheets turned. The mystery got deeper and deeper.

By lunch time I spotted something. Thank God Fionn, I got something to work on. Sheets twelve and two were designed in New York. These sheets were the actual metal frame. This frame consisted of a solid outer shell with a hidden track to leave the cogs turn. The reason the track was hidden was for health and safety reasons. Now Fionn, the problem identified was the same for model aircraft or anything else constructed in America for European markets. The Americans have to change European millimetres to American inches. Whoever designed this part hadn't converted the millimetres into inches correctly. That had to be it. So, by two-thirty I prayed like a lunatic that this was the solution. But I had to be cautious. So best not to check until my shift was just about to change. Main reason Fionn, was that if I were wrong, I could do a quick runner out the gap and home.

So, at three forty-five we all stood in front of the main roller puller at the first junction where the main roller parted into four smaller rollers. A group of electricians, fitters and management watched. The Owner cast an eye over the whole scene.

So, I asked a fitter for a lump hammer. All stood shocked wondering what I was going to do with a lump hammer near the most expensive machine in the factory. The Owner decided to leave the circus continue. A large lump hammer was produced and Bang, Bang, Bang, Bang and a moan. A low moaning of metal against metal. It got louder and sweeter. The rollers moved once in rotation and then a little bit more. Lights flashed as the whole line started transporting metal from the back to the front of the factory.

They all stood in silence and stared at the floor. A long scratch mark showed where I had hammered and moved the offending part of the line. Hands darted out to shake my hand Fionn. All the ass lickers had to admit I was right. Those two-faced bastards nearly made me sick. I was some hero.

Mr Lucey spoke to me like an adult and never held back on the facts. So, Mr Lucey starts telling me things that you won't confide in a priest.

"Twelve thousand a year I averaged including overtime before tax. That worked out at sixty thousand in cash the owner gave me, imagine that Fionn, seeing all that cash in one go. My wife was dumb struck. We sold the two-bedroom semi and bought a three bedroom semi out, here next to ye. Now my little boy didn't have to share his sister's bedroom anymore. After the move we still had thirty-two thousand pounds left. Common sense was the order of the day. Sure, we had people asking for loans and in fairness to my wife, she suggested that we don't loan people money, no, she actually gave three close friends a thousand pounds each as a gift."

Mr Lucey sat and looked vacantly out the window into the distance. He talked and talked but must have forgotten it was me he was talking to. Because he didn't leave any details out, not one. As he explained to me his life I sat like a statue, didn't want to miss any of this.

"Now it's a classic case of be careful of what you wish for Fionn. The new house meant new neighbours and one of these neighbours was a woman that lived with her sister, a few doors down from us. She clicked straight away with my wife. They golfed together at Ashmore and enjoyed the ladies' mornings, walking and talking around the course. Pretty soon they were spending all their spare time together. Often the children would have to wait for me to do the dinner as their mum wouldn't come home till all hours. These late home comings were the fuel for the first of countless arguments. I never laid a hand on her, God forgive me, but maybe if I did, she might still be here?"

We both watched the sky through the filthy kitchen window while Mr Lucey lit up another cigarette, he choked and choked as he dragged in the smoke. Thought I heard a sneaky fart. Oh no, what a disgusting smell. Something must have crawled up inside him and died. He horsed the smoke back into his small frame. Mr Lucey wasn't tall and broad like my dad. He was my height and appeared to be lighter in weight than me. One thing struck you when he looked at you, his eyes, they were the bluest eyes I have ever seen. Granny often joked, "What the fuck was the great Lord God thinking giving a pisshead like him the most beautiful eyes in the world."

He continued wheezing out the words.

"Three days a week Mrs Lucey worked in the local supermarket. You know Fionn when you have money, money seems to follow you, one of life's mysteries. In this case all the meat, vegetables and fresh products were sold to staff at half price the night before their best by date. In one stroke, our shopping bill was halved. For the first time ever we were cash rich. Amazingly our savings actually began to grow, and the future was bright, very bright. We didn't live in fear of bills or strange knocks at the door. What I noticed most is that I didn't borrow, just say, tools off people for jobs, I went out and bought them."

The corner of an empty packet of cigarettes was torn off. He started to clean out his teeth with it. Another full packet of cigarettes was opened, and he constantly held either an unlit or lit cigarette between his fingers. Must be a nervous thing, his hands seem to move independently of his body. The energy used up by the adjusting and readjusting of his fingers seemed to calm him down! Can't believe it! Another cigarette was lit, and he continued.

"One Friday night I knew that I wasn't imaging the change in my wife's behaviour. She had begun to wear more and more expensive tops. As I was fixing a light in our bedroom, I watched her pick out her clothes to go out for a drink with her new friend. All this fussing around wasn't for my benefit."

He flicked ash off his cigarette into the overflowing ashtray. He got serious, very serious.

"Something wasn't right, something didn't make sense, and something couldn't be said. No, that would frighten her. I knew that I would have to leave things continue and all will be revealed. Work carried on as normal and the kids settled into their new schools. But still I sensed, no knew, something wasn't right. When you live with someone for fourteen years, Fionn, you notice the smallest of things. Anything that isn't the normal routine stands out. It was getting out of control. Sweetest Christ, she took thirty minutes to get ready to go and collect a Chinese takeaway one night. She spent half of the time choosing the right sweater. Then she stopped eating junk food altogether. We only ate the stuff once a week. She would get us the takeaway and then only eat a salad herself. All this watching how she dressed and how she ate wasn't for me. No, it wasn't and well I knew it."

Another orange is peeled. His hands are dripping with juice. He cleans them off his pants and wipes his mouth with the sleeve of his jumper. No orange is offered, maybe the fact I didn't want any earlier confirmed to him I wasn't an orange type of person. The orange peels join the cigarette butts in the ashtray. The journey to the bin seems to be a step too far. Mother of God, another cigarette is in his hand unlit. As he speaks, I can see all the pieces of orange stuck in his teeth.

"So, when I started piecing together this jigsaw, I saw a picture I didn't like. She was having an affair. Had to be. Now my problem was to figure out how to handle it? What could I do? Who could I turn to? Only person I could think of was her new best friend. Please God she will be able to help me out.

So, one evening while Mrs Lucey was doing overtime, I walked the short distance to the house. Stood there and rang the doorbell three times. Nobody seemed at home. But I could hear music. It was coming from the back of the house. Might as well go around! No side gate and I just wandered up to the kitchen. The kitchen window blinds were up, and the light lit up the whole garden. At first, I thought my mind was playing tricks. My wife was sitting on her friend's lap while her friend's sister poured out wine. This wasn't teenage girls being all pally pally. What I saw was raw affection."

Just then Harpo comes into the kitchen and is surprised to see me. Fuck him, he came in at the crunch time in the story. Mr Lucey rises and vanishes into the hallway. "Thank you, Harpo, I just missed out on a great story, you absolute bollocks. Fucking Thanks."

But a week later I got my chance. Had to take this opportunity to find out what had happened to Mrs Lucey, or my mind would explode. He sat, full of beer, holding a small glass of whiskey. My dad the selfish bastard was well on for a Friday night. He went out to some work to do at three o'clock in the afternoon and was now pretty smashed at ten. He tried to follow a quiz programme on TV, but I kept interrupting him. Granny was gone to bed and Paul was working at Hillside. I had the prick all to myself. How do I bring up Mrs Lucey? I decide, go straight in for the kill.

"Dad Mr Lucey told me about how he caught his wife cheating on him. Is it true? Sounds a bit far-fetched?"

Before he could lift his head, I plonked a few ice cubes and more whiskey into his glass. Got to use the right bait when catching the big fish. His bleary eyes roll around and stop at me.

"Say that again boy!"

Being very careful with my words I throw out my line.

"Mr Lucey told me about his wife's carry on."

The fucking idiot took the bait, hook, line and sinker.

"Pretty heavy. Wasn't easy on him."

The glass went up to his lip. A large amount of the gold liquid found its way down his throat. It seemed to lubricate his mind. Carefully I refilled the glass.

"Could you just imagine seeing what he saw? What he witnessed that night would push a saint over the edge. He let me in on the whole sordid disgusting episode one night. You know, God forgive me, but a separation is worse than a death. Because in a separation you still see the other person. Hold it, one second, that's that not strictly right in this case because his wife ran off for good."

The ice cubes rattled at the end of the glass. How much of this poison can he drink? Again, he tries to protest as I refill his glass, but I insist telling him to chill, he hasn't any work tomorrow. Without any encouragement he continues.

"Mr Lucey saw more than enough that night. He was broken. You see Boy, the heartache turns to shock which then slowly turns into anger. What could he do? What could he say? No matter what is said or done, the fact remains that his wife likes women! It was all too much for any man to handle. He decided to wait a week and when his mind can process what happened a bit better, he will confront, no, ask her what was going on. Believe it or not Mr Lucey isn't stupid. He works things out by not rushing in. So, the way he saw it, was, that, it was a phase! That it's a phase. She was experimenting with her sexuality. No need to rush to any conclusions. Wasn't the first woman to try something different? After all she was a mother to three beautiful children. Common sense will win out."

"In a strange way Mr Lucey had sailed his boat straight down the river of 'Denial'. By tossing the truth about what he had seen up in the air countless times he was catching and turning the facts to suit himself. What he saw now became, what he thought he saw. He didn't, no couldn't, understand what he saw. Leave it be for at least a week or two. Boy, he had convinced himself that everything would work out. Poor bastard."

The self-righteous asshole swirled the glass in a clockwise fashion and watched the ice cubes chase each other. This was the most he had spoken to me in a hell of a long time. He must know how deeply I hate him and everything about him. But still, he tells me things when I ask him. Don't know whether he tells me things to make our family look more 'normal' or is trying to be friends with me! He coughs and continues.

"Around February his marriage fell apart. Mrs Lucey had a plan in motion. You see Conor Flynn sold her girlfriend The Neighbour a policy and a fat cheque landed on her doorstep. The seeds of separation were planted. You see Boy one person's dreams can be another person's nightmares! Some women being the heartless bitches they are, will knife you in the back, take the knife out and then ram it through your back again and again."

Slowly and carefully, he shook his glass and the ice cubes rattled. The whiskey was gone. I did a super quick refill. He seemed to enjoy telling me what he knew.

"So, one night when the kids were sound asleep. Mr Lucey decided to talk to his wife about what he saw. Gently he tiptoed around the topic of her sexuality. Believe me that took some restraint. When finished they both knew what was being said and what was seen. A lot of men, no, most men, would have been nasty or even violent. Mr Lucey remained the perfect gentleman at all times. So much so that for reasons of sanity he only mentioned once about the one girl actually touching her. He wasn't opening that can of worms tonight. Let's be honest it was a no-win situation. He told me she defended herself vigorously and violently by shouting at him."

"I deserve to be happy. At the end of the day, she makes me happy. Why can't I be happy?"

"But Boy, Mr Lucey was sinking fast. Nothing he could say was going to change her mind. But God love him he did try and try. He pleaded with her."

"Happy, we have three lovely kids, a top class home paid for, money in the bank. What do you mean happy? We have to just get on with it. Raise our three children and do the best for them."

The more he argued his point the bigger the hole he dug. Without realising it Mr Lucey just made her point for her by omitting both of them from the list. It didn't go unnoticed, and she hammered him for it.

"Where do we come in that list? Way down with the new carpets? Or the new dining room table. Spare me…"

"In life Boy, some people talk a problem to death, others shout the problem thinking if its loud enough it might make more sense, others leave the problem fester where it is and pretend it doesn't exist. Mrs Lucey got up and left. Why bother? No amount of talking was going to stop her being happy. As well as that she had the whole thing planned out. No woman would ever leave a man without a backup plan."

My ears took in every single word.

"So that night Mrs Lucey vanished. Sneaked out the back door. Mr Lucey knew it won't be long before she is cuddling into her neighbour and planning out their new life together. It was an escape from the boring life that she felt trapped in. The family life was smothering her. Both women had the money to leave and add to this the fact that their little secret was out in the open. Not once did they consider the hurt that would be caused to those poor kids."

"I know you're young, but a relationship should be equal, fifty/fifty commitment. But this one was far from equal, sure no way was Mrs Lucey wasn't giving up the chance to be happy with the neighbour."

One morning when Mr Lucey had gone to work and their children to school, she packed her suitcases for the trip. Over the years Mr Lucey told me that Harpo nearly drove himself mad reliving that morning. He knew that he was right but couldn't be honest enough to admit it. His father hugged and kissed him, put his lunchbox into his bag while all his mum did was rub his head. Rub his head like a dog. The very last time he would see her and all she did was rub his head! His two sisters feared even worse, if that was possible. All they got was a 'see ye later' down the stairs. That's what hurt the children more than anything else. The fact there wasn't even a pretence. Just a cold goodbye. Their mother never did anything unless it suited her. Typical woman.

Tell you one thing Boy, before she and The Neighbour ran off, they dropped into the bank. Mr's Lucey had forged her husband's signature on their joint account and wrote in a sum of sixteen thousand and four hundred and thirty-seven pounds. She wasn't going to be petty down to the pence taking half the money. The house was his and half the money. She took only what belonged to her. Not once did it occur to her about the children, their needs and how any of this would affect them. By God she was ruthless.

Off to Dublin, fly to Heathrow and onto Toronto. This life wasn't going to be easy as neither of them had a qualification. What a joke.

Next day I had to call to Mr Lucey while delivering the post. He invited me in after taking a packet from me. He sat, it was like someone had ripped out his heart. He focused and focused on a piece of paper that lay on the table. He handed the note left by his wife to me and asked me to read it. It simply read – 'Gone to Canada, need to be happy'. That was it, no sorry, no if's, no buts, nothing about the kids, no mention of him…just seven words. Seven words to sum up her role as a Mother and a wife! He had no time to get angry the kids will be home in a few hours from school.

Next day I bump into him by the green. He looked half dead with the worry. Boy he told me that when he sat down with the kids he gently and easily explained that Mummy was gone. The kids thought he meant 'gone' dead. They were inconsolable. May and June broke down in hysterics while Harpo sucked his thumb. The room descended into chaos, so he had to scream at them, "Gone away."

Everyone fell silent. The tears stopped, Harpo took his thumb from his mouth. He asked his dad, "Gone where? Work?"

After losing control of the room once Mr Lucey couldn't risk it a second time. Honesty was the only policy. He had to tell them the truth.

"Canada. She's gone to Canada."

June stood up and ran upstairs. May put her head into her hands. Harpo reasoned and turned to his dad.

"With whom?"

That moment Mr Lucey decided to answer all the kids' questions but not to tell them anything that they didn't ask.

"A neighbour."

Basically, drip feed them information and to do his best to stop the family sinking into madness. The madness started that very first night. May didn't eat her dinner, June wet the bed and Harpo slept with him. By the end of the week all three children crammed his bed. Trying to set a routine was getting impossible. It dawned on him that the kids were terrified that he would leave. They whispered nonstop when he left the room. Their behaviour had weirdly improved. Gone were petty squabbles and shouting matches to be replaced by a deafening silence. If one of them did something wrong the other two would scold them and then shun them. It was getting out of hand. In the space of a week his children had grown up. A certain innocence was gone replaced by a distrust and a nervousness that would never leave. Boy when your mum died, I was spared all the emotional turmoil because you and your brothers were so young.

So, Mr Lucey found himself dealing with all kinds of craziness, from all different angles. A few days later and he gets a phone call at work. The bank queried him that due to the large sum of money that was changed into traveller's cheque did he have any problems cashing them. His jaw dropped.

Not once did he think of 'how could she afford to go to Canada'. So, in fairness to him he bit the bullet and let on he knew about all the money taken out of the account.

"No problem. Thank you."

The person from the bank informed him that the cheques could be cancelled within twenty-four hours.

"All sixteen thousand and four hundred and thirty-seven pounds can be returned to your account if any problems arise. Thank you."

For a second, Mr Lucey was going to cancel them. But being a problem-solving kind of person, he knew that this would give her a bigger reason not to return. Money was only paper and if she wanted to leave, she would leave. Just say she did come back if he cancelled the cheques, it could mean she might take everything next time, every last penny. He was smart enough to know that she wouldn't listen to him in their own home, she sure as hell wasn't going to listen to him on the other side of the Atlantic. That was his plan, come to think of it, he hadn't any other options.

Well life went on and on for a couple of years. Before one Christmas Mrs Lucey popped back up and upset the whole house. She rang one Saturday morning. I think Mr Lucey said it was May who got to the phone first. "I can't tell one of those girls from the other. Like, they should wear name badges. Anyway, anyway, give us another drop, go on Boy."

The glass was refilled with ice and whiskey. What worried me now is he hasn't had a piss in ages. So, if he gets up at all he will go to bed. So, I only half fill his glass with whiskey and fully fill it with ice.

"You see Mrs Lucey's accent was completely different. It had to be, otherwise no one in Canada would understand a word she said. She didn't recognise her own daughter's voice. Those three innocent children clustered around the phone. They each spoke around ten minutes to their mum. All asking the same questions. All getting the same tale about her happy fairy-tale of a life. Then she was gone, promising to ring again soon. Now Boy! The Mother was obviously lonely and decided to mess with the kid's heads. Sick that's what it is."

"Mr Lucey was out the front washing his car and sensed something wasn't right. Silence, the house was too quiet. The kids must have gone out. Then a clatter of excited chat. They were all in the hall, out talking each other. Louder and louder, it got and then nothing. They ran out to the driveway to tell him what had happened. Mr Lucey stood glued to the spot. He never expected this, he should have, but he didn't. Each of his children took turns to inform him what their mum had said. He soon realised that it was the same story rehashed over and over. Their mum was doing great, missed them, missed Ireland and missed the weather. No mention of her husband or no apologies. As the kids retold the conversation with their mum certain truths appeared. Truths that only appeared in word and not in thought. The thoughts of the children were clouded by emotion. Mum must love them why else would she phone! Whereas the words spoke for themselves. Their selfish tramp of a Mother never once gave an inkling she was coming home, the words said by all carried a simple theme. Mrs Lucey never asked her children much about themselves, no, the opposite, all she kept telling them was how 'happy' she was. Why the hell would you ring to tell your kids that you're happy, after deserting them? Boy, learn from this, learn, because this is how life is."

He was actually upset for the Luceys, this didn't make any sense to me. Or was he just deflecting from all the heartache he has caused under his own roof.

"Mr Lucey, Boy, he knew this was trouble. That night the bed wetting returned, the loss of appetites and the dreaded silence of worried and scared children. By the second night his bed was full again of restless bodies. For a year and a half, he had held what remained of his family together. Things were starting to level out, a normal had returned. Granted it wasn't the normal he wanted but it was normal. Life can be built around normal. Kids crave normality. Scars were now re-opened and sore to touch. All the healing was undone. His children were now being infected once more by that woman's unloving touch. A simple thirty-minute phone call had thrown the whole house into chaos. The most frustrating thing was Mr Lucey didn't get to speak to his wife. If he did, he could have asked her some basic questions about her plans. Was she ever going to visit the kids? That was all he wanted to know. He still loved her, the poor bastard, a sin that's what it all is."

"But I tell ya Boy, she was far from finished with messing with their heads and hearts. I was on a van delivery on overtime one Saturday leading up to Christmas. I had a massive box to deliver to the Luceys. So, I knocked on the front door and Mr Lucey carried it into the kitchen with me. Well, it was plastered in Canadian stamps, so we all knew who it was from. Mr Lucey threw on the kettle for a cup of tea for me."

"I stood and watched him open the Parcel for the three kids. They were wired with excitement. He pulled out three black bags. They all had the same items. A blue sweatshirt with 'Toronto Maple Leaves' written in blue on a white maple leaf. Under this sweatshirt was a neatly packed red sweatshirt with Canada emblazoned across the front. The kids loved them. As the red sweatshirts were lifted, more excitement ensued as a red and white scarf with Canada stamped on it fell out of the sweatshirt and on examination a matching hat was found. No doubt about it these were expensive and classy items of clothes. As the kids tried them on, they found that they were a little large. This was ideal as they will get more wear out of the clothes by growing into them. Mr Lucey's eyes filled with tears, he glanced at me. He kept it together. He had to, he was the Dad.

How could she be so stupid, so thoughtless and so bloody selfish? Because now staring at us were symbols of Canada where his wife ran off with The Neighbour. His kids for all purposes appeared like they were proud, yeah weird as it was, proud their mum was in Canada. Fickle as kids can be, they never realised that all this Canadian gear would draw a lot of unwanted attention on to the family. Honest to God Fin that woman is a nasty piece of work.

So, Mr Lucey and I went out to the garage. In there all alone he cried. Palms against his face he pondered that he couldn't take anymore. When was it going to end? What next? As he dried tears from his face, the phone rang. This was getting way out of hand when he was terrified of the sound of his own phone. Thank God it wasn't his wife.

It was their Auntie, all three kids excitedly waffled on to her about their presents. I followed him back into the kitchen, didn't want to leave him in a destressed state. Mr Lucey then spoke to his sister. Love is a powerful thing and in the right hands can reduce any of us to humble onlookers in life. She offered to collect the children and insisted on all of them spending Christmas in her home. Shocked, Mr Lucey thanked her. One whole week of mental and emotional rest. He sighed with complete relief.

Later that afternoon, the kids ran into their Aunties house wearing matching red Canada sweatshirts. As he walked home, he stopped, flickering Christmas lights caught his eye and the merriment within The Horseman. Staring into the Horseman pub, Mr Lucey needed some distraction, something to take his mind off things. He said hello to me and commented that it struck him as odd how full the place was at 5pm. A seat by the TV was free. Picking up a newspaper he ordered a stout. Six stouts later and he made the journey home. Boy, I never saw him drink before. No, never once.

Sure, he stopped me out delivering the post next morning and confessed to me he wasn't really a drinker. His head was dull, and stomach upset. The taste of the stout didn't appeal to him or the routine of having to pee all night. Neither did the company. Mr Lucey was a shy man, really shy and resented the fact that having a drink on your own meant that he was easy company for the losers to latch onto. These so called regulars were nothing better than Bar Flies. The shite they spewed out frightened him, especially the way humourless stories were repeated till the laughter stopped. Could you imagine living with these failures, he joked to me? Their wives must be delighted that they were out in the pub and not at home. But the writing was on the wall. For a smart man he didn't see that he had a lot more in common with the Bar Flies than he realised.

By four pm that very afternoon I saw him ordering his first pint. He was back in the pub again. This boiled down to only one fact and one fact alone. Take all of this on-board Boy, listen to your Old Man. With all his dislike of the taste, smell and feel of the pint it still did something for him, it lessened the pain. All the negative effects of getting drunk were greatly outweighed by that one simple fact. Last night was the first night in a year and a half that he slept straight through. His wife and the neighbour never entered his head. The alcohol had given him the peace of mind he craved, it was a pity he had to drink so much of the stuff to get the effects. Granted, I was in the pub too. But I only had two pints before tea and two pints after. The pub to me was for the craic."

Even during this story, he has to make out that he is some sort of fucking angel. The self-righteous prick continues.

"That night in the pub and seven pints were drunk. Free hot whiskeys were on offer, but he declined. It was whiskey that drove his father mad. His late mother always warned him to stick to the pints and he would be okay. The craving for the beer was in his blood. So, the more he drank the more he wanted. Not having the kids to take of was a massive relief.

By night three and he had eight pints and read two newspapers. Carefully, he thought he was crafting an image of a man just out for a quiet drink and a read of the newspaper. To the rest of us in the pub, he was an anti-social drinker who hadn't the decency to even acknowledge the bar staff. Like, I saw a side of him I didn't like. He ignored nearly everyone around him. Drinking is supposed to be a social event and it doesn't kill you to be nice."

Sitting straight up my father the know-all points and warns me.

"You never breathe a word of this to Harpo, you hear me, but that night was the first night Mr Lucey sleepwalked and peed on the landing. We were talking out the back of the bar and he told me that the next morning he stood confused as to why there was a damp patch in the middle of the carpet. That happens when you are a kid, I have done it, but not cool as an adult. Well, he knew when he woke up something wasn't right as he didn't need to go for a piss. Speaking of pissing, one drop for the road Boy. I need to use the bathroom."

Super quick, I fill his glass with whiskey and add water. Lots of ice is thrown in. Don't want him too wasted. This is getting too interesting for him to slip off to bed. I wait, I wait, thank you God he's back.

"Good Boy, hey, hey, you filled my glass up. Where was I? Oh yeah, Christmas day, hungover, he barely ate a morsel of dinner at his sister's house. What comes with drinking heavily is a false sense of reality. Mr Lucey spent a lot of his life in denial. Just deny what is happening. Deny that his wife doesn't love him anymore and everything will work itself out. Deny that he is drinking too much and also that won't be a problem. The first steps of becoming a heavy drinker are easily taken by most and helped along by many. His sister saw he had a hangover but didn't say anything. Her brother had never before arrived so dishevelled like this. He wasn't a drinker and she, in her innocence, thought he was just blowing off some steam. What helped Mr Lucey become the complete pisshead he is now, is that he wasn't an awkward drunk, not far from it. He was a touch ignorant but not nasty or bad tempered. Therefore, like a true pisshead, he handled his hangovers with patience, a bit like dealing with a child teething, plenty of patience and eventually the screaming in his head will stop. Signs were there from the start but no one near him could read them. Biggest sign was when he asked his sister to care of the children for two more days. She was ecstatic, not having children of her own meant more time loving her brother's beautiful bunch. By eleven o'clock New Year's Eve Mr Lucey had ten pints and was fairly tormented looking. I mean he was pitiful, talking to himself under the TV. So wasted that he collapsed and slept straight through the midnight celebrations."

"This New Year like so many more in his life would be greeted through blood shot eyes. All that mattered now to Mr Lucey was killing the pain. The more being drunk meant the more pain been subdued. His whole physical being was slowly crumbling. Like Boy, he was quiet a good-looking bloke. First to go was his boyish smile to be replaced by a constant frown. Next his skin turned from a white to a creamy flaky texture. A once straight back now stooped and hands constantly trembled. After a year of drinking every night, he was a mess."

"There were serious consequences. Three months of Mr Lucey missing days, lateness and heading off home earlier, tested the patience of all his work colleagues. Help was offered. But it's impossible to help someone, who doesn't want to be helped. Fired – after twenty years fired. He couldn't care less."

"One night in The Horseman, he was having a cure. He whispered to me that a bank statement had landed on the hall floor that morning. It confirmed his expectations. With a pen in hand, he calculated that he could get seven years drinking from that amount. Plus, the job agreed to give him a redundancy package if he agreed to instantly resign. I sat there gob smacked thinking about the amount of money he had. The Gods had arranged it that if he wanted to drink so be it. The children didn't feature in his plans anymore. They didn't feature in anybody's plans. After a year and a half of watching their dad getting drunk, sick and wetting himself, they had seen enough of life. The kids had gone very quiet at home. But from the outside, I could see that they had retreated to places in their minds that they hoped, no prayed, that no one could ever find them. Mr Lucey never once was abusive to them, he just didn't see any of them ever. It was like they were invisible to him."

This all made sense to me, often over the years I had seen him bounce in the front door and collapse in his favourite chair. Well favourite chair sounds a bit romantic, it was the chair that he wet himself in most, Harpo, May and June wouldn't sit in that chair if you paid them. By the time he woke next morning the children would be gone to school.

"You see Boy by sticking together they learnt to survive. But surviving wasn't going to help them bloom in life. All they wanted was the madness to stop.

Here's one, Boy, for you, this will put a smile on your face. The Horseman pub heaved with people, European soccer was on the TV. Very busy for a Wednesday night. Among the drinkers, one drinker stood out. A fine tall cut of a man held court. The locals couldn't get enough of him. The whole place knew him except Mr Lucey. Boy, he could drink, pints disappeared pretty quickly from his large hands. No matter what he said people listened and he worked the audience professionally. He made a point of listening to people and smiling back at them when they answered his countless questions. Calling me over Mr Lucey inquired as to whom this man was?

I told him Conor Flynn, he used to work for the bank. He now had a face to the name. Within an hour I saw Mr Lucey chatting to Conor. They clicked instantly. Conor could disarm the shyest person. Something about Mr Lucey didn't sit well with Conor. Because, Boy, Conor Flynn won't be sitting with you round after round if there wasn't something in it for him. In his experience, loners who drank in pubs tended to have cash squirreled away. The signs were there, Mr Lucey didn't drink the cheapest beer, and he stayed out of rounds and wasn't mean. Far from it, he insisted on buying Conor a pint back every round. No, this man had money. Equally something about Conor struck Mr Lucey. This guy was no ordinary man.

Weeks later and Mr Lucey asks me in for a tea. The post is light, so I say thanks. He tells me about the events of the week, he is a broken man. He saw his life for the disaster it is. Boy, the last nail in the Luceys coffin of misery was firmly nailed home by their mother. As she drove the nail home the kids gladly encouraged her to do so. Once again, they were at home alone watching television. Phone rings. A whoop electrified the house."

"Mum's coming home."

"Each child started shedding tears. Mum was coming home to end all this madness. She would save them. Mr Lucey saw all this unfold around him. In a moment of clarity, he knew that he would have to get help to stop drinking. Now he saw the misery that he had inflicted by the expression on the kids' faces. Simple things like dinners, they would have proper dinners again. And lunches for school, beds will get clean sheets and the smell would leave the house. The phone call ended, and they all jumped around with relief. The nightmare for all of them was going to end.

Boy he was a mess, his head was melting from all the pressure. Mr Lucey had reasoned correctly that he was failing in taking care of them and the kids knew he would frighten Mum from returning. He saw by his kid's reaction to the phone call a weird kind of logic. They wanted their mum back so badly it seemed their dad was the root of all their problems.

Who ever said that absence makes the heart grow fonder really understood life. The longer the Mother was in Canada, the more the anger towards her lessened. On a daily basis they were exposed to the pain caused by Mr Lucey and his drinking. This pain ranged from not being loved, to hunger, it covered every emotional and physical need imaginable and all only a hundred yards from our front door. You have a good idea what he put them through.

Having boys is a holiday compared to having girls. May had just started puberty and needed a Mum now more than any other time in her life. She needed a Mum now more than ever. The main thing wearing May down was she was rearing her two siblings. At thirteen, she found herself a mother figure constantly dealing with washing, ironing and organising meals. More than anyone, the very child who barely held it all together, needed her mum back.

Days rolled into weeks, which turned into long months. No Mum, no phone call, no letter, nothing. The normality of despair continued. Each child had whole stories made up in their minds as to why their mum never returned. The longer they waited the more fanciful the stories got. Without knowing it, all of their stories had a similar ending. Their mother must be dead, how else could she forget them."

Silence, silence, a snore. Damn it, he's asleep. Sneaked off to bed and left him there. Paul can wake him up when he comes in. About five minutes later I heard the front door open. Then Paul helping Dad up the stairs. Within a few minutes Paul was getting undressed next to my bed. His jacket and jeans were bone dry. Very unusual as it was bucketing rain all night. His boyfriend, the doctor, must have dropped him home.

It's the following morning and Dad is walking across the landing. He shouts down the stairs to see if anyone is in the kitchen. I know he wants someone to put the kettle and toast on for him. Quietly I slip out the back and out across the green. He can make his own fucking breakfast.

Chapter Twelve
The Big Question

During the school year, the weeks blend into each other and life stumbles on, one soul destroying day to the next, from Monday to Friday. Weekdays mean nothing to me. I live for the weekends. Friday afternoon, the gloom lifts. Six o'clock on a Sunday, it starts to reappear. School isn't for me. I don't like it and it sure as hell doesn't like me either.

It's Friday evening, so I head over to Harpo's house. We talk in the kitchen while May and June prepare dinner. They are doing some kind of a stir fry which smells really nice. I'm relaxing into the weekend, quietly enjoying the view of the girls' sexy asses, when I hear something. It sounds like a quick knock at the front door, followed by someone coming into the house. The kitchen door opens. Standing in the doorway is a woman holding a cute little black boy by the hand! We all stare at her, stunned into silence. Who is she? She seems as surprised as we are. As if she had walked into the wrong house by mistake.

Harpo is about to speak when the woman smiles. "Ger is that you?" she asks.

Harpo's eyes get even wider. "Mum?" he stammers. No one moves. No hugs or kisses. Not even a 'hello'.

"How are you darling?" asks Mrs Lucey.

Harpo is dumb struck. What is going on? Is that his mum with a black kid? The kitchen is silent. May and June exchange a quick look and walk out of the kitchen. Mrs Lucey smiles as they brush past her.

"Who are your friends?" she asks, as if this is all completely normal. She didn't recognise her own daughters! Harpo looks disgusted.

"That was May and June who just walked past you," he spits back.

I can tell that the smell in the house is getting to Mrs Lucey. The fact her own daughters have just ignored her, doesn't seem to bother her as much.

"What is that smell? Its stomach churning," she says, twitching her nose.

The little black boy is glued to the spot. He can't take his eyes off Harpo. Maybe he's never seen a ginger before.

"Mum, why are you home?" Harpo whispers.

She brushes it aside. "I just am." It strikes me that Mrs Lucey isn't a nice person. She is very, very attractive, but not nice.

"You staying here?" Harpo asks.

"I don't know yet. Where's your dad?"

"The Horseman."

Mrs Lucey looks surprised. "What is he doing there?"

"Drinking."

"Your dad's out drinking?" Mrs Lucey repeats, adding "Drinking what?"

"Stout. It's a bit early in the year for lager," Harpo answers. Mrs Lucey looks confused. It's like she doesn't speak English. Harpo seems to have recovered from his shock. He winks at the little black boy who is still standing there staring at him. "Who is this little fella?"

"Your brother, Joel," she replies as if she'd just been asked what day of the week it is. Mrs Lucey tugs on her little boy's hand and turns to leave. She has one last question: "Are my bags safe here?"

We both nod feeling insulted. Who does she think we are? She is out the door in a flash.

I look over at Harpo. He looks angry. He's not talking. He has no idea what I would give for my mum to walk into my kitchen. I know that I should be delighted for him, but jealousy is eating me up. He's got his mum back. Harpo gets all the breaks. He gets all the attention from girls. He's tougher than me in a fight, and now his fucking mum is back. If I am no better than Harpo, then I must be at the very bottom of the pile of shit that is life. Simmering with envy, I make some lame excuse and fucking leave.

I sprint home and blabber straight out to Granny what just happened. I don't get it all out because my prick of a dad arrives in from the pub. He looks like an excited schoolgirl who is bursting to tell us the latest gossip.

"You are not going to believe this! I was standing by the door of The Horseman, and who walks past me, but Becky Lucey. I say 'Hi, Becky' and she barely says hi. You won't believe it, she has a…"

"A black kid!" Granny, and I exclaim at the same time.

"She asks me where her husband is," he continues, not missing a beat. "I point him out through the packed crowd and follow her. I wasn't going to miss this. Mr Lucey has been pinting away for hours. He can't believe his eyes. She has no shame after all she has done. 'Hello', she says, 'we are home for a visit'.

Lucey asks, "What do you mean 'we'?"

"She meant her son," says Granny.

"She did! How do you know that?" says Dad. Not waiting for an answer, he keeps going. Lucey looks her square in the eye and says, "Your son lives with me, remember?" Then he notices the little, black kid hiding behind her legs all along. That gives him a real fright. He's white as a sheet. He composes himself, drains his pint and asks, "Where did you get him from?"

Granny and I are transfixed. This is too good to be true.

"Same place I got the other three," she answers him, all spit and venom. "I'll tell you one thing – she hasn't any time for him," Dad says. "Bold as brass in front of everyone in the pub, she tells him that they need a bed for the night."

Granny and I wait for the conclusion. I'm a bit disappointed. No fist fights. No new revelations. Dad finishes off by telling us that Mrs Lucey is staying at Harpo's with Joel. I yawn and stretch. Granny starts to tidy up. Dad has lost his audience. Then he remembers something:

"I almost forgot. The little black kid is really cute. His name is…"

"Joel," Granny and I shoot back.

Granny wags her finger at Dad and me, "Both of ye stay the fuck away from her. Do ye fucking understand? She is trouble with a capital T."

We nod. Dad is out of steam. He gets up and puts the kettle on. I go into the front room and watch whatever rubbish is on TV.

We sit on the wall, as Harpo tells me about his mum moving back in. He says they slept in the front room which isn't as dirty as the rest. After eating breakfast, and dressing Joel, she started to clean the kitchen. She spent the whole morning cleaning the kitchen. The girls are still ignoring her. At round three o'clock, she asked Harpo where his dad was.

"I told her that he'd be in the pub. Where else would he be on a Saturday at three!" Harpo explains. "Still the penny hadn't dropped with her. So, Fin, I was getting tired of her all-innocent routine and decided to give her a few facts. What do you think happened when you ran off? I asked. Dad fell apart – that's what happened."

"What did she say?" I ask.

"She told me to take my brother down to the park, because he could do with a bit of fresh air."

I shake my head in disbelief.

"But you know what? I took him to the park. He's a really great kid. We had fun. And when we came home the kitchen was clean, and bright, and shiny. It smelled fresh. She'd been to the shops and coked a stew. Only Joel and I ate it. May and June went missing. It's not perfect, but it's a start."

The days pass. Every time I meet Harpo, he fills me in on what is going on. In the morning, Mrs Lucey tackles one of the rooms in the house. The backroom was first to get a makeover. Plaster was stripped off the mouldy walls, carpet ripped up and the room laid bare. She says that she is waiting for the bank in Canada to forward her savings over here. Then she'll move out to her own place.

I can see that Harpo's resolve to not like his mum is beginning to crumble. He is dotty over his half-brother Joel. They go to the park together every day. Harpo tells me that Joel sits outside the bathroom door every time Harpo goes to the toilet, and that he creeps into his bed for a cuddle when he has a nightmare. Even May and June can't help noticing their baby brother, though they still ignore Mrs Lucey.

Harpo sensed that Mr Lucey didn't buy into any of it. He wasn't stupid. All this redecorating and tidying up wasn't for their benefit. No. His wife had some kind of a plan, and he would bet his last penny it didn't include any of the family. Harder and harder she worked. The bathroom was transformed and still only Harpo made any effort to get on with her. I could see after a few weeks that Mr Lucey had decided to leave his wife run the house the way she wanted. It was at this time with Mrs Lucey at home, I got to see how selfish Mr Lucey was as well. Her very presence in the house constantly highlighted his constant absence. It was becoming more a case of – she wasn't what they wanted but she was all they got. Mr Lucey even got Harpo and me to help him with Joel's new pets.

The wire was nailed tightly to the frame and that was it. We stood back, a pretty impressive rabbit hutch dominated the garden. Two small rabbits squeezed into the corner of a cardboard box as Harpo and me got the bus home from the pet shop. This was a surprise for Joel. Mrs Lucey asked Harpo to help Joel to feed and clean out the rabbits. The cardboard box was put by the back door. Mr and Mrs Lucey watched Joel jump with joy as he opened up the box to find two little rabbits staring back at them. One pure white rabbit and one jet black rabbit. No huge leap of imagination was made, as the black one was called 'Sooty' and the white one 'Snowball'. I laughed to myself that the rabbits were like the Luceys black and white.

The back garden was walled in so the rabbits could be left to roam around at their leisure. Drama ensued, as we ran forever trying to catch them and return them back to their hutch. It was all good fun. On the second day, Harpo and I left them out to run around on their own. We watched them playfully sprint around the edge of the garden. They smelt everything, nibbled everything and constantly pooed. Snowball seemed to be adventurous. He wanted to examine every plant, bush and tree. The phone rang and Harpo knowing the rabbits couldn't escape ran in to the hall. I stayed by the corner of the garden and spotted, couldn't be, it was, Vincent. Hadn't seen Vincent in God knows how long.

Vincent watched, that's what he did best, watched. Below ran two little shapes, one was black, and one was white. Tiny, curved backs straightened when they ran. They were quick, very quick and they jinked, ducked and dived when frightened. Having seen enough, Vincent jumped up and onto the massive chestnut tree and watched the kitchen door. All he saw that caught his attention was a pair of shoes. They were Harpo's, he had taken them off when he ran in to the phone. Mrs Lucey's new rules on cleanliness were being followed by all. One shape froze, clung to the earth, a noise frightened it. The rabbit's eyes at the side of his head gave him a panoramic view of what was all around him. Vincent's eyes in the front of his head focused in on the white. His long tail slowly stretched back. It would take a jump to catch the white. Both rabbits nibbled at some long grass next to the wall. Again, the supreme killer in the cat emerged. A deadly combination of patience and a sixth sense for predicting his prey's movements, gave the white shape no hope of escape. Down. Shapes break into opposite directions. Vincent's body lengthens, paws are pushed against soft earth. White shape runs, sprints, dashes but can't get evade Vincent. The very wall that is supposed to protect the rabbits is now trapping them in. A claw makes the slightest of touches against white fur. That's all that is needed. The rabbit is hurt. It rolls and regains its legs but can't accelerate fast enough. Snap…needle sharp teeth grip the white shapes neck.

Shake...the life ebbs as Vincent runs straight up the wall. He now sees me watching him from the shadows, he moves.

I climb the wall and watch Vincent. Beneath the trees and undergrowth of a rundown garden a few houses away, he slowly and carefully begins to eat Snowball. A small hole is surgically created in the rabbit's white fur. Very little blood appears as Vincent starts to eat the tastiest organs around the stomach first. His looks really hungry. The Luceys were convinced that some other families were feeding him and therefore they only feed him when they see him. And they haven't seen him in months. So, Vincent when the chance arises will gorge on whatever is on offer, be it titbits from neighbours, birds, mice or small furry family pets.

Harpo returns out the back. I know that I have to tell him that Vincent took Snowball otherwise I might get the blame. He doesn't seem to be that pissed off and tells me to keep it to myself.

Joel can't find Snowball. Mr and Mrs Lucey check the garden. No rabbit. Confusion sets in. We all combed the surrounding gardens searching for Snowball. They are all mystified except Harpo and me. The rabbit seemed to have vanished into thin air. Joel was convinced that Snowball was going to suddenly arrive back in the garden. Mrs Lucey suggested that a magpie might have taken Snowball, to which we all just laughed. She was a lot closer to the truth than she could imagine.

I showed Harpo where Vincent took and ate Snowball. Vincent had left only the shell of Snowball's body after dining on all the meaty parts. Two grey crows waited patiently for him to finish. He was full. Vincent saw us coming. He knew he had done wrong. Within a few seconds he was gone, up and back on top of a southerly facing garage roof. Time to snooze. The grey crows hopped excitedly around the carcass. Within a couple of hours Snowball was no more.

Mr Lucey was really angry, he didn't like to be made stupid and the rabbit vanishing did just that. He kept checking and rechecking the garden for an escape route. How the hell did the rabbit vanish? No way could he have got out of the garden. The side gate was padlocked, which meant that no one could have taken Snowball. Only one thing to do. Watch the other rabbit the next day and see if there is a way out of the garden that they don't know about.

A night of rain left the grass soaking. Next day Harpo and I watched Sooty. He ran and sniffed at the ground. All the rain had removed the rabbit smells left behind the day before. He seemed nervous, his movements were very jittery. The senses that nature had given Sooty told him that whatever took Snowball was around. He could tell it was near, very near, too near. Sooty sprinted, then bolted in circles around the garden. Even though it was Mr Luceys first time keeping rabbits, he knew this wasn't normal rabbit behaviour. The poor animal was a mental wreck. Not one blade of grass touched Sooty's mouth. His nose twitched uncontrollably. His eyes didn't see anything unusual. His ears didn't pick up anything unusual. His nose did, that scent was here. A sixth sense warned him that his life was in danger. Big danger, real danger, the scent got stronger. The three of us stepped back into the kitchen and watched.

The front doorbell rang. Mr Lucey left his spot at the kitchen window and went out to the hall. Where is the rabbit? Where is he? No way can he have just disappeared! There he is. Harpo and me both focused and we could barely see Sooty at the Back of the Hutch. We began to notice that the rabbit wasn't moving. Come to think of it…

As Harpo opened the backdoor, we spotted Vincent scaling the wall with the half alive rabbit in his mouth. A holler from Mr Lucey, Vincent turned to see a rake miss him by an inch. Dropping the rabbit, he made his escape. Sooty fell, his eyes were half closed, and his legs were kicking fresh air. Still with the rake in his hands, Mr Lucey unlocked the side gate and decided to pursue Vincent. There wasn't any pursuing to do. Vincent had disappeared, gone, not a sight or a sound of the ginger tomcat. Still red with anger, Mr Lucey returned into the kitchen. He gave us a bollocking for not stopping the cat.

He rushed back out into the back garden, Sooty was gone. We could all see Vincent, running across a neighbour's wall, heading towards the bulb fields, a large nursery where all sorts of flowers were grown. Once he got that far, it would be impossible to spot him. Little legs kicked and fought. One last tight squeeze and Vincent dispatched Sooty. Harpo and I sprinted keeping Vincent in our sights the whole time. Through the bulb fields he ran, up a narrow lane and taking two steps at a time, he entered the Old Mill. Carefully Vincent followed the crumbling rotten beams, till he reached the top part of the roof. We gazed up at him. Relaxed, he shunned us, hung the rabbit over the beam and snoozed. This meal will be enjoyed later. Harpo loved that manky horrible cat so much. He was so excited to see Vincent it was unreal. We returned back to the Luceys.

Mrs Lucey swore she would kill that disease ridden cat if it were the last thing she would do. What was going on? Her so called family couldn't keep two rabbits alive more than twenty-four hours. She screamed that it must be a record in bad pet keeping.

Two days later I run in the back door. Granny and my dad sit at the table drinking tea. I let it all out in one go.

"Mrs Lucey is gone!" Neither one of them show an ounce of interest. I continue announcing my ground-breaking news. "No bull, there was war. Harpo said she left today after all hell broke loose in the house. May and June freaked out! They said she was carrying on with some man. So, she packed her stuff and left."

"Stay out of it, Fin. She is fucking lethal." Granny snaps at me, but I have to get the story out.

"Granny, Harpo said she was making a right tart of herself sneaking out late at night and everything. May and June caught her red handed. When Harpo was babysitting Joel, she was carrying on."

"So where has she gone?" asks Granny, showing only mild interest. My mouth is on fire.

"London. She fucked off – sorry, sorry – she *left*, this afternoon. Harpo said she had a handbag full of cash."

"Sure, it's none of our business where she goes," says Dad, putting his two cents in. "What has it got to do with us?"

I keep talking. I can't stop. "Harpo is like a mad lunatic. He said that he will smash the guy's face in. The one she was with."

Reining me in Granny shouted.

"Here now!" Granny shouts at me. "What's all the talk of violence about!"

"She might still be around," Dad states in his matter-of-fact voice. "Why come all the way home just to leave again. We don't know what went on. All you're telling us is hearsay. It can't be that bad."

"It is. Trust me it is. Harpo called her a 'whore'. She caught the bloke she was with for a lot of money. That's why her handbag was full of cash. By all accounts, she made a right fool out of the poor idiot. All I am telling ye is what I was told. Like that she was hoping to sell the family home! Harpo said their mum's cousin actually came around to check the house out."

Granny doesn't believe any of it. She gets up with a sigh. "Fin, your dad and I are tired. This is all he said, she said, they said. It's an entertaining story but, it's late. I think Harpo has an overactive imagination."

Dad gets up and says goodnight. That's it. Maybe the story wasn't all that ground-breaking. Maybe they had heard it all before.

Today is Friday, the last day of school. Glory, glory the weekend! Harpo walks home from school with me. He looks like someone has ripped out his heart and tried stuffing it back in.

"The bitch, Fin. Like, can you believe it? To plan to sell our home? I wanted her back all those years, and now I hope that I never see the Bitch again. You know what? I feel sorry for Joel. He has to deal with her all alone."

I keep quiet, knowing deep down that if my mum could come back, she wouldn't be a complete Tramp like Harpo's. We get to my house. We say nothing. I walk to my door. Harpo walks off alone. I decide to stay home and watch TV. My only comfort in life is that Harpo's pile of shit is way bigger than mine.

It is so annoying being woken by voices in the middle of the night. Paul is peacefully snoozing above me. Silently, I make my way out of the room and down the stairs, to the sneaky step, which is the fifth step from the bottom of the stairs. This is where you can sit and listen to what's going on in the kitchen without being spotted. In Harpo's house the sneaky step probably smells of piss.

Granny sounds distraught. "Jesus Christ, tell me I am wrong. Christ, please tell me I am mistaken." Granny rarely takes the Lord's name in vain. Taking the double barrel name means something really bad has happened. "Tell me, it wasn't you."

There's dead silence. Then Dad speaks up, "I'm sorry."

"Sorry? You're fucking sorry? You couldn't leave her alone. Like a stray fucking dog, you had to chase around after her. Sorry! We will put that one on your headstone."

Silence. I stuff my fist in my mouth to stop me bursting out laughing. I wait for the Mad Mullah to appear. It doesn't take long.

"That woman doesn't know whether she wants a man or a woman. Fucking hell, talk about confused! What did she do when she met you? Decide that she was back on dicks again. That family have lost their mother again over the likes of you. Don't say 'Sorry'. I am fucking warning you!"

I sit giggling to myself. The dirty bastard must have been riding Harpo's mum. You couldn't make it up.

"So, May and June caught you two together? Where?"

"Dropping her off home. They only saw us kissing."

"Only fucking kissing. Sure, what harm can kissing cause, you dumb bollocks? You were only fucking kissing? That's wonderful. Two mature adults! Can you tell I am being sarcastic?" I can hear Granny lighting up a cigarette.

"What Fin said about her selling the house? Was that also true?"

"I don't know. It was news to me," Dad mumbles. He is unusually sheepish. He has backed down to the Mad Mullah.

Granny bangs on the table. "Well, twenty-four hours ago you didn't know fucking anything. Spare me the bullshit. You will only admit to the stuff you are caught out on. You are a fucking idiot. We agreed not to talk about the night, my daughter died in that hospital. But you swore to me that there was nothing between you and Becky Lucey, when we both know you were with her the night my little angel died."

"Don't fucking go there!" Dad yells.

"Don't fucking go there? Believe me, this time I will ram the potato peeler through your nuts while you're fucking asleep. You were out with Becky Lucey drinking, while my daughter bled to death." I hold my breath, waiting for Dad to say something. Granny storms around the kitchen. Silence and then a bombshell.

"Where did Becky Lucey get all that money? I thought about that today. So, I checked the Credit Union savings books. Couldn't find them. Why's that?"

It takes forever for Dad to reply.

"It's all gone. Every account is empty. I will pay them back. Honest I will, just don't tell the boys. Trust me!"

Please God no! All my savings to help me leave Cork when I grow up, are gone. My 603 pounds are gone. All the money Granny saved for all of us every day since we were born is gone. He gave Harpo's mum all our savings. What a scumbag.

"That's nearly twenty thousand pounds in total," Granny yells. "You gave that tramp our twenty thousand pounds. For fucking what?"

"The money was for a house. She was going to buy a house under my name and live there. If she bought it with cash, the price would have dropped and then we could afford it."

"We? Who the fuck is We? You have a fucking family here, remember? There is only one 'we' and it's your family."

"I just wanted Becky to be happy. She was so upset," says the prick. I hope his heart is broken into tiny pieces. Mine is. The Mad Mullah is in full swing. I hope she decks him.

"Are you winding me fucking up? Happy? What's all this happy shit about? We all want to be happy, you fucking selfish prick. But you can't be happy all the fucking time. People who are happy all the time are fucking mad. Yes, fucking mad, like that tramp Becky Lucey. Happy? She has four kids to rear. She should be fucking happy doing that, or learn to cross her fucking legs."

Dad is pleading, the pathetic prick. "I am sorry. Truly I am." The Mad Mullah is having none of it.

"Sorry? We are gone from happy to sorry. Fuck off to bed! I can't stand the fucking sight of you."

I run up the stairs and back into bed. Paul wakes up as I was slipping back under the covers. I tell him that I was in the bathroom. He goes back to sleep while I silently cry for my stolen money.

Chapter Thirteen
Lives of Constant Sorrow

Granny was picking at her ear. Actually, rooting around for something that was irritating her. It was freaking me out how she could happily fit so much finger in that small space. The Mad Mullah is back at her maddest. What humiliated me the most was, we were in a queue, and she didn't care who watched her picking her ear. Well, I don't know if queue is the right word! A long black line waited to pass Cousin Jimmy's coffin. All around me wore black, I was in my favourite blue shirt because in an hour I was off to the local Disco. Boredom. Only for the coughing, the place would be like the morgue they took him from. Hushed whispers, offered words of condolence for his parents. The whispering gave the impression that no one wanted anyone else to overhear their opinion on Jimmy. If I were in that coffin, I would want people to talk loudly and let the whole world know I was a great guy.

Granny extends both hands and hugs both his parents at once. Very impressive piece of theatre. A double hug is not for the faint hearted. Then the coffin. Granny leans into my ear.

"Never seen the mad bastard so quiet or still. He was off his snot."

With that she rubbed her eyes. They were bone dry but to the assembled blackness she appeared like an older relative eaten up with grief. I loved Granny; she was such a pro. Hold it. Peering into the coffin I get a fright. Jimmy is wearing the same blue shirt as me, my spine shivers. On his jacket lapel he has a Pioneers total absence Association badge, the guy was either stoned, drunk, or stoned and drunk as long as I can remember. Usually, he wore a yellow and blue badge with 'Never mind the bollocks', written on it. Our Jimmy was a punk. Tough as concrete and just as thick. It's a terrible thing to say, but hey, I wasn't the one who 'borrowed' my dad's car and drove full force into the back of a truck. Maybe that's why they are all whispering, with embarrassment.

Out the front we stand. Nods and winks replace 'hellos' as all enforce this uncomfortable silence. The shiny coffin gently sweeps above the crowd. The pall bearers are young, they must be his friends. A selection of black suits and white shirts couldn't hide their anguish as they carried their friend's body. Feet shuffle as the coffin is lowered into the back of the hearse.

Controlling the whole scene is Fr Collins. He is smiling. In fact, he is the only person in the whole place with a constant smirk on his face. No matter what sacrament is being administered, Fr Collins chuckles and gives off warmth. It's pretty unnerving. Be it a wedding or funeral, his face would be one big beaming bright white toothed smile. The fact that God is present through him, gives him a natural high. Or could it be that he wanted to be the bride at every wedding and the corpse at every funeral? Earlier, he eulogised about Cousin Jimmy like he was his son. Jimmy was lots of things in life but being a religious person wasn't one of them. He wouldn't darken the door of the church from one end of the year till the next. Come to think of it, if Fr Collins saw 'Jimmy the punk' walk down the street he would gladly put his head down and walk past him. But here, right now, Cousin Jimmy was a soul that has to be saved and if being saved meant creating a 'New Jimmy', well so be it! What exactly was Fr Collins role in all of this? It appeared that he didn't just help the dead to find their way to heaven! No, he actually convinced all of us that this person belonged with God. To be seated next to God for all eternity. Fr Collins only buried saints. For everyone who rested beneath him was now an angel of God. The manner of death confirmed this to all who stood before. Lamenting, Fr Collins proclaimed that, "Jimmy was robbed from us." Well, he got the robbing part right. Cousin Jimmy's criminal record was bigger than his record collection. As Granny warned all of us every time Jimmy called, "Don't leave him alone, for fucks sake, he would stick the television up his jumper if he thought he would get away with it."

The television reference was part of a classic tale which will last the test of time. Jimmy, off his chops, robbed his own house. Yeah, you read it correctly, his own house. Hid all the stuff in a friend's garage, went home and put on an Oscar winning performance, when his parents broke the news to him that the house was burgled. He even cried with shock to discover that his mum's jewellery was taken. All went to script, until the Neighbour who never smiles casually divulged to the Guards that she saw Jimmy coming to and fro from the house all evening with a friend. The Guards drove around to the friend's house and got a full confession in a less than a minute. Here now, is the reason according to Granny why he was dead. Cousin Jimmy's parents were too soft on him. They should have kicked some sense into him after the 'robbery', but no, instant forgiveness was all Jimmy got. Granny believes religious people are weak. In her eyes holy people are spineless cowards who are solely responsible for most, if not all of the world's problems.

So next to me was my Granny whispering, "He was a waster," – and ten feet opposite was Fr Collins mourning – "we were robbed." Somewhere in the middle was the truth as to why Cousin Jimmy died. All that really mattered was that he was going into a hole in the ground. The crowd of black started to break up and head towards the Church. Eyes met that didn't need to meet. Fr Collins and Granny journeyed into each other's souls. Only God knows what they saw. The man in black made a bee line for us. He was short, fat and waddled like a penguin who was just hit by a car. Come to think of it, I couldn't see Fr Collins ever actually doing a real day's work. Here he is.

"Hello Granny, can I call you by your Christian name?"

Granny looks down on him.

"No thanks, Father, Granny is who I am. Lovely words you delivered earlier. Pity you actually didn't know our Jimmy."

Fr Collins had a God given ability for just ignoring what was actually said to him. With a sorrowful whisper.

"He was taken too quick Granny. Poor child."

Granny wasn't having any of it.

"Not quick enough, maybe his parents might get some well-deserved peace and quiet now."

Turning and facing me head on, he pleaded.

"We've all got to be more compassionate and understanding."

Fr Collins aimed these words directly at me. He felt uncomfortable with Granny not towing the 'we were robbed line'. Once dead, the Church were extremely forgiving on past sins. In fact, it seemed rude to mention that when someone dies, they could have been a complete and utter bastard.

Out of line with the Vatican, Granny persisted.

"Lovely, Father, easy knowing he didn't rob you blind for drink money. Jimmy was a scumbag and all the pine and brass on that coffin won't hide that fact."

Our Fr Collins was wasting his time.

"Try to be more forgiving…"

Granny introduced some common sense. But religion and common sense don't mix.

"It's hard, no impossible to forgive a person unless they ask for forgiveness, Father. I don't ever remember Jimmy ever saying sorry."

Fr Collins towed the party line unashamedly.

"Only God knows, Granny. He and only he knows, it is not for us to pass judgement on Jimmy."

Her patience was gone. Granny lit up a cigarette and coughed out the smoke all over Fr Collins.

"Spare me, Father. The 'God only knows crap'. It's a great get out clause to every argument. Pity God didn't know about the truck Jimmy rear ended. He could have warned him."

Fr Collins chuckled. This chuckle was a signal that he couldn't care less what you thought. His chuckles said so much. Just to torment Granny he continued.

"God loves you, Granny. You mean so much to him."

Flicking her cigarette ash in his direction.

"That's reassuring, Father. He must have feck all else to do with his time than worry about an old woman in Cork. This God of ours could be better employed feeding the millions starving in Africa, or the hundreds of millions suffering under communism. Or is it just first world white people he cares about?"

They both needed each other to test their faith. Fr Collins needed Granny to reassure him the world had sinners that God could save. Whereas, Granny needed Fr Collins to strengthen her underlying belief that God did exist but had a shower of clowns running the show. Both were afraid not to believe. Fr Collins grinned that annoying grin and made his excuses.

"I must go to the Church. Would love to see the pair of ye at mass. All are welcome."

Fr Collins leaned and gently whispered into Granny's ear.

"Please don't curse in front of the boy."

Granny took a step closer to Fr Collins.

"Sure, God had me forgiven before I even asked for forgiveness."

That was it, I could head off to Hillside Tennis Club to enjoy the underage Disco. Striding like a man on a mission, I get to Hillside in record time. Standing next to the door and larger than life was Gerry the Gorilla. He was huge, arms wider than my thighs and hands like shovels, the biggest neck I have ever seen on anyone, it was like a tree stump. Even his face was chiselled, black eyes perched under a forehead like Frankenstein's monster. Come to think of it, all Gerry the Gorilla was short was two bolts in his neck. All this muscle was completely undermined by a squeaky girlie voice. Every time Gerry stammered, people had to stop themselves from laughing. If that weren't bad enough, he couldn't pronounce his 'R's'. When God was finished sorting out the starving and the communists, he might spare a second and fix Gerry's vocal cords. The door was his domain and Gerry took being a bouncer very seriously. He treated the underage crowd the exact same as the over eighteens which meant he stammered to us like we were adults. Puzzled, he inspected me from head to toe.

"You okay?"

Catching me off guard, I reply, "What?"

He was now squaring up to me and eyeballed me with suspicion.

"You okay kid? Take it easy. No acting the bollocks."

I was late so it was just me and Gerry at the door. He wasn't leaving me pass. All my friends were on the other side of that door. Now I started to plead, hoping he would move out of the way.

"Yeah like, I'm not going to act the maggot. Can I go in please?"

The annoying monster wasn't leaving me past.

"You're sweating kid, you on something?"

Dumbstruck I question him back.

"What?"

This bouncer thing has gone to Gerry's head.

"You have sweat rolling down your face."

Now I can see where the halfwit is coming from.

"I hurried to get here. Was at a removal."

Gerry spoke.

"A rrrrrremoval?"

My mind threw out the facts.

"My Cousin Jimmy Reardon he died in a car crash."

Surprised, he continued.

"You know Jimmy Rrrrrrreardon?"

So, I kept explaining.

"They are not strictly my cousins, more my Granny's relations. You know we call them cousins, but they are probably third or fourth relations."

Gerry was forcing it all out.

"Jimmy Rrrrrrrreardon, many a night I had to throw him out this very door. I ain't leaving you in kid, if you're like him!"

Gerry the Gorilla towered over me. Just to emphasize his words, he took an unnecessary step closer. Having sweat running down my forehead and a nutter for a cousin weren't going to help me get in. My night seemed doomed. With a polite wave, he bid me farewell.

"Sorry kid, you have to leave."

No point in arguing. That muscle bound freak will always be at this door for every occasion, discos, parties and social nights. Best plan was to just go home. Then the seriously weird happened. The door opened and out popped my brother Paul with a mug of tea and a sandwich for Gerry. Seeing me leave, Paul screams.

"Fin, where are you going?"

Gerry answered, this was what he got paid for.

"Home, he's not allowed in."

Paul pleaded with Gerry.

"No, no, no Gerry. He's my brother."

It was hard to tell on a scale of one to ten how surprised Gerry actually was. This was because he looked twice at Paul and then straight at me. He stumbled around in his mind to find a word that could sum up his confusion.

"Rrrrrreally."

Proud as punch Paul explained.

"Yeah, he's my baby brother."

Paul ushered me in as Gerry leaned against the window ledge and sipped his tea. Five minutes earlier I would have sold my soul to get in, now I just wanted to go home. Entering the hall, I was hit by a wall of sound. Just in case that wasn't enough to disorientate me, bright lights blinded me. My two most important senses were disabled for twenty to thirty seconds. When I adjusted my eyes, I could see Sharon Lyons with a group of girls. She saw me and I half waved. While my hand was still waving, she turned and cut me dead. Was I seeing things? Sharon Lyons cutting me fucking dead? There ten feet behind her was Harpo. As I walked past Sharon, she took the opportunity to ignore me again. She blanked me and posed with her friends. In a room full of people, I felt so alone. Sometimes in life, our deepest and most private feelings are only exposed in crowded rooms. Sharon wanted to disown me and the easiest place to do it was in front of our peers.

"Over here, thought you would never make it."

Harpo put a brotherly arm around me. He looked well. Then AC/DC came on and we formed a circle. The air guitars came out and we tuned up to the opening chords of 'A whole lot of Rosie'. Next was Saxon 'Wheels of Steel' and the night was heating up. While the hardcore enjoyed the heavy metal, the chips and sausages were being handed out at the bar. As the dance floor thinned out, I spotted Paul heading straight for me with a large basket in his hands. Harpo saw Paul too and realised what was happening. Harpo patted Paul on the back.

"Well done, Paul."

Fingers came out of the darkness and plucked sausage after sausage from the basket. Two cold bottles of Coke were pulled out of Paul's jacket for Harpo and me. Even after all this kindness Paul had shown me tonight, I still despised him for what he was. People around could see his campiness, they would want to be blind to miss it. I hated him for being what he was. Had to get rid of him.

"Thanks Paul, these are my friends, fuck off."

He got the message, everyone within hearing distance got the message. Paul smugly gestured back.

"They're hardly my friends, Fin!"

With that, all around me laughed. Paul was extremely quick witted, he needed to be, to defend against the armies of bullies that surrounded his world. Paul loved Harpo because he didn't judge him. In fact, Harpo treated Paul with the utmost respect. An unholy alliance built up between them over the years. So much so that Harpo didn't tolerate the slightest belittling of Paul.

"You can be some asshole Fin. Cut the guy a bit of slack. He is after sorting us out with drinks and food."

When you don't give a shit about someone, you don't give a shit about them, so fuck Paul. Disco Dave talked between every song. Boy did he love the sound of his own annoying voice. He was the local DJ on Cork Hometown FM.

To be honest he played great music, even though he was my dad's age. But he dressed like he was eighteen. The requests were his downfall, they were endless, and all for the best boyfriend/girlfriend / husband/wife…they were never ending. Just like Fr Collins, Disco Dave didn't know anybody who wasn't a saint. According to Disco Dave every couple in Cork were madly in love. His smooth, steady voice echoed around the room.

"Here's a slow set. Let's start with Foreigner – Waiting for a girl like you."

The volume went down in sequence with the lighting. The only person in clear view was Disco Dave, who was under a bright light. It all seemed surreal, a middle-aged man creating the atmosphere for all these teenagers to start kissing and fondling! My eyes peered into the darkness, Sharon was out dancing with some tall bloke. That was the end of my chances with her. As I turned to tell Harpo, he was gone. There he is, with God knows who!

"How come you're not dancing?"

Kelly Burke. A girl who lives around the corner. We grew up together. I acknowledged her out of politeness.

"Not in the mood."

She stood her ground, knowing full well that I had no one to dance with. Kelly stood there hoping, no praying I would ask her out to dance. That wasn't going to happen. Not tonight, not any night. Since we both could talk, I have being steering well clear of Kelly Burke. The main reason is that she's completely and utterly uncool. Granny cruelly remarked to me one afternoon as Kelly walked past our house. "Holy fuck, she is one horse of a girl."

"Here Fin have a gum. Take away the taste of sausages if you get lucky."

This was the killer, even though she knew I didn't want to dance with her, she still thought it important I have fresh breath for someone else. But the niceties of Kelly Burke weren't going through my brain right now, no, the fact she made it appear like we were together, was seriously damaging my chances with other unknown girls, who might think we were a couple. Maybe that was Kelly's game, maybe she told her friends that we were an item, maybe I was being set up. This had to stop before it got out of hand. What could I do, she was mad about me? I had to do something, so I called her close.

"Kelly."

She leant in towards me.

"You have to go, people might think we're together."

She fumbled, turned and left. What the hell! First Paul, now her. This was proving to be a very exciting night! Three slow songs later and I had to move. The slow set didn't go on longer than five songs. That was it, I had to move. Circling the crowd, I started to calculate my chances of pulling a girl. The odds were getting greater against me minute by minute. The girls who were here to be picked up, probably were already gone by now. This left the remaining girls undecided which meant they were fussy bitches who were very, very picky. Being the realistic person I am, I know that I am not the standard that fussy bitches aspire to? Add to this the pool of girls that no self-respecting bloke would be caught dead with, and you now have a situation fraught with danger. Her, yes, her, I tap her on the shoulder, and she turns. My jaw drops, from behind she has the most beautiful hair and body. From the front she is an angel, a fallen angel. Before a word could be said, we are in a tight embrace slow dancing to Diana Ross and Lionel Richie's 'Endless Love'.

She snuggles into my neck. Tight hands pull me closer. Her chest feels soft like a pillow. A sweet scent whiffed from blonde hair. A nibble by my ear. My resistance was crumbling. Something was said and I just nodded. Next thing I knew, a tongue was parting my lips. My head rolled back, her mouth got closer. A slap on my back.

"Watch out."

Throwing my head back, I hit the girl behind, her boyfriend was unimpressed. I mumble.

"Sorry."

The blonde hair spoke, or should I say shouted.

"Why don't you go and fuck yourself, ya stupid tramp. It was an accident."

We were all in shock, me more than anyone else. No need for hostilities. I was in the wrong.

The couple stared. They stared a second too long and a fist caught the boyfriend's nose. Now his head rolled, a stagger and a second punch floored him. Suddenly the dance floor cleared. A hand grabbed the blonde hair and lifted her up.

"Rrrrrrregina, you we're warrrrrned to behave."

Gerry appeared out of thin air and escorted Regina to the door. Doing my best to melt back into the crowd, I sought out Harpo. Mind racing, I explained to him what had happened, and I that I was bricking it in case the bloke she floored would come after me. Harpo broke down laughing.

"Chill boy, that's Regina Deasy, the maddest family in the Southside."

Lost and confused, I didn't know what was going on.

"What?"

Putting his arm around me Harpo kept laughing.

"Fin sometimes I wonder do we actually live in the same city? You were kissing 'Regina the Renegade'. Maddest bitch on the Southside. You're class boy."

A hand grabbed my elbow and scared me shitless.

"Fin, you okay. What happened?"

It was Paul like Mother Goose running around the place. Couldn't take any more of this.

"Fuck off, Paul. Please just fuck off."

Harpo having had enough of me picking on Paul gave me a bollocking.

"Give him a break, Fin. I am not asking you, I am telling you to stop showing him up in here."

Knowing this battle wasn't worth fighting, I back down and apologise to Paul.

"Okay, okay, sorry Paul."

It was too late, thankfully Paul just left.

Sharon seemed to ditch the tall bloke and was now flirting with Harpo. She did like him. He gave off an air of not giving a 'fuck' about anything. Girls found something in him that I couldn't see or understand. This might sound confusing coming from his best friend but for the life of me, I didn't see any outstanding characteristics in Harpo. Sharon and Harpo chatted while I sulked. All week, the hours were counted down to the disco and since getting here it's being a complete fucking nightmare. Cousin Jimmy's removal was more fun. That girl is back and now Harpo is kissing her. Noooo…the tall bloke is back, and Sharon is…kissing him.

Disco Dave kept the tunes coming. I have had enough. Need to go to the toilet. Through a mass of people, I wade and enter the gents. There is noise, shuffling, I step back and watch. Some guy has Paul by the throat up against the filthy tiles. No one sees me. They are terrorising him about his shoes. Paul always wears really gay, cream-coloured shoes when going out. It's now very serious. One shoe is taken and then the second. They are thrown in the urinals. Laughter erupts. Then one guy threatens to piss on one of the shoes. Paul stands his ground and refuses to bend, buckle or break. I need to go, this isn't my fight, and after a lifetime of watching him being bullied I slowly turn to leave. The door opens and in walks some bloke. He sees instantly what is going on. Ignoring me he wades in.

"Leave him alone."

They all stand back. But there is always one hero who won't or can't shut the fuck up.

"Why, what will you do abo—"

A kick into the nuts was landed with a fistful of hair dragged down to waist height and a foot slicing through the air into a face. The rest stood back. No one else was going to risk a similar fate. Quiet. We all focused on him. As he turned to watch the group break up, I get a clear view of him. He has the brownest eyes I have ever seen. Head bowed, Paul thanks him and leaves upset.

Ten minutes later Harpo is giving me hell for not protecting my brother after finding out what happened.

"Why didn't you help him, Fin? He's your brother!"

Couldn't care less who kicked the shit out of Paul.

"Why should I? I am sick of that drama queen."

Harpo knows me long enough not to take any of my bullshit.

"He's your brother Fin, if you don't stand up for him, who will? Show a bit of family loyalty."

Tired and fed up with it all.

"Fuck off Harpo, give me a break…"

The goodness in Harpo won't be silenced.

"Give you a break, you're no better than those assholes beating him up."

My mouth goes into overdrive.

"Well, I don't love gays the way you do…sorry."

Now Harpo is in my face.

"What does that mean? What are you on about?"

Turning, I left Harpo to be swallowed up by the crowd. Paul had headed into the private members bar, where I could see Dr Hughes comforting him. It was a pantomime, with Paul now playing the Dame and me the Villain. Thankfully, the night was nearly over. No, please God No. She was back.

"How is Paul?"

After arguing with Harpo, I just wanted peace and quiet.

"Good thanks, Kelly."

She stepped closer.

"Can we have one dance Fin? I would love to have the last dance with you."

This was all I needed.

"Sorry, Kelly. I am not in the mood."

Her hands came out to me.

"Please, Fin, wouldn't kill you. I…really do like you."

Fed up with everything, I crumble.

"I don't even like myself, Kelly. So, I find it hard to believe anyone else would like me!"

Disco Dave played his last request. A song that has helped a million teenage boys pull a million teenage girls. The sweet tones of Jon and Vangelis – 'I will find my way home' squeezed the couples closer together. I waited.

Turning, I went to find my jacket to head off. The lights came on. Sharon was leaving with the tall bloke, Harpo was leaving with the flirting girl, and I was leaving with self-pity. Off down the road I strode, ready to burst.

Halfway home and a figure caught my eyes underneath the chestnut branches. Bold as brass, he sat on the edge of the footpath eating chips from newspaper wrappings. He looked deep in thought. He looked hungry. He looked very cosy. This was my chance. Slowly, step by step I neared him. The battered fish had him well distracted. Happily, he nibbled at crunchy shell covering the white meat inside. He stopped. I stopped. He dropped his head and continued munching. I drove my foot full force into his side. It caught him square in the ribs. He rolled in pain. I stamped my left foot on his back. He escaped the impact only to see a pair of boots closing in on him. Turning, he decided that he wasn't leaving his food behind, no way was he walking away from the first decent meal in days. Back arched, tail bent at the very tip, head down, he spat at me. Vincent had me now in his sights. Rogue Tom Cats are a law onto themselves. This Rogue was an outlaw. Panicking, I tried to frighten him.

"Shoooo…fuck off"

Nothing. Vincent hissed. Shit. With a dash he ran straight for me. Jumping up and out of his way I felt a warm blow hit my leg. Blood. He cut me cleanly through my jeans. Again, he got his bearings, again he hissed and ran at me. My lungs released pain.

"Aaaaaaaggghhh…"

A second blow caught me just below the last one. My jeans were soaked in blood. Again, he came back. I ran but felt him close in on me. Turning, I released a kick into thin air. Miraculously, it found Vincent's stomach and flung him out onto the road. A skid. Dr Hughes BMW went completely over Vincent. Silence. Hidden in the shadows Dr Hughes and Paul couldn't see me. They were puzzled as to how a cat could suddenly fly out from the darkness into the middle of the road! Vincent ran from under the car into the night. His only hope now, bruised and badly shaken, was to get to the safety of the old tower in the fields where Harpo and I saw him last. Into the night he ventured. To get there, he would have to take the lane by a cottage with trees. But he was hurt.

Dr Hughes parked around the corner from my house. Paul covered his face with his hands. Hidden in the darkness, I stood within five feet of the car. I could hear every disgusting homosexual word being said.

Paul unburdened all his fears and feelings there and then. He started blabbering to Dr Hughes that he hated himself for what he was. That's what upset him so much. How could he change? In this horrible world, Dr Hughes was the only one who understood him, who listened and who cared. The tears ran down his cheeks as Paul expressed his innermost fears. Was his whole life going to be spent being bullied? Would he forever be living in fear? Why was it always him, that boys took an instant dislike to? Dr Hughes listened. He hadn't the answers to Paul's questions. So, all he could do was just be there as a shoulder for Paul to cry on. My brother, the queer, mentioned the elephant in the room, obviously a pink elephant!

"Can you tell I am gay?"

Then Dr Hughes lied back.

"No, Paul."

Paul's tears got louder.

"So why can so many other people see it?"

The Dr continued lying.

"Paul, you being gay isn't an issue. Just try and be yourself in life. Not what other people want you to be. It's important to know who you are and where you are going. Life is a journey, Paul and it's not where you are going, it's how you get there. Be the best you can."

But Paul wasn't giving up.

"Journey, where to? I hate going outside the front door! The whole world can't stand me. I can't stand me! What can I do to be normal? All I want to do is fit in. My dad can't stand to be near me, my Granny treats me like a leper and my brother probably secretly wishes I were dead."

An arm went around Paul's shoulder followed by more filth from Dr Hughes.

"Don't say that."

I could tell Paul was loving all the attention.

"It's the truth. Can't I say the truth? It's the truth. I wouldn't like me for a brother, so why should even my brother like me?"

My leg hurt, stung like crazy. The bleeding stopped. Vincent had made at least seven long insertions on my thigh. Never expected the ginger bastard to stand and fight. I needed to get home. Thankfully, it was a thirty second walk.

Pain. It hurt all over. As I walked around the back, I noticed two cut sunflowers that were well dried out, left on one of Granny's flowerbeds. A nibbling started and finished, over and over again. I stood as still as a statue. Brown fur released kernel after kernel. Then with a couple of seeds safely tucked into his mouth the wood mouse ran into a crack in the wall. After a few seconds he returned to collect more seeds. The garden is littered with sunflowers dotted all around it. Does Granny actually realise the amount of mice she would attract into the garden by growing them?

After slipping in the backdoor, Granny spots me from the hall. She flipped. The Mad Mullah cornered me and demanded to know what had happened to my brand-new pair of jeans. When I left her at Cousin Jimmy's removal earlier that evening, I was perfect. I explained about the cat. Only when I pulled down my jeans to show the long thin cuts, did Granny finally believe me. My thigh was completely red. Pain. Out came the TCP and a firm but loving hand sterilised my wounds, while I held in the screams.

There by the door stood Paul silently gazing at me. He didn't want to miss the drama, so he closed his eyes to all the blood and stayed silent. Standing, sweating, stinging skin cleaned. Granny scolded me.

"That fucking cat. You did kick him good?"

Proudly I boasted.

"Ya Granny caught him a beauty with one kick."

Her hands dabbed on disinfectant.

"You're fucking lucky you don't need stitches Fin, fuck it, very lucky. We have to clean out each cut, in case of infection. I don't think you will be taking on that fucking cat again."

Paul spoke and then wished he hadn't.

"That cat ended up out in the road in front of the car. Dr Hughes thought he had killed it."

Granny was waiting a long while for this opportunity. She wasn't going to leave it pass.

"Dr Hughes and you are great buddies all the same Paul! How come he didn't drop you to the front door?"

Not a word said.

"Are you fucking deaf Paul? I asked you a question!"

Still nothing. By arguing with The Mad Mullah, Paul would be giving her more fuel for future arguments. She would never listen to him the way Dr Hughes did. All Granny ever said was 'try and fit in' or 'everything will be fine in the end'. Meaningless words.

It became obvious to Paul from an early age that Granny didn't warm to him. He wasn't her type of boy. He really wasn't anybody's type of boy. She preferred the 'Fin's' of the world. Boys like me with imperfections and flaws not just on show but proudly displayed. Boys who would grow up into men that led lives of constant sorrow. This very sorrow was never really their fault. God no. The whole world conspires against them. Men designed to repeat the same mistakes as their fathers and feel secure in the fact that, yes, they didn't become better people than their peers. This lack of ambition would always make them more lovable and non-threatening. Failure was seen as bad luck and any good luck was wrongly mistaken for fate. No, this family would never celebrate Paul's excellent school reports, outstanding sporting achievements or his dedication to work. Why should we, he's a fucking queer!

Success by Paul was seen as easy. All his hard work was dismissed as 'naturally smart' or 'he has the brains'. Not once did Dad or Granny ever think past their limited frontiers and acknowledge the amount of study he had done. This family, his family only recognised the mundane. Any other family would be pushing Paul to do medicine or law. God no, his own father one night after coming home late from the pub, suggested that bar work would be an ideal job for him. Even adding that within a few years, Paul would make management! Managing a bar or anywhere else with the best grades in his year! A normal

Dad would be suggesting, no, demanding that he would own a string of bars by the time he was thirty. The better he did, the less respect Paul was given. It was taken for granted that he would do his 'best'. The same 'best' I did but never got the marks he constantly achieved. That was the bottom line, all Paul wanted was recognition. As he got older, he was beginning to realise that this was never going to happen. Our family celebrated being average because it made everyone feel safe and secure in their own average worlds.

Two days later and Harpo has me out rummaging through laneways for Vincent. He is really worried about that flea ridden bag of fur. Harpo couldn't stop laughing when I showed him my thighs. He didn't believe for a second that I was an innocent victim. So, I went along hoping to settle a score with Vincent. We walked forever until we hit fields.

Lifting my head, I cast an eye towards the countryside, to my right I saw a cow lying surrounded by more cows in a meadow. To my left was the edge of a wood. Focusing, I made out two women in the woods. They were jogging into the open laneway. In the very far off distance were cottages. A few hundred yards away, we could make out a woman feeding chickens.

A steep embankment blocks our way. Up carefully, avoiding the thistles, onto the ditch. Pain, two thistles prick at my sore spot. I see chickens happily pecking at the ground. This countryside is a dirty filthy fucking place. Right in front of us is a marshy landscape, knots of grass dot a massive bog. Hopeless! No way am I going any further. Beyond that is a farmhouse among trees. Shit, there is barking coming from that direction. Don't think my cut legs would get me very far if chased by a dog! But just like 'Little House on the Prairie', a miracle happens. Right here, right now. Harpo leaves out an excited.

"What the! Fin, over there."

A bundle of foxy fur in the distance. There by a wheat field with a lark, rising and rising electrifying the crisp air with high pitched chords, sat Vincent. In a few minutes we were by Vincent's side. Harpo was a cat person and as soon as Vincent flinched when he touched his side, he knew there was a problem. Very slowly, very carefully he picked Vincent up and comforted him. The cat must be in serious trouble as he doesn't even glance at me. I was secretly delighted the little bastard was in pain. Harpo had turned into Florence Nightingale in the space of ten seconds.

"I will look after you. Hey, hey you thought I forgot about you?"

Vincent now cradled securely in Harpo's arms as we walked back into the woods and towards the city. The countryside wasn't for him, better off in the city. Snuggling into Harpo's chest, Vincent got the much needed warmth his body desired. The pain was eased by the support Harpo's arms gave him. Within minutes he was asleep. By the time we reached Harpo's house his arms ached.

Carefully, he placed Vincent on the floor. Vincent stumbled, meowed and rubbed his body between Harpo's legs. Instantly Harpo starting fussing over Vincent. Vincent had Harpo well sussed out as a soft touch. Worried, Harpo examined his manky coat.

"Fin looks like tissue damage to me. Pity he can't talk and tell us what is wrong. By the way, he his holding himself, it's like something has hit him hard."

Oh yeah, left out the part of my story about me kicking Vincent. So, I do what I do best, bullshit.

"Like a car?"

Examining Vincent Harpo sighs.

"No, if it was a car he probably wouldn't be standing here! Something has hit him! But not a car. This little guy badly needs a good meal."

As Vincent sat, Harpo started to tidy up the kitchen. He moved the basket of apples and the basket of potatoes, his dad bought the night before down the Horseman, from under the table. Now Harpo is moving quickly and starts to make Vincent a bed from a cardboard box and an old pillow.

The kettle was put on. A tin of tuna left behind by his mother is opened and the brine released down the sink. The smell got Vincent's attention. A quarter of the tin was broken up with a fork on an old saucer. Vincent's head rolled up and down Harpo's leg. Saucer placed in the middle of the floor. In a ball, he sat silently devouring the fish. We both watched him with deep interest. I moved to make the tea. A hiss. Quickly I sat back down with fear. Harpo pointed out the blatantly obvious.

"Ha, ha, Fin he doesn't trust you near his food."

I protest. "But he was cool with me next to him earlier!"

Harpo wipes his face and proudly explains.

"Of course, he was. If we didn't help him, he would probably starve. Cats aren't dogs. They will only love you to get what they want. He has what he wants now, so stay back till he is finished."

The old pillow was lovingly adjusted and readjusted in the cardboard box. The last of the tuna was licked from the saucer. Vincent scoffed it down in one go. A sore hurt body made an indent on the pillow. Carefully, the most painless position was found. Sleep. An awkward silence descended. I could feel that Harpo was thinking hard about why Vincent would scratch me.

A tiny movement under his armpit. There again. He didn't know what to do. Now one at his stomach. What the hell is it? Another one. Two more. He involuntarily smacked his leg. Hand under jumper. He got it. A small, tiny little insect in reddish brown colour was between his fingernails. In disgust Harpo crunched it.

"Shit, Fin. Fleas, the little guy has fleas."

I instruct him.

"Go out the back and shake out your top."

At the backdoor he violently shakes his jumper.

"How come you didn't get them?"

Sarcastically I answer.

"I didn't carry the filthy little maggot for miles!"

He needed to pee. Stretching. Soreness. Out of the box he crept. When a cats got to go, he's got to go! Out into a bright hall. Need to pee. In here looks good. Into the front room where Mrs Lucey slept, he crept. I followed his every move while Harpo cleansed himself of fleas. After years of living ferally, Vincent has got used to going to the toilet wherever proved to be the most convenient. That gap between those two chairs fits the spot. The rooms unused, not touched since Mrs Lucey and Joel vanished. A vase with dead leaves rests on a small table. A glass with roses perches on a thin shelf. Hanging on the main wall was the scariest picture Vincent ever saw, a flying fox and it seemed to glare down upon him. In the corner was a vase with carnations and above them was a massive glass bowl with chrysanthemums. All the flowers were dead and dried, all flowers Mrs Lucey had bought to brighten up this shithole.

Under the main chair were three pairs of shoes left behind by Mrs Lucey. Vincent sniffed them, the scent of human was still present. But what really got his attention, was the large glass tank with the two black shadows swimming to and fro. Have to investigate this. Up and confused. Vincent went around the tank, over and under the table that held the tank up. He couldn't figure out how to get into it. Blissfully the two black shadows swam around a large stone skull, skirted around a red plastic crab on its back, and then like flying arrows aimed themselves to the surface for air. His eyes zoned in on their every move. Dropping down towards the glass corner, they nibbled around a half figure of an angel buried in multi-coloured gravel. They were oblivious to his presence. A noise.

"There you are, Vincent. Fionn, where did he come from?"

My Lucey patted me on the back. I couldn't tell whether he was going to the pub or coming back from it. His blood shot eyes took in the cat and the fish tank. Before I could speak, Mr Lucey ignored me and gave Vincent his undivided attention.

"Now Vincent, what are you doing staring at Guinness and Murphy? You are an adventurous little guy! Who is a busy boy? Mrs Lucey got Joel those fish to keep him company after you ate his rabbits. Vincent, well what can you do with two goldfish in a tank? Can hardly talk to them or throw them a stick!"

Mr Lucey inhaled and panted. The cigarette dangled from his lip. A shaking hand hooked and picked up a tiny little net. The lid of the tank was opened, and a black shadow scooped up. Flipped from the net right down in front of Vincent. The horrible flea ridden bag of fur was perplexed.

"Try a Guinness, Vincent you mad bastard. It's supposed to be good for you!"

Tail smacked the floor as Guinness's head moved in circles gasping for water. This was an alien environment for the goldfish. Vincent glanced at me and then Mr Lucey, was this a trap? Lighting quick Vincent locked onto Guinness squeezing his head between his pin sharp teeth. In a second, Guinness was crunched and swallowed. Mr Lucey wrung his hands over and over with excitement. The net was produced again.

"Did you like that, Vincent? Here, let's try a Murphy's."

He threw Murphy up into the air. Halfway down and Vincent caught him before he even saw the ground. Crunch and swallow and Murphy joined Guinness swimming around in Vincent's stomach. Then, to show his delight, Vincent made a figure of eight by constantly going in and around Mr Lucey's legs. Mr Lucey bent over till his and Vincent's eyes met and spoke to him as if he was a child.

"I never liked them, Vincent. Sneaky little things watching me. Every time I came in or out that door, I could see them watching my every move."

After tea I called back over to Harpo. He called me into the kitchen. Backdoor opened and flea powder gently brushed into a ginger coat. All this attention Harpo was giving Vincent reminded me of his relationship with Joel. It was weeks since Harpo felt needed. It was years since Vincent felt needed. Bonds were forged from necessity. He rested, Harpo fretted. The soreness was still there when he brushed his side. Not a flinch, not a murmur. Be brave for Harpo.

The back garden was long and narrow. In the distance we could see the head of a man in another garden. It went to and fro to the sound of a lawnmower. It was Sharon Lyon's dad cutting the grass. The wind toyed with a willow tree, frightening two white butterflies out into the open. They danced on the breeze before landing on some wild roses.

May and June came around the back together and got a surprise. June, with ruffled hair from playing soccer, bent and gently played with Vincent. There was a time when the old Vincent would run and hide. Not now, he stayed still pretending to be asleep, hoping they would leave him alone. They stayed too long, too noisy and too late. But a cat got to do what a cat got to do to survive.

Chapter Fourteen
When a Small Fire Starts It's Always Best to Extinguish It Straight Away

Granny, Dad and Auntie Mary were talking. Paul was the topic of the day. They were all in deep discussion regarding his behaviour. The same questions kept coming up as how best to handle him. Standing back and maturely analysing the 'problem' was the last thing that any of them was going to do. Handling the issue of a queer in the family was uncharted waters. So, the best way of solving this dilemma was the 'blame game'. Little jibes were swung between Dad and Granny as to whom was at fault for his gayness. Granny decided to get her jibes in quickly.

"It wouldn't have killed you to have spent more time with him growing up. You're never short of time for your fucking birds!"

Dad protested back.

"For the love of God I tried, but we have absolutely nothing in common."

She was fighting her corner.

"Always an if, but or a maybe from you. Always a reason not to do something. Fuck it, you're a genius at talking yourself out of doing something. All I am saying is a little more time with Paul wouldn't kill you!"

Dad wasn't backing down.

"Actually, it would, he is hard work Granny. To be honest there isn't a thing in the world I could talk to him about."

Granny fought back with sarcasm.

"Try talking about yourself. That's a popular conversation piece with you when you are out there with your lady friends. Tell him the bullshit you would be filling up those sluts with."

Auntie Mary asked for calm. Too late, twenty-five years too late.

"Can we stick to Paul please? This won't get us anywhere. The boy is going through a tough patch at the moment."

Granny's patience had dried up.

"Tough patch? Unless you can't or won't see it, he is gay with a capital 'G'. Mother of fuck. It is out there for the whole world to see. We have no way of hiding it."

Dad grasped at straws.

"We don't know for sure!"

Granny scolded Dad.

"It's as clear as the nose on your face. Remember when he was five, we had to stop bringing him anywhere near girls because all he wanted to do was play with dolls. Then he started robbing and playing with my makeup. Fuck it, the signs were there from day one. The kid is queer, and we have to figure out what to do."

Surprisingly Dad fought Paul's corner.

"We do nothing Granny. He is a good kid and that's all that matters. Let's be honest here, it's that mad bastard Fin we want to be discussing. He is on the road to nowhere."

A sharp tongue cut the air. Granny was angry.

"Why the fuck did you drag Fin into it? Leave him out of this."

Dad tried a different approach.

"We all know that in a few years' time Paul will be gone to live his life somewhere else. Sure, we all know that London is over filling with Irish gays."

But Granny wasn't having any of it. She wheezed back.

"Never knew you were so familiar with the gay scene in London."

Granny coughed. Dad in desperation ranted.

"Stop trying to wind me up. Unfortunately, I can't wave a magic wand and cure him. God knows I would love to. So, give me a break."

Maybe it was because Auntie Mary was there, but Granny won't give Dad a break.

"No, I won't, sort something out to at least curtail his behaviour. Sometimes it's like living with the Village fucking People."

Dad pleaded.

"Granny I don't know why you're treating this as one big joke? One of your brothers was a full-blown queer!"

A line was crossed, no rubbed out. Dad had enough of Granny belittling him. He wanted her to stop. Granny growled.

"You are a smart fucking asshole all the same. He wasn't Gay. No, he wasn't. So don't say it."

A crack was found, and Dad widened it.

"Well, your daughter said he was. The facts speak for themselves, no kids, separate bedroom from his wife and oh yeah, spent all his spare time in the golf club surrounded by single men. Bingo…that's seems to describe a queer."

Unwittingly Dad had just described Auntie Mary's husband Dr Hughes. The atmosphere was getting nasty. Not to be left out, Auntie Mary chirped up.

"This is getting us nowhere. Paul is a lovely kid who needs to be loved…"

Granny had enough.

"Will ye stop? He is loved, that's not the problem. It's him being fucking queer that's the issue. And the person who donated this gay sperm should grow a proper pair of balls and take responsibility for bringing a fucking queen into the world. Thank God my daughter isn't here to witness this. Thank you, God."

The mind is a terrible thing. Especially when it's attached to a cold heart and a sharp tongue. Hurtful does what it needs to do to win the day. Uncaring words are damaging, uncaring facts are life changing. Releasing these facts into the open can be at the best of times careless and at the worst of times criminal. But facts being facts, speak for themselves. Dad had enough. He held firm.

"He isn't my son."

Granny and Auntie Mary knew that this was for real. Dad's tone stayed solid, again he said the line.

"I am not his dad."

A single voice shot out from the kitchen, it was Granny.

"You're fucking mad, mad as fuck. He is not your son. What the fuck are you on about?"

Never heard Dad sound so tranquil after saying something so life shattering.

"Granny, I know you know! When Paul was born, he nearly died. Remember. That ring any bells? So, your precious daughter told me about her fling. She was out of her mind on medication and worry. Would you believe she begged me to stay in the hospital and then she demanded me to bring Paul's dad into her room to see his child, in case Paul died? All she kept saying was 'go and get him, just call him'."

Then silence. With a roar Dad reinforced the message.

"He is not my son and well you know it."

If Granny stayed silent, she would have shown an innocence. But she spoke too quick and too concise. Auntie Mary was silent.

"You know nothing. Absolutely nothing about my daughter. So shut your filthy fucking mouth."

Dad had made his point. Anymore said would just weaken his position. In typical fashion my family went out to solve one problem and ended up creating a whole new fresh one. Granny thought that the boys were out of the house, so she had the freedom to vent and rage.

"Tell Mary you're lying. Tell Mary now."

Dad remained silent. Granny still shouted.

"Tell her that my daughter didn't have an affair. Tell her the truth you fucking bollocks."

My head was full of confusion. As Granny and Dad spoke, they planted the ripening seeds of despair within our minds, that fell from their darkened hearts. Every family crisis big or small ended with failure. This failure started the minute Granny, or the odd time Dad, tried to show authority.

Even if a household job wasn't done, the fallout always got nasty. To show what a useless child you were, Granny would make comparisons with Dad. Now the task that wasn't done to her standard would be blamed on him. Whichever one of us boys that offended her would now have to go through five minutes of Dad bashing. I grew up listening to my dad being torn down a peg or two daily. With two boys doing jobs around the house there were bound to be mistakes, which led to Granny ranting on and on about 'how only a pathetic Dad can produce such fucked up kids'. When your dad is portrayed as a failure and your Granny mad, it's a given us kids would end up with problems. Granny still screamed at Dad.

"See Mary, he's a fuckwit. A lowly fuckwit."

Dad stayed silent. Something had caught Auntie Mary's attention. In her life she would have heard millions of words being spoken, sung and whispered. But within all these millions of words lay one sentence that would forever change her life. It wasn't the actual words being said, no, it was what was inferred. Granny knew what Dad meant; he knew what he meant. The comment passed by Dad to Granny was meant to go over Auntie Mary's head, but it didn't, the words landed, and she took them at face value. An argument was going on between the two of them, next to her, but they dropped a bombshell without realising it. They both honestly thought they were being smart, really smart, and so smart they got careless. Auntie Mary interrupted the mindless ranting going on around her and spoke softly to her brother.

"You said, 'she begged me to stay in the hospital and then she demanded me to bring Paul's dad', that was an unusual thing to say."

Dad was surprised.

"Why?"

I realised that Auntie Mary was livid about something that was said. Their best form of defence was unity. This would have worked normally but this wasn't normally. But Auntie Mary wasn't giving up.

"You said, 'she begged me to stay in the hospital and then she demanded me to bring Paul's dad'. This means that Paul's dad was in the hospital already. By begging you to stay in the hospital meant that you could find Paul's dad, by leaving the hospital meant that your wife wouldn't have been able to contact him for whatever reason! So, you weren't asked to stay to be of comfort, you were asked to stay to be of use."

Granny cut Auntie Mary clean off.

"I don't understand, Mary. It's a bit confusing."

Exasperation from Auntie Mary.

"Confusing? Both of ye knew your wife had an affair. That's quite obvious. So therefore, if she did have an affair, which means that there is a man involved. For some strange reason I am kept in the dark about who he could be?"

When a small fire starts it's always best to extinguish it straight away. Out the flames before they rise out of control. That's the wise thing. Even though Granny tried the wise thing, she grabbed the nearest liquid to quench the flames. Petrol instead of water was thrown. The effect was explosive. Granny picked the wrong sentence at the wrong time.

"Mary, it has nothing to do with you. By—"

Auntie Mary fought her corner.

"Nothing to do with me! Well, I think it has. Why else would ye be all cloak and dagger. Something doesn't make sense and my brother has put his foot in it by trying to be smart."

Auntie Mary's days of being treated like a moron were well over. Again, she poked her brother to get a response.

"You sit there lying to your own sister to protect your mother-in-law. A woman right next to me who has never once shown or given you thanks or respect for putting a roof over her head."

Dad wasn't for breaking ranks with Granny on this one.

"Mary, sit down. Granny's right, there is nothing to tell."

Auntie Mary was getting angrier.

"Spineless that's what you are. Afraid of her and…"

Granny fought to regain control of her kitchen.

"I am still here Mary. Do you mind? You need to sit the fuck down."

The shouting got louder. It was all kicking off.

"You washed up old bag. Go on say the name of your daughter's lover."

Once again Granny threw more petrol on the flames.

"You're fucking mad girl."

Auntie Mary showed a side I never knew she had.

"Mad!"

Mary was aggrieved, the words came out and she continued speaking.

"My husband spoke a lot in his sleep. One thing he…"

Dad now cut her off.

"Very riveting, Mary. Granny and I have had enough."

Auntie Mary made her point.

"You will listen. Both of ye will listen. I am not going mad."

The atmosphere was charged.

"As I was saying. My husband told me one night after a lot of drink on our honeymoon, about the time Paul was born. He had been an intern at the hospital. It all makes sense now. He got well wasted on shots in the hotel bar. Boy did he throw them back…"

Granny pleaded.

"Mary, love, don't do this."

Auntie Mary ignored Granny and carried on explaining her story.

"There's drunk and there's drunk but he was gone past the stage of making the slightest bit of sense. Two barmen carried him up to our room. Threw him on the bed and left. Those were the days that I thought I was madly in love and so I lay next to him and watched television while he slept. About an hour later he started to cry uncontrollably. From a deep sleep to bawling crying in a second. Something was eating him up. Over and over, he ranted that he 'wanted his boy'. He wanted him so bad. To be honest it freaked me out.

Within five minutes he started talking clearly in his sleep. Then something he said has stuck in my mind all these years, 'I only got to hold him for a minute'."

We all knew what was coming. It was only a surprise to Auntie Mary to actually hear it said out loud.

"So, you confirmed to me that my husband is Paul's dad. After all this…"

Granny cut in and even at this final hour she strived to control what was left of the situation.

"For the love of God, Mary, get a grip. Would you…"

Dad demanded.

"Quiet. Leave her talk."

A calm voice kept speaking. The words being spoken actually brought calmness to her.

"Granny it had to be my husband. I couldn't visit my sister-in-law to see Paul. She wasn't allowed any visitors. That meant the only man in the hospital who knew her, was my husband, a doctor. Three weeks later, he left his job in the hospital and took up some dead end position in a family practice. Why else would one of Cork's youngest and brightest doctors pack up a promising career?"

When the mind is right it can't comfort the heart. It's like they are strangers. The clarity of honesty can be sometimes too heavy for the heart to hold. Auntie Mary now saw her marriage in a bright light. The shadows of deceit were driven away by the sunlight of truth. Anger replaced upset and the tears started. I was stunned.

"That's why he married me. That's why. That's why. To be near Paul. Please God no, it was his idea to get Paul the job in Hillside. Oh, sweetest Jesus they had lunch nearly every day together. Right under my nose! Never made any sense of it till now. The whole of Cork was convinced that I caught him…ha ha…When I think back how weak I was to believe him, the millions of times he told me when we first met that he loved me. What a dumb blonde I was! And then he would invent reasons to come over here and collect Paul. He didn't hesitate once to come here to pick up his son and bring him to work."

With the facts out in the open the reality was now exposed in its rawness. The tears flowed freely.

"My own lying brother with his lying mother-in-law has lied to me for the past God knows how long? It all makes sense."

Then a shattering shriek from Auntie Mary.

"My husband's son is being reared by ye."

The silence from Granny and Dad was deafening. They didn't need to hear this. All that was being said wasn't new to them. Best to leave things the way they always were. No amount of talking will fix this broken mess. Auntie Mary wasn't finished yet, her tears got sadder and sadder.

"That makes me Paul's auntie and stepmother!"

Granny panicked.

"The boys will be in any minute. Got to prepare a dinner."

At this stage they all had enough. Granny lit another cigarette and seemed to be lost in another world. She was getting too old for all this hassle. A younger Granny would have controlled this mess, not leave a stuck-up cow like Auntie Mary run riot with her 'Facts'. Time to prepare a dinner. Each of the three will now have to deal with their own feelings. One thread did join them all together, each had a loved one lie and deceive them with life changing consequences. As they parted no one mentioned Paul, he had become an afterthought in their selfish lives. Kitchen emptied.

Paul, who had been sitting outside the back window next to me, stood up. He didn't say a word. What could he say? Me, well I was extra delighted it wasn't me in Paul's bastard gay shoes.

****

Food was great, bed extra comfy, house warm, but the noise was a little bit too much. Well, it can't be perfect. Vincent curled up next to Mr Lucey on the sofa. As usual the television was way too loud. He had to pee. Off into the front room. That's better. The old table leg fitted the task perfectly. Even though Vincent had to walk around the litter tray his conscience was clear. He's a Tom Cat and Tom Cats do what they want. Anyway, it's chilly outside.

Mr Lucey sat down and welcomed Vincent onto his lap. He was better now but lazy. This home life was taking its toll. Out there in the darkness some unwanted cat would be scenting his territory. Worse, still could be lots of cats taking little pieces from the edge of his vast domain. Bastards the whole lot of them. Again, he snuggled into Mr Lucey, they were in love. The relief Vincent experienced since the flea powder was applied was unreal. Well, at the start it wasn't. The fleas gravitated to his ears first, for warmth and safety and then around his ass. The itching made him angrier than usual. He even scratched May across the hand when she rubbed him. The blood flowed free and fast from her hand. She went apeshit demanding that the cat be got rid of. Took Harpo and Mr Lucey all week to talk her around. They argued rightly, that Vincent wouldn't last long outside the house. That's all in the past now. I sat next to them waiting for Harpo to come downstairs.

Mr Lucey rose and prepared supper for the both of them. He asked me would I like a sandwich, a polite 'no' from me. A sandwich from a guy who pisses at the end of his stairs. Mr Lucey and Vincent became inseparable. Sitting by his feet Vincent waited patiently. This was a lot easier than hunting to get fed and a lot tastier. Head bowed into spider like fingers, Mr Lucey whispered, he was saying grace. Then pieces of ham were carefully dropped for Vincent to eat. Never once did Vincent leave the table hungry. If anything, he was putting on weight steadily. At first it was well needed, the weight lately was slowing him down. Why worry? The Luceys are the best meal ticket he ever had. Now the radio was blaring.

I went back into the dining room to wait. Vincent wandered in after me and up onto the sofa. Our differences seemed to have been forgotten or at least tolerated. Above the television was a painting of a shepherd with a flock of sheep. Something stopped him getting comfortable every time he entered the room. Two stuffed birds peered down at him. On his right the Kingfisher and above him, the Green Parrot. Both brought in a second-hand shop by Mrs Lucey. All Vincent's natural killing instincts told him to attack and kill them.

Mr Lucey said goodnight and climbed the stairs. Vincent ran out and followed him. Gripping the banister, he sings gently to Vincent, "The man is at sea, the man is at sea." Over and over, he sang that line. They climbed the stairs, under a painting of men drinking, how ironic? Another 'bargain' Mr Lucey had bought in The Horseman.

Next day Harpo called to me with a packet of cigarettes. It was ages since we had a smoke. Off out the back of his house we headed. Vincent like a puppy followed us.

We strolled through a field with yellow flowers. We stopped and waited till the woodcutter took a break, eating his lunch next to the pine tree trunks and dandelions. If he saw us, he would tell us 'to clear off his land'. The three of us sneaked down the lane with our backs to the ditch. Hurried through undergrowth, till the mill was back in view. We stepped into the mill. Vincent started scouting his old domain, a scent was discovered. Over on the window ledge and he sniffs all around. Sitting up, something caught his attention. Two rabbits tearing at some tree roots.

Harpo laments.

"Vincent knows he is too slow, too fat and too old to chase and catch them now."

Old age was catching up with Vincent. His hunting now will be restricted to pouncing on unsuspecting prey. Gone are the days of hunting down his meals by running them into the ground.

Out the back, under an orange sun watching life go by Harpo passes me a cigarette. A noise. Gone. No, back again. Up. Staring towards the two poplars on a road through the hills, something under the trees catches our attention. I couldn't see anything. The lovers stopped, glancing at Vincent. They were distracted. Stillness. They sat next to some tree trunks with ivy. They kissed. Harpo whispered.

"It's Sharon Lyons with that tall guy she met in the disco at Hillside."

Harpo had to call them both over to us. Sharon waved at Harpo and walked over to join us. Vincent seemed constantly distracted by all the scents and sounds. I made my excuses and left. Wasn't going to stand there like a spare prick to be ignored by the likes of Sharon Lyons and her new boyfriend. Harpo called me back, I just walked homewards. My world was shrinking fast when the likes of Harpo were said 'Hello' to before me.

The light coming into my bedroom got weaker and weaker. The door opened. Paul got a surprise when he saw me lying on my bed in the semi-darkness. He started to talk, not to me but more at me. He needed to unburden himself.

"I called to him. He invited me in, don't think he was too surprised to see me. So, I offered to make him tea. Would you believe he attempted to tell me how to make his tea? I have made him enough tea over the years to know how he likes it. We sat there in silence just drinking our tea. My patience was gone, and I needed answers."

There was a silence and then tears. Tears of pain. Paul buried his face into his hands and wept unashamedly. He sounded angry.

"Couldn't tip toe around this one. So, I dived straight in. Well, aren't you the busy boy with all the secrets! You kept the one about having a son, very quiet. Proper little secret agent, aren't we?"

Paul inconsolable pressed his face up against the window. A full moon lit up the garden. He walked around the bed like he was lost. The tears fell from his chin. I was so grateful it wasn't me dealing with this shitstorm.

"He at least tried to explain. At least he didn't lie. He admitted that it happened, he fell in love with a married woman. We should have been more responsible and mature. These things happen. Its life, sometimes…"

Blowing his nose, Paul stopped. Time didn't matter. He continued.

"I know I shouldn't have got angry, but I did. I had to let somebody know how I felt. I screamed at him, so for years and years you looked at me every day and kept this to yourself. What kind of a bastard does this?

He didn't back down. He fought back and coldly explained to me like I was a patient of his."

"What could telling you achieve? This was hardly going to solve anything. What help would that be! Well please tell me because I would like to know! Come on tell me what good opening up a can of worms like this would do?"

Paul sat next to me on the bed, and I just wanted him to stop annoying me. I had enough of my own problems.

"I blew it, Fin. I acted like Granny would and shouted at him – 'For such an intelligent person you're really fucking stupid. Deep down stupid. The kind of stupid that is convinced no matter what anyone else says, you are always right. The big man because you're a doctor. You must have done your medical exams in crayon'.

He asked me to sit down and be quiet. My ears couldn't believe it. He was talking down to me. I flipped.

Don't tell me what to do. You're not my real dad."

"Fin, I didn't know why I was saying all these things. It was like Granny had taken over me. I wasn't there to throw dirt. All I wanted was a hug and an apology. In all fairness to him he tried to explain but I wouldn't have any of it."

"I am truly sorry. I am. I never wanted it to come out like this. I…"

And Like Granny Fin I didn't take any prisoners.

"Lot of fucking 'I's' there doctor, sorry to drag you away from yourself, but where does your son standing in front of you fit in? All that I know is that you're covering your ass. Let's be honest here you don't give a fuck. You didn't give a fuck yesterday, today and you won't give one tomorrow. We are talking about real people here, not patients, real people with real feelings. And all you can say is that 'you're truly sorry'. Spare me the bullshit."

And then he decided the best form of defence was attack.

"Okay, you tell me what to do."

Fin, he had said the worst possible thing he could have at this time. Still, I fought back for no reason than to hurt.

"That's your life in a nutshell, isn't it? Somebody else taking responsibility for your actions. Beautiful, here take my life and tell me what to do. What me, act like a man? God no! You have me for a son and you only worry is yourself. He just sat and said one word."

"Sorry."

"Sorry…yeah"

Had to go. Had to leave. As I stormed out the front door there was only one thing left to be said.

"Goodbye, Dad."

Dr Hughes didn't get the opportunity to say another word. By the time I got home it dawned on me that I had made it all about me. "Fin, I have turned into the nasty short tempered spiteful person that is our granny."

Keeping in a smile, I stay quiet. What a drama queen. Last week he acted like he wanted to ride Dr Hughes and now today he wanted to play Father and Son. I was just in shock that Dr Hughes wasn't a queer!

Paul then did the 'wish I was dead routine'. Prancing around the bedroom he wailed like an old woman about how cruel life is. That was my cue to go and watch TV.

****

Next day found Granny standing among thousands of tons of cold smoothen stone. Her eyes focused on the statues among the semi-darkness. It never seemed to be warm in here. Never a comfortable warmth. You wouldn't come in here on a cold day to escape the chill. Draughts freely wandered between pews changing direction and temperature randomly. It was years, too many to count since the last time she came here to pray. There were countless funerals, first holy communions and confirmations but no praying. Now it was time to seek out divine intervention. Any help will do as long as its help. Standing gazing at Christ she prayed and begged for the strength to keep her family together.

Out the back window, movement. It couldn't be! I adjusted my eyes. Vincent was peering in at the canaries. Brazen, bold and broken he crept past the bird room, towards the garage at the side of the house. A woman walking in a garden nearby sneezed, she spooked him. Running…bang…he stopped and retreated the opposite direction. I heard the noise too, time to inspect.

Granny lit the tiny wick and carefully placed each candle into the holder. One candle for every troubled soul she knew. Fin, John, Dad, now Paul. "Ouch." The candle beneath that was lit for Fin burnt her hand. Down the candle fell. Her hand hurt, she was angry at being so stupid. Paul's candle turned upside down and the yellow flame vanished replaced by a thin black line of smoke.

Turning, facing the garage I stopped myself shouting. Legs kicked and kicked as the life began to leave Paul. He was hanging by the blue rope Dad used to tow any friends' cars that broke down. His eyes hunted down my soul. The kicking got quicker and more violent. As the life left Paul, I stared back at his face changing shape. His neck was stretching as the rope tore into the flesh at the base of his skull. What could I do? What could I say? What I did was run and run into town.

Chapter Fifteen
The Dark Corners of Our Minds

All afternoon I wandered around Cork city, too afraid to come home. What had I done? It was wrong. No amount of throwing it up in the air and praying that it lands correctly will ease my conscience. I had left my own brother hanging in the garage. He might have tied the rope and kicked the chair from beneath his feet, but I guaranteed he wasn't getting a second chance by deserting him. Running off like the spineless coward I am. Yeah, I panicked but you know what, fuck him.

Not a sound to be heard as I stood outside the front of my house. Calm. Opening the front door, I stepped into a full house. Surrounding me was a wall of grief. In among the weeping and wailing stood Dr Hughes. Ushering me aside, he explained that Paul had a seizure in his bedroom and died about an hour ago. My first reaction was bewilderment, last time I had seen Paul he was hanging from a rafter in the garage. So, what happened now? He had a 'Seizure'? Granny threw her arms around me, and I couldn't tell you who was comforting who. Not a single tear left my eyes. All that mattered to me was that something happened, and all around me were people creating a monster of a lie. So big that it was invisible. What unsettled me was who knew what? Who started this lie? Who is in on it? Who isn't in on it? Do they know I know?

Had to take control of the situation and begged Granny.

"Can I see Paul?"

Granny wheezed and rubbed my cheeks.

"It would be too disturbing, Fin. Best to remember him the last time you saw him."

That line swam around in my head refusing to drown. I remember him as his legs kicked trying to grip a ground three feet away from him, his eyes cried out for me to help him. It was a look of complete desperation. 'remember', it's impossible not to.

Orange lights flickered around the front room. At the front door two ambulance men listened intently to Dr Hughes. Instructions were given and clear orders were to be followed. Paul's body was carefully stretchered out into the back of the ambulance. He was gone. I didn't get to see his body properly as Granny had us all distracted in the kitchen. That was it. Dad kept mumbling about that he should have tried harder. He kept repeating like a mantra 'that he never saw it coming'. In among all this mayhem I actually began to wonder what was for dinner. Will we be getting fed? I kept trying to convince myself that it was the stress playing with my mind, but no, I am really hungry and wanted dinner. Granny must have read my mind and suggested that I be sent to the chipper. This idea was shot straight down by Dad.

"What would people think? Pauls gone and we are eating chips! The neighbours would have a field day."

Granny persisted.

"The boy has to eat, sure it would only take Fin ten minutes. We have to keep our strength up."

Hunger proved more important than mourning and off I was sent to the chipper. Place was empty. Ideal. Order was given. Waited. Then disaster. The over friendly lady behind the counter spoke.

"How's your Granny?"

Do I or don't I tell what happened! All I could offer was—

"What?"

But she wasn't just paid just to serve chips. No, she also had to be the friendly face of 'A Chip in Time' Corks newest and cleanest chipper.

"Your Granny. How is she?"

Please God would she shut up.

"Fine…thanks."

The friendliness continued.

"Good, tell her I said hi."

Head down I mumbled.

"Okay."

Still, she shuffled in front of me. Her back stooped over the boiling fat. She rose her voice because the fryer was getting louder.

"Chips will be a few more minutes. Sauce on the burgers? Oh yeah, your brother in the tennis club. Don't tell me, yeah, one second, Paul that's it. He left his jumper here last week. It's out back, I will get it in a minute."

Lucky, she had her back to me otherwise she would have seen my face drop. Trying to keep it together I keep it simple.

"Thanks."

She still keeps blabbering the nosy fucking cow.

"How is he? Nice kid."

Can't tell her, not here, not now.

"Fine."

As the extremely over inquisitive lady vanished to get the jumper, the door opened. Harpo, speechless, stuck out his hands and said how sorry he was. There was real hurt and pain in his voice as he hugged me. Come to think of it he was the first person so far who had expressed any genuine heartfelt feelings about Paul.

"My dad saw the ambulance, we thought it was Granny, but the driver told him it was Paul. Some kind of seizure! What? How the fuck could that happen? He was the nicest guy you could meet. This is so unfair, Fin. He was so good to everyone. Many time that…"

She was back and loud.

"Here's Paul's jumper, might smell a little bit of chips, so tell him I'm sorry."

My hands reluctantly stretched over the counter and bundled the neatly folded jumper down by my side. Harpo just stood there frozen. He hadn't a clue what was going on. She pointed at my burger.

"Onions on the burgers, love?"

Super quick I shout back.

"Yes, please."

Chips and burgers were wrapped in newspaper super-fast. Harpo had followed me up here to show his respects. I hadn't time for it. Keeping the grieving to a minimum, I left Harpo to mourn alone. Running, running as fast as possible without dropping anything, I get home. Visitors have arrived and the chips are laid out on the table still in the newspaper. Hands constantly dip in and out of the newspaper, seeking out the crispest chips first. The room fills with small talk. Silence. Couldn't tell how long Fr Collins was standing by the door observing the scene, but he was long enough to know this wasn't the normal behaviour when a loved one passes away. Granny had her back to him munching on a battered burger. A small smile creased Fr Collins lips as he tried to make God relevant in our kitchen.

"God be with us in this time of need."

Eating stopped, but the chewing continued right up to the second blessing. Fr Collins opened his hands showing his milky white palms that never did a day's work. Just then it struck me that he was the only one in the room that didn't have a chip in his hand or mouth. He concentrated on summoning God.

"Please God, protect and take care of all present, that they will get through this time of need."

Granny took back control. Mouth still full of batter burger, she thanked Fr Collins.

"That was lovely, Father. Thank you. Would you like a batter burger or a chip perhaps?"

Fr Collins had a role to play and true to form he wasn't going to let any distraction like food get in the way. Zoning in on Granny, he begins to weasel his way into the mind-set of our family.

"It's terrible, Granny. Really terrible. How are you and the boy coping?"

Granny knew the score and brought the conversation back to her. She would carry the shield to defend her boy against God's wrath.

"Not easy, Father, we got to be strong for the child. It's very hard on him. We did nothing to deserve all of this. What it is all about, Father? How can an all loving, all caring God do this to us!"

As she spoke, an eye was kept on the chips. Since she was speaking to Fr Collins, the eating continued and with all freely munching away there wouldn't be many chips left in a while.

Knowing that trying to explain or defend God's plan at these times could be counterproductive, Fr Collins distracts the faithful by sticking to the basics.

"I will go through the arrangements later with you. He was such a lovely boy."

Truth be told, Fr Collins would find it hard to tell me and Paul apart. He was at this game long enough to know the drill. Got to hand it to him, he was good, very very good. A true professional of Christ.

"Would you have a picture of Paul? It can be put on the table for people to share a prayer over."

The only picture of Paul on his own to be found was his confirmation photo. His hair was shorter, face thinner and he looked fed up. Granny cleared the newspapers off the table. The photo was given pride of place. She silently fumed, the chips were gone!

Fr Collins relieved that he could now add a face to his prayers, lamented.

"Why oh why? Such a handsome young man taken. Was it a seizure, Granny?"

A voice spoke from the hall. Dr Hughes was out talking to Dad.

"Yes, Father, he didn't suffer, thank God."

Fr Collins shuffled his awkward little frame over to the kitchen door.

"I didn't see you there, Doctor!"

An uneasiness developed between the man who cured souls and the man who cured bodies. An awful lot of what Fr Collins refers to as 'Gods will' can be easily explained medically by Dr Hughes. Equally Fr Collins can just as quickly dismiss the short fallings of medical science. Both men lived off reputations for fixing souls and bodies. Both men strived to be unapproachable in their fields of expertise. Both men knew they were always one person away from failure. Both men buried their mistakes. Fr Collins wasn't sharing the misery with anyone, least of all a doctor.

"Granny, prayer will help you. Would you like to pray?"

Lighting her cigarette by the back door Granny coughed.

"Now?"

A bewildered Fr Collins smirked.

"Yes."

With that we all knelt for a decade of the rosary. Fr Collins mumbled out Hail Marys and actually winked at me during the prayers. He was loving it, everything around a death ensured the priest got prime position. No jostling with brides or screaming babies being baptised. No, this was his show, and no one was going to take that away from him. For Paul to get to heaven, the ass kissing had to start here. The journey to meet God in far off universes takes a lot of fuel and the greatest fuel of all is prayer. The right prayers in the tank and Paul's soul will coast past black holes and meteors. He will be at God's side by teatime tomorrow. Only problem was that Fr Collins was the only person who knew the right mixture of fuel and how much was needed. He wasn't leaving the crowd slip through his clasped fingers.

"Wasn't that lovely, Granny! Paul in all our thoughts and deeds."

Granny stood back up wondering, was he trying to wind her up? Fr Collins started mingling with the mourners.

The hall became as busy as Patrick Street on a Saturday evening. Granny stood by the kettle constantly making tea while Dad handled the alcohol. By eight o' clock the whispers were becoming laughs and by nine o'clock it was hard to tell whether people were grieving or having a good time. Dad filled his glass to the brim with whiskey. Cousin Jimmy's parents arrived stunned by what greeted them. Dad, taken aback by their distraught appearance, tried in vain to explain the merriment.

"We are celebrating Paul's life, he was the greatest kid you could wish for."

Without realising it Dad began to indirectly compare Paul and Cousin Jimmy. The fucking idiot of a man ranted and raved how Paul 'never doing anything out of the way' to 'he was a quiet as a thief, sure you wouldn't even know he was in the house', made Cousin Jimmy's parents extremely uncomfortable. All they wanted to do was share a bit of Dad's limelight and misery. Being addicted to misery, meant Cousin Jimmy's mum and dad became regulars on the circuit of death. A family member's sudden departure from this world would give them a certain kind of high that ordinary deaths lacked. Blood is thicker than water and tears for family members are saltier than the norm. This was the first death that Jimmy's mother didn't get to dab a tissue against the corners of her eyes for the night. There was dabbing, Granny placed a cloth in her hand and asked politely if she would wipe down the table. Jimmy's father was sent to the off license to get more drink, a long list of beers and a fist full of notes were pressed into his hand. Confused, he followed out the instructions only to discover that he didn't have enough money to cover half the cost. Not being a drinker himself he wouldn't even get the satisfaction of enjoying one of the beers. Why not treat himself! A large bottle of Coke was placed in among the beer. Returning, he was struck by the noise coming from the house. A party was after developing, the curtains were open for all to see the drinking and storytelling. Every minute or two, loud laughter would erupt. The beer and Coke were placed on the kitchen table. His wife now stood by the sink, drying the mountain of cups, glasses and plates that were constantly building up. Excusing himself, he had to use the bathroom. Returning he was horrified to discover the bottle of Coke gone. Politely room after room was checked, politely he was told it wasn't there. Every glass was eyed, still no sign of it. By the end of the night Cousin Jimmy's dad became more annoyed at the Coke vanishing than Paul dying!

With the lateness, came the hardcore drinkers whose thirst surpassed their dignity. First to arrive was Harpo's dad. Funny thing about alcoholics and their relationship with free beer, they morph into whatever they need to be, to fit in. At this time of night Harpo's dad is usually a self-righteous bastard whose ability to listen is strongly contested by his ability to talk. In plain English, he's a fuckwit who can't or won't listen to anyone. Put some free beer in front of him and suddenly you have a Buddhist monk who not just listens but cares. Cares in such a way, that all around with listen to his words of wisdom. The crowd is fooled momentarily into thinking that the drinking has helped him on this quest of wisdom. That the beer contains little nuggets of hope and understanding, which if drunk enough of, will empower the individual onto a higher level of understanding. Keep filling his glass and the words of wisdom might cease but his very presence gives comfort to all those who see him. By the end of the night, Harpo's dad will be recast as the victim in life and the very beer he craves, the abuser. Forget about his kids, forget about his home, forget about his job, and just remember that he is the victim. Do it enough and before long you will be as bad as he is. Don't ever forget, the sound of the drink talking can be very seductive, easing you into a false reality where the whole world is chilled and lies are easy to swallow!

A voice echoes down the hall. It's midnight, I cower. The voice greets all present. He says the right words to the right people. A bottle of beer is placed in his hand. The green glass is nearly completely hidden by massive fingers. His head has to be bowed walking into the kitchen. Excuses are made to his lateness. None of the adults' mind, they are grateful that he has arrived. All the younger people are baffled as to why he was out drinking till midnight on a Wednesday night in the first place. Beanpole smiles and talks to Granny.

"Lovely kid your Paul. A touch of the genius. What an athlete. Gentle soul. Wouldn't hurt a fly. He had some future ahead of him. Seizure? I keep forgetting your first name Granny!"

Granny stopped, stood and snapped. She got her blow in.

"Granny's fine, ye had a colourful history that for sure."

With that she vanished out of the kitchen.

Beanpole squeezed in next to Harpo's dad. I went to the kitchen for a drink of water. It was just after midnight and there sitting talking to Granny and

Aunty Mary was Dr Hughes. He seemed really cut up about Paul's death. The conversation ebbed and flowed until Granny and Auntie Mary agreed with Dr Hughes on something about the coffin. Listening…Auntie Mary spoke.

"It's for the best Granny. You couldn't have an open coffin with Paul's face all contorted. People will remember him looking like a freak and not the handsome young man he was."

Sipping my Coke from a mug, I thought, how convenient, what about the burn marks around his neck from the rope? Was this chat for my benefit? Or was it real? Granny spoke.

"Ask Crazy Ken to tidy up Paul's hair. He will rest easier with a proper haircut."

Crazy Ken didn't just cut hair, he trimmed back people's personalities. Walking in the front door of his hairdressers, was like dancing through a minefield while smacking a metal bar off the ground. Something was going to explode in your face no matter how lucky you felt. The line of patrons waiting to get their hair cut was Crazy Ken's captive audience. It was an old school men's salon with no frills. Just pictures of guys with prefect hair, who looked like gay porn stars on the walls. These pictures gave me the willies. Excuse the pun, but they did. Having to sit below those creeps made me feel extremely uncomfortable.

While Crazy Ken cut your hair, he started a question-and-answer session which ran perfectly parallel to the amount of hair being taken off the victim's head. It was like he had a set amount of questions to be asked in a set amount of time. These would range from 'how was school going?', to 'when's the last time you got your hole?' A lie would be smelt out. He had the memory of an elephant and the tongue of a rattle snake. In between lisped sentences his tongue would smell the air. No shit, as he cut your hair his tongue would shot in and out involuntarily. It was this quirk of nature that turned his tongue acid. You see Crazy Ken didn't wait to find out if you liked him or not. God no. Everybody he ever met, he treated like an asshole, and hey if you were nice, then you were a nice asshole. The method to his madness was self-protection. Liked a wounded lion he battled with all around. Obviously, Crazy Ken knew he was crazy and learnt to completely ignore that fact. He was big, pretty big and had long jet-black curly hair which he tied into a ponytail. A thin moustache ran over his top lip. For all the world he looked Mexican! One thing is certain, he sure as hell didn't look like any of the gays with the perfect hair hanging on his walls.

Crazy or not he had a beautiful wife, drove a souped-up Golf GTI and lived in a nice part of town. Him and Paul didn't get off on the right foot but ended up being as thick as thieves. It was a Saturday when Paul and I strolled into Crazy Ken's for a haircut. I was two seats behind Paul and had to watch how these two clicked. It was Paul's first time coming here. Granny sent him as Crazy Ken's is cheaper than all the other hairdressers. Paul spoke out of turn and put his foot in it straight away.

"I need a haircut."

Without looking back Ken instructed.

"Well, if you're looking for lamb chops, you're in the wrong place! Take a seat kid."

Paul in innocence rambled, where angels dare to thread.

"Thanks, my Granny sent me. Are you Crazy Ken?"

Remaining calm and focusing on the head under his fingers, he brushed Paul off.

"Yes Ken. You can call me Ken."

Crazy Ken was taken aback. Who is this Mummies Boy? Who does he think he is? Calling me Crazy Ken. Time to question the little shit. Not one person in the line of boys waiting for a haircut felt safe. Whether this kid is dumb or mad something was going to kick off. Three heads of hair were dispatched with sharp words and sharper cuts. Crazy Ken kept looking at Paul. Just when Paul got up to take his turn on the chair, the penny dropped.

"Okay kid, what do we want?"

Paul, loud enough for the whole queue to hear, quipped.

"Two lamb chops please."

Crazy Ken was taken aback, this kid is funny.

"Okay smart ass, I meant your hair."

Proud as punch Paul requested.

"New Wave please, like Spandau Ballet. No too loud, but loud enough."

A hand went around the back of Paul's neck, gripping tight enough to be felt, a tongue licked the air within an inch of his ear, a voice.

"I know who you are."

Not one-bit fazed Paul giggled. I loved every second of it. Crazy Ken didn't know I was Paul's brother.

"Hope so, you have been grilling the last three boys ahead of me. Crazy you don't do whispering."

Going red, Crazy Ken had to regain some respect.

"Say Crazy once more and I will stick this pair of scissors into your neck."

A hand gripped the flesh on the neck tighter. Paul had him rattled. A lisp voice continued.

"Saw you last week carrying shopping, yeah it was Friday around noon. With some old guy."

Paul stared into the massive mirror in front of him.

"Oh yeah the guy with the jam jar glasses! I play him in chess."

Crazy Ken wasn't giving up.

"Is he any good?"

Bored of waiting Paul threw out one word.

"Yeah."

Still not one hair was cut. Crazy Ken kept interrogating.

"Bullshit kid. Don't bullshit me."

Flustered and annoyed Paul snapped.

"No, I'm not."

Pointing the scissors at Paul's reflection in the mirror a threat was made.

"Yes, you are. Oh yes you are!"

At this stage Paul was well pissed off.

"How would you know?"

As loud as his lisp let him shout Crazy Ken barked.

"He's my grandad and even though I'm thick stupid, I would still beat him at chess."

The captive audience laughed. Crazy Ken learnt from an early age that jokes aimed at himself guarantee a laugh no matter who hears them. Back within an inch of Paul's ear.

"So there, Mr Bullshit."

Still waiting for a haircut, Paul snapped.

"So there what?"

The lisp got wetter and as Crazy Ken spoke, he dampened Paul's neck.

"So there, there."

Paul didn't grasp the mechanics of slanging. You know, you give a bit, take a bit, till the joke is worn out. So Crazy Ken's method of intimidation couldn't work on Paul. Standing back styling, it stood out that this kid was a loner. All he wanted was to be left alone. Put him out of his misery. Crazy Ken opened up to Paul.

"The old man is my grandad, and he tells me you play him down in the community centre. Well, play is the wrong word. You leave him win some games."

Paul relieved, let out a laugh.

"Ha-ha."

The scissors started clipping hard.

"Yes, you do, he says you're lighting quick. Never shuts up about how nice you are."

Flattered, I could see Paul going red in the mirror.

"Thanks Ken."

A smile and a rub of a brush across the neck.

"Call me Crazy."

The most unusual friendship developed, one that defied logic, one that surpassed reason. When Paul went to pay Crazy his money was refused.

"You will never pay in here kid. That's for putting up with that grumpy old Grandad of mine. Come in every two weeks for a fresh cut."

Paul, loving all the attention, kissed ass.

"Tell you what Crazy. You cut my hair and I will teach you all the moves you will ever need to know in chess."

A firm handshake.

"Sounds like a deal to me."

That was probably the most important friendship Paul ever made. Paul's hair was constantly preened within an inch of its life and Crazy slowly, very slowly, became the chess player he always wanted to be. Crazy had a great natural chess, brain but an instinct to always go for the jugular was his downfall. By constantly attacking, he left himself wide open for counter attacks. This worked great when arguing with people, they would retreat hoping he would shut the fuck up. But on a chess board that type of intimidation didn't or couldn't work. As the games got longer and longer, Paul began to open up more and more about himself. Crazy listened and that's all Paul needed. He didn't need someone to agree or disagree, no, just listen. Paul told Crazy his inner most fears and the constant dread he had of the world. Crazy opened up to Paul about how deeply embarrassed he felt that he never really did his best at school. Yes, the hairdresser was doing well, but sometimes when he cuts old school friends hair he can see them laughing at the way he conducts himself. The class clown who never grew up. Both identified with each other through their weakness, and both used their strengths to cement a friendship. Crazy became super protective of Paul. One day as Crazy cut happily away, the teenager in the hot seat, was a smart ass. Gazing down at Paul and me he smugly remarked.

"See that tall guy at the end of the line?"

Both looked at Paul. Crazy listened, snipped and combed as the kid spoke.

"He's a queer, serious, I heard he is…aaaaahhh shit."

Glaring into the mirror Crazy apologised.

"Sorry there, boy. You moved your head. It's only a small bit of blood. Your ear will be fine. Don't move your head again…thanks."

****

Mr Lucey took two large spoons for the kitchen drawer. Harpo often told me his dad played the spoons, but I never saw it. Thought he was lying but obviously he wasn't. A click and clatter as he warmed the spoons up. Mr Lucey spoke, and the kitchen filled to overflowing.

"A song for the lad. This one is for Paul, God be good to him."

The spoons moved faster than his fingers against his thigh. Once everyone's attention was on him, he started singing, *The Curragh of Kildare* by The Johnston's. Mr Lucey was some singer and set the tone by delivering the opening lines in a heart-breaking tone.

"The winter it has passed.

And the summer's come at last."

I gazed around the room and could see that our souls were like ships with no sails. Paul was in everyone's thought and heads bowed in shameful reflection. Beanpole didn't look so big now. Dad leant against the sink and looked into his glass for comfort. Cousin Jimmy's parents held hands. But the figure that that stared straight at the spoons freely dropped tears onto a chest full of pride and not enough love. Granny was holding it barely together, but the last lines echoed and echoed around our consciousness till it stung.

"That's your hearts are full of woe,

It's a woe that no mortal can cure."

The spoons stopped and silence.

Climbing into bed, I could hear all the chat below. A light sleep arrived. Paul was calling me. Turning away, I wouldn't answer him. Screaming at me. Still, I ignored him. Then slowly I turned, he was hanging, but not dying, no, he was doing the moves to YMCA by the Village People, his favourite song. He gestured for me to join in. Floating in mid-air he sang and danced to his heart's content. As my eyes stared in disbelief, he turned his back on me and danced away. Next morning Granny stood in the kitchen ironing shirts for the removal. The day passed with blurred reality. Was this really happening? We should be all at school today? A knock on the door. A Frown stood and offered sympathy around like chocolates. If you wanted a little or a lot, he's giving it out at a cost. The Frown was our family undertaker and boy did he take death seriously. Words were used sparingly and strategically. The best of everything for Paul at a price that the family wouldn't resent. He had an ability to look straight through you. All this grieving and pretence at grieving had worn down his soul. The conversation would rise and fall around issues like – type of wood for the coffin to Paul's favourite jumper, the Frown stayed the Frown. Even when Granny asked him about his own children, he still was the Frown.

A knock, a tear, a hug, a heartbroken man. Crazy Ken came to offer his respects. Over an hour he had spent down at the funeral home fixing Paul's hair the way Paul would have liked it. It took an outsider and a demented outsider to be the first person to grieve openly for Paul. His face dropped and hands shook as he broke down crying in the kitchen. You would want to be blind and heartless not to see that this man's world had been shattered. Constantly he referred to Paul as one of the best friends he ever had. A friend he loved and admired. That it was impossible to believe that Paul was gone. After talking for ten minutes Crazy Ken could see that none of us had held Paul in the same high regard that he did. Less and less, he spoke as it began to dawn on him that we weren't really interested. Granny thanked him and walked him to the door. When Crazy Ken left, we all went back to remembering Paul in the dark corners of our minds.

The removal took forever. Afterwards we were left on our own to say our goodbyes to Paul. The coffin was opened for a few minutes. Paul had a look of pure horror moulded onto his face. All our heads changed angles to try and get a better view. But no matter which way he was viewed, it looked like he hated us. As a final farewell, Paul made sure we all knew what he thought of us. Then Granny kissed his cheek, this was the cue for the rest of us to follow suit.

When my turn came, I cried, leant over Paul and kissed his marble cold forehead. Tears dropped onto his face and stuck. They never ran off his cheek. My tears just formed little liquid bumps that reflected the little lights in the ceiling. It was like Paul was telling me that my tears weren't good enough to run down his face. His favourite woolly jumper came up his neck to the bottom of his ears. He looked like one of The Beatles from the cover of a Hard Day's Night.

That night, a pattern started developing. Again, Paul came to me in my sleep. He wanted a loan of my favourite coat. The navy one with extra padding. He was frozen stiff in the coffin and needed something to keep him warm. I pretended not to hear him. This irritated him and made him shout louder. I turned my back to him. Paul screamed at me that he would 'ask someone else and that he didn't want anything from me'. Turning to tell him take the coat, Paul was gone.

Next day, we put Paul in a hole in the ground. The same dark hole that contained our mother. Dad spoke at the graveside that now Paul's mum would look after and protect him in the next life. As Dad rambled on more and more about the next life, he seemed to show up our failings in supporting Paul in this life. For all the world it sounded like that now, Paul was getting a second chance through death, to be the person he should have been when he was alive. All the while Fr Collins stood there with a smile like the Mona Lisa, from one side it looked like he was happy and from the other he looked like he was sad. The Frown organised the throwing of earth down onto the coffin. People whispered and wandered back to their cars. Granny, lost for words, tried to hold it together, we barely held onto whatever reality was supposed to be. A cigarette had been in her hand constantly for the last three days. She coughed and wheezed out.

"He will get to spend real time now with his mum. Something none of ye boys ever had the luxury. They will do things now that they missed out on. They will have a lot of catching up to do."

We all looked at each other in shock. What was Granny on about? She made it sound like they were off clothes shopping or going out for a meal. "He nearly died when he was born. Frightened the life out of her. They are together now and—"

Dad cut in sharply and not a second too soon.

"Shut up Granny. They're dead, they won't be going anywhere."

For ever we stood at the graveside, looking at the headstone, half heartily whispering off prayers. This headstone would become a part of my life for years to come. Every Sunday, Granny would press gang me into visiting the grave and praying for her daughter and grandson. The more we went to the graveyard, the more we resented it. Every time we walked away from the grave Granny would promise to return as soon as possible. This meant that she often would go on her own. She would vanish for hours at a time, staring at the writing on the headstone. Now Paul's name had been chiselled into the granite. Reading off the dates of birth and death like a prayer. One evening, in deep reflection, she sensed a presence near her. Somebody watching from a respectful distance. Her eyes cracked open, and a voice floated towards her.

"Come on, I will walk you home. You aren't doing yourself any favours here."

Granny felt her prayers were answered. Her daughter and grandson had sent someone to look after her. She smiled, the first smile in months, a warmness filled her. Locking arms, they walked silently down the footpath and home. Conor had come back to look after her.